Freeing Abigail

by

LuAnn Nies

Published by
Melange Books, LLC
White Bear Lake, MN 55110
www.melange-books.com

Freeing Abigail ~ Copyright © 2013 by LuAnn Nies

ISBN: 978-1-61235-653-2 Print

Cover Art by Stephanie Bibb

Freeing Abigail
LuAnn Nies

Abigail Pendergrass's dreams are destroyed when an accident claims her best friend's life, leaving her emotionally and physically paralyzed.

Beauregard Winkelman, her new physical therapist, is a tall, sexy Texan whose career is on the rocks due to his scandalous past and indiscretions.

Beau's last chance depends on getting Abby back on her feet. Her last chance for a real life rests in his trained hands.

Tension enough without Dr. Voight threatening Beau's career and Abby's recovery.

Dedication

Writing Freeing Abigail was a labor of love and commitment that took four years to complete. A lot of research went into getting the story as accurate and believable as possible. I'd like to say thanks to everyone who had a hand in giving Abigail a reason to fight back and to give life a second chance.

My critique group is the best. They have taught me how to craft the best story that I can by digging deep into your character's psyche to find what really makes them tick. Thanks, Denise Devine, Lori Ness, Robin Nelson and Chad Filly for having faith in me.

Honorable mention and many thanks to:

Rick and Kathy Ellis, Innkeepers at the, "Old Thyme Inn" for their help and information on Devil's Slide and Half Moon Bay.

Realtor, Ben Heinrich for answering questions about the types of houses found around Big Sur.

Emergency room nurse and friend, Karyn Olson, without her help and guidance Abigail would have never made it to the hospital or through the surgery.

Physical Therapist, Sharon DeValos, who answered numerous questions that enabled Abby to walk again.

I'm sure there were more who helped and I'm sorry if I didn't mention you, but I appreciate everything you did to help this story along. I am truly blessed and surrounded by wonderfully talented people.

Chapter One

"Slow down!"

Abigail Pendergrass braced her hand against the dashboard and glared at Carolyn who reached over and turned up the radio, cutting off any of her further pleas. Drawing in a deep breath, Abby gazed out the window.

She enjoyed the drive up to San Francisco in Carolyn's new red Corvette and the day of shopping, but the drive back to Big Sur was starting to resemble a roller coaster ride. The speeding sports car cut around sharp curves three hundred feet above the jagged rocks lining the shores below.

Abby leaned toward the middle of the car and swallowed hard as the guardrail flew by in a blur. She didn't like arguing with Carolyn, but Abby was upset. Carolyn planned to transfer to Michigan State to be closer to her new boyfriend Josh. Abby felt betrayed. Since the age of thirteen Abby and Carolyn made a plan. They would graduate, spend a couple years exploring Europe and go to the same college. Then they would marry brothers and become real sisters.

But Carolyn had changed since she met Josh.

"Carolyn, please slow down. There could be rocks on the road. You know Devil's Slide is notorious for landslides."

She tried again to get Carolyn to stop. "Let's stop in Half Moon Bay at that little open-air café. We haven't eaten for hours. What do you

5

say?"

"No, I want to get back as soon as I can."

"It won't take long."

"No!" The tires squealed as they rounded another curve.

"What's the big hurry anyway?"

"I want to spend time with Josh tonight. I didn't think we were going to be gone so long."

"You hardly know this guy. I can't believe you're going to throw away all the plans we've made."

Carolyn tossed her sunglasses on the dash, her blue eyes bright with irritation. "I don't expect you to understand right now, but someday you'll meet someone, and you'll want to spend every minute with him. Then you'll know how I feel about Josh."

Abby doubted it. They entered the village of Half Moon Bay, and she relaxed back into the seat as the car slowed. They coasted through town, but it wasn't long before they were speeding again along the steep rocky terrain of the San Mateo coastline.

"I don't understand," Abby said. "How can you just pick up and leave? You don't even know anyone in Michigan."

Carolyn didn't respond. Abby crossed her arms and glared straight ahead. It wasn't long before the rocky reef that flanked the Pigeon Point Lighthouse came into view.

They approached another sharp curve. Pinned to the door by the car's momentum Abby instinctively searched for the passenger side brake pedal. "Slow down! It won't kill him to wait a few extra minutes."

"I'm not going that fast," Carolyn said, turning toward Abby. The back wheels of the Corvette caught gravel. Carolyn cranked the wheel, sending the car into a spin and smashing through the guardrail. Dirt, grass and gravel flew into the air. Airbags ballooned from the dash.

The engine roared as the car bounced and rolled. The sound of crunching metal was deafening. Shopping bags, purses, dirt and debris riddled the air. Pain shot through Abby's head as it shattered the side window. The car slid on its roof for several feet before coming to a stop.

Trapped in her seat belt, Abby hung like a fly in a web. Terrified, she called out to Carolyn, but the only sounds she could hear were the spinning of the tires and the pounding of her own heart.

Abby woke with a gasp; sweat covered her body, the nightmare fresh in her mind. *Will I ever have a night of peace!* She stared at the colorless ceiling. Swallowing, she blinked several times as a tear slid down her cheek. How many tears could a body make?

At the sound of chirping birds, she turned her attention to the open window. Their carefree songs floated in with the early morning breeze and rustled her bedroom curtains. She sighed and turned her face away from the window.

I'm only twenty-three, and my life is over. I'm a prisoner of my body with no chance for parole.

Why did I debate—no, argue—about something as insignificant as which school Carolyn wanted to attend? It wouldn't have mattered if she wanted to move to China. She *would still be alive, and we would still be friends.*

A sob tore from Abby's lungs. Carolyn's death was her fault, and that guilt held her hostage. Unable to speak and paralyzed for the rest of her life was her penance.

* * * *

George Pendergrass paced to the wall of windows overlooking the Pacific Ocean. His head pounded. His mind reeled with frustration. His sister Lily stood in the doorway.

"I can't help her if she won't help herself," he said as he came to a halt in front of the windows.

"George," Lily said, wringing her hand. "You can't give up on your daughter!"

"Don't you think I know that? What am I supposed to do? Abby just lies there and stares at the ceiling. We've tried everything the doctors advised. She's been to the finest institutions money could buy, and still there's no improvement."

Closing his eyes, he massaged his temples and heaved a heavy sigh. The accident never strayed far from his mind. His baby, his only child, had been left paralyzed. "She hasn't spoken for months," he murmured under his breath. "What if she's done permanent damage to her vocal cords?" He turned to see his fears reflected in his sister's eyes. "What if she never speaks again?"

"Don't do this to yourself." Lily rushed to his side and placed her hand on his arm. "You've done everything humanly possible."

"My baby's shut me out completely." He collapsed into a chair, dropping his head into his hands. "I just don't know what else to do."

Lily squatted next to him and placed a hand over his. "We'll just have to keep looking. Someone has the answers." She squeezed his hand. "Don't give up yet."

Raising his head, he said, "What would I do without you, Lily?" Years of wisdom and faith shone in her loving blue eyes.

"Well, I'm afraid you'll never find out. You're stuck with me," she said with a forced reassuring smile. "We'll figure this out. I promise."

The specialists had informed George that Abigail had a good chance of making a significant recovery. Yet after months of therapy her behavior suggested that she had given up. Her surface injuries had healed, however, George feared her mind and spirit never would.

"I really thought once we brought her home she would at least try to make an effort," George muttered, shaking his head. "Was it a mistake to bring her back here?"

"You had no way of knowing she would shut down."

Only a miracle would bring his little girl back to him. His gaze traveled around the great room, which had been decorated with expensive artifacts from his travels to the Far East and covered the seven and a half foot long Steinway. He sighed. Even with all his money he couldn't buy back his daughter's health or peace of mind.

* * * *

Abby heard her aunt's soft footsteps on the hall carpet long before the woman approached the room.

"Good morning, dear!" Lily entered and placed a breakfast tray on the bedside stand.

"How are you this morning?" Adjusting the bed, she raised Abby to a sitting position. While she fed Abby, like every other day for the past few months, she shared the daily news and any juicy gossip she had heard from the television or the tabloids.

"Guess what I heard? Your cousin Patty is going to have a baby. Isn't that wonderful?"

A baby? Abby's stomach twisted in to a knot of jealousy.

"The weatherman says it's going to be eighty-two today. Maybe Doctor Voight will stop by for a visit. He has Fridays off, doesn't he?"

Lily's head tilted slightly, her nose twitched, and her eyes sparkled with mischief. "He could carry you downstairs. We could sit on the patio and have some iced tea. A little change in scenery would do you good. You would enjoy that, wouldn't you, dear?"

Abby replied with a sigh. Her aunt continued to chatter. Her words blended together as usual, and Abby tuned her out. Her life had consisted of the same routine every day for the past several months. Her aunt climbed the stairs and fed Abby her meals. She would clean her up and then administer a couple minutes of therapy followed by a rub down.

Although Lily helped with the housework, she insisted on taking care of Abby personally. Abby loved her for that. She didn't want strange people touching her. She just couldn't understand why everyone didn't realize that the therapy was a waste of time.

She glanced over at the antique hutch and its curved glass door, which held her porcelain doll collection. She couldn't see them all, but she knew their names, how they were arranged and the occasions on which she'd received them. They were her most prized possessions. And just knowing they were there gave her comfort since she had returned from the hospital.

The walls in her room were painted a light creamy yellow, which brought out the honey tones of her rattan wicker bedroom set—except her beautiful queen-sized bed had been replaced with a hospital bed. Her gaze swept across the room to the shelves that displayed her tennis and swimming trophies. She had worked hard to win those trophies. Now it hurt to look at them.

They're just another reminder of what I've lost.

* * * *

Lily entered her own room and collapsed into a chair. She pulled a tissue from her pocket and wiped her tears. She loved her niece, and she loved feeling needed, yet it was tearing her apart to watch Abigail lay there day after day without any improvement. Before her accident, she had been so full of life. Now the girl lay dormant some place far below the surface.

Abby's skin had once been healthy, tanned to a golden brown from hours spent outdoors. Now she looked pale and gaunt. Dark circles shadowed her beautiful blue eyes. Her long brown hair had been cut short, and the shine had faded away along with the girl's spirit.

Lily tucked the tissue away in her pocket and sighed. Each morning their routine stayed the same, and each day her niece refused to participate or respond. She would let Lily move her arms and legs but refused to follow any directions.

She's a paraplegic, not a vegetable. But if she doesn't start helping herself she soon will be. If only she would speak again she could continue her sessions with the psychologist.

Lily and George weren't qualified to perform her physical therapy or to deal with her emotional issues. She needed professional help. She needed to fight to get her life back.

Lily dragged herself to her feet and crossed to the double doors, which opened on to the terrace. "What a beautiful day." She stared into the bright blue sky. Her faith was all she had left to offer. "Lord, I know I've used up all my favors in my sixty-eight years," she prayed "But I'm not asking for me. I'm asking for George and Abby. You know she's not getting any better. And George, well, he's almost at the end of his rope. I've lived a long full and happy life. You've been more than generous to me. You've given me three wonderful husbands and many years of happiness. I only ask that you give Abigail the same chance for happiness. I'll accept anyone you send. We've done everything we can. Now it's up to you." The potted palm at her side swayed in the morning breeze. "Oh, one more thing, Lord. Please hurry."

* * * *

Beauregard Winkelman awoke and struggled to pry open one eye. Excruciating pain shot through his skull, and he winced. "Hmmm." Someone had filled his eyes with sand and his mouth with cotton. Mentally hitting rewind, his mind replayed the sketchy events from another wild night at the Brass Rail. Just the thought of the loud music and alcohol intensified the pounding in his head. *If I keep up at this rate, I'll be dead in a couple of months.* He pinched the bridge of his nose, but the pain didn't subside. "Hmmm."

"Hmmm! You awake, Sugar?" A warm naked body snuggled up against Beau's side. A mass of red hair washed over him as soft kisses were placed across his chest. His eyes shot open, and he scanned the room, trying to get his bearings.

"Your apartment is so much nicer than mine," she said, propping her chin on his chest. "You hungry? I'm starved."

"Oh! Ginger ... Morning." The thought of food churned the acid in his stomach. "No! Don't move," he said before she had a chance to rock the bed.

She cuddled closer and purred, "Whatever you say, Sugar."

Beau closed his eyes and tried to relax. *Something has to change in my life.* The money he was making as an apartment superintendent wasn't adding up quick enough for the down payment needed to start his injured athletes physical therapy clinic. He would be fifty years old before he had enough money saved up to print business cards. And he could pretty much toss the idea of owning his own house in the trash with all of his other dreams. One way or another he had failed at everything he had done. He was a has-been college football player and then almost lost his physical therapy license. *Face it, Winkelman, this is your life. Gram would be proud.*

* * * *

Sarah Winkelman, Vice President of Marketing for Miller Electronics in Fort Worth Texas, perched on a paisley sofa in the lobby of Pendergrass Technology Incorporated. The marble floors were polished to a high sheen, the walls painted gray with stripes of various shades of blue. Sarah had been in some nice buildings in her life, but none compared to this one. Tropical plants, potted bamboo, and cat palms surrounded the enormous fishpond and fountain located in the center of the lobby.

Reaching up, she touched a leaf to see if it was real, then glanced up to find the sober looking woman behind the reception desk watching her. Sarah smiled and shifted in her seat.

She had heard stories and rumors about Pendergrass Technology Incorporated or PTI, which had been referred to in the business world as "Pillage The Innocent." She'd heard Mr. Pendergrass was a take-no-prisoners kind of man which meant since he purchased Miller Electronics her position could easily become a casualty of this takeover. But she was confident that he would like and accept the proposal she had spent three stressful months working on.

She wasn't only worried about her position and future but also that of her marketing staff. Would he keep them? Or would he install his own people in their positions?

Sarah checked her watch. She had arrived early—he was late. Crossing her legs, she smoothed the skirt of her new lavender suit and willed herself to relax. Her foot bounced like a metronome due to her anxiety.

From her research, she recognized the tall middle-aged man with a slight dusting of gray at his temples the minute he entered the building. His gait was strong and steady, and she couldn't help but admire the way his dark gray suit hugged his lean athletic body.

Without a word, he proceeded past the waiting area and reception desk to the elevators down the hall.

Willing herself to appear unaffected by the handsome millionaire, Sarah checked the contents of her purse while keeping a wary eye on the receptionist. The woman's dark hair, eyes and fuchsia lips were in stark contrast to her pale skin. Had she escaped from a display window on Saks Fifth Avenue?

After several minutes, the phone at the reception desk rang. The mannequin-like secretary hung up the receiver, and in a monotone voice stated, "Ms. Winkelman, Mr. Pendergrass will see you now. His office is on the third floor."

Sarah stood, offered the woman a bright smile and said, "Thank you," then strolled toward the elevators. As the doors slid shut she thought, *I've made it past the gatekeeper. Now to face the dragon.*

* * * *

George stared through the French doors, oblivious to the beautiful seascape below. As owner and CEO, he prided himself on being a problem solver. However, no amount of money could make his daughter want to get better. He rubbed a hand at the tension building at the back of his neck.

I've built this business from the ground up and conquered every obstacle thrown in my way. I've succeeded as a businessman but failed miserably as a father. He sighed.

A sharp knock sounded at his door. George reeled in his thoughts. He wasn't in the mood for this meeting even though he had received several faxes from Miller Electronics in Fort Worth praising Ms.

Winkelman's work.

"Come in." His administrative assistant Paula stepped into the office and held the door open. A willowy blond gracefully stepped around Paula and held out her hand as she approached his desk.

"Mr. Pendergrass, I'm very pleased to meet you."

George drew in a sharp breath and hastened around his desk like an infatuated youth. Offering his hand, he said, "Ms. Winkelman, very nice to meet you. Please have a seat." He gestured to a chair positioned in front of his desk.

"Thank you." She smiled. "Please call me Sarah." Her southern accent floated in the air.

George glanced toward his assistant who stood poised at the door, one jet-black eyebrow arched in objection. "That will be all, Paula."

The woman hesitated, and he struggled to keep a poker face. He wished he could have witnessed Paula's expression when this beautiful southern belle strolled off the elevator.

"I've brought the proposal," Sarah said, breaking into his thoughts. She opened her briefcase and after handing him a folder gracefully lowered herself onto the chair. As if in slow motion, she crossed her right leg over her left, causing her skirt to hike up. He admired her shapely legs and dainty feet. Her blond hair curled under to envelop her slender neck, and wispy bangs were brushed to one side of her face. He swallowed hard.

Taking the folder, George forced himself into his own chair and tried to focus though he would have liked to study her long slender legs a bit longer.

His gaze scanned over the papers. "Very impressive. You've put a lot of time into this project, haven't you?" She shifted slightly, and the scent of jasmine wafted across his desk.

"Thank you. Yes, I have."

"You're very efficient." He shuffled the papers and from under lowered lashes watched her tug on her skirt.

"Thank you." Her voice was confident yet shy. She reached up and nervously played with one earring.

Her action jolted George back to a former time and place. His vision blurred as he pictured his daughter on the high dive, giving her right ear a quick tug, a secret signal between father and daughter. He was surprised that after occupying his every waking moment Abigail had vanished from his mind the moment this woman entered his office.

"Mr. Pendergrass? Are you all right?"

He glanced up. Her brows were arched in a slight frown, her forehead creased with concern.

"Is there anything I can do for you? Should I get your assistant?" She started to rise.

"No, I'm all right." And gave himself a mental shake.

"If this isn't a good time we can reschedule," she offered and reached for her briefcase.

"No, it's fine." Her kindness and concern for him was refreshing. Her brown eyes were dusted with amber flecks, giving them the color of expensive aged whiskey. He wanted to immerse himself in those eyes and drink from their depths. Under their influence, he found himself confiding in her.

"My daughter, my little girl, was injured in an automobile accident a year ago."

"I'm sorry. I didn't know." She shifted forward in her chair, and he copied her movement.

"It left her partially paralyzed, and I'm afraid nothing short of a miracle can help her now." What was it about this woman that made him feel so at ease, so comfortable? He hadn't felt this way in a long time.

"I'm sure you're getting her all the help she needs," Sarah reassured with a slight smile.

"That's the problem. Her doctors claim she could make a significant recovery if she'd follow through with physical therapy." He stood and paced across the floor. "But she refuses to cooperate."

"What do you mean?" She swiveled in her chair to face him. "Doesn't she understand she could get better?"

"I don't know what she thinks anymore. She quit speaking to anyone several months ago." He wandered to the French doors behind his desk and stared out over the empty horizon.

"Is she in a hospital?"

"No, she's at home. We've been to hospitals and institutions all over the country, but she fought everyone who tried to work with her. After several months of getting nowhere, the doctors thought she might respond better at home. She's made it impossible for a therapist to deal with her. I'm afraid my little princess isn't the easiest person to get along with."

"Pardon me for asking, but what does her mother think about all of this? Surely she doesn't allow this sort of behavior?"

Turning around, George shook his head. "My wife passed away several years ago."

"I'm so sorry. All of this must be terribly hard on you."

"My sister lives with us and works with her, but Lily's sixty-eight years old, and it isn't easy for her to move Abigail around."

George's head pounded. He returned to his desk and sank into his chair. The stress of the past few months weighed heavily on his mind. How had he let the meeting get so far off track? What must she think of him?

The room fell silent as George reached for the proposal papers. *Focus*! He told himself.

* * * *

The door opened, and the woman who had greeted Sarah when she stepped off the elevator rushed in. "Sorry to interrupt, but I have a message from your sister. I thought it might be important." She handed Mr. Pendergrass a folded piece of paper.

He opened the note, snickered then stuffed the note in his desk drawer. He glanced up at the woman who had been giving Sarah the once-over and said, "Thank you, Paula." The woman frowned, turned on her heels and sashayed out of the office.

Had she been only marking her territory? The glint in her eye had plainly stated, "Back off, Blondie—he's mine." Sarah couldn't blame the woman for being protective; the infamous Mr. Pendergrass hadn't turned out to be the cutthroat pirate she'd expected. If she was willing to admit to herself, and she wasn't, she wanted to comfort him … whatever that might entail.

"If there's a problem I can reschedule," she said, slipping her purse strap over her shoulder. A strange expression hung on his face for a fraction of a second.

"No, we're fine. Your proposal sounds intriguing. But I'd like to look it over again. Run some numbers."

Sarah rose, handed him her business card and said, "That's fine."

He stood as well. "Thank you for coming in. I'll be in touch."

"Thank you. Very nice to meet you." She shook his hand, and it took all she had to not race for the door. Stiff legs carried her out of his office. She closed the door behind her and leaned against it for support. Thank goodness his guard dog wasn't at her post.

Had Mr. Pendergrass sensed her attraction toward him? *I'll never get the job if he thinks I'm attracted to him. I bet he has several women beating a path to his door.*

Once settled safe and sound in her rented yellow Honda Civic Sarah couldn't shake the image of his troubled face. *What a terrible thing for a parent to go through. His poor little girl, paralyzed.*

Why would she refuse help? The poor little thing must be so confused and terrified with no mother there to love and comfort her. Sarah lost her parents at a young age. But this little girl still had her father, and his love for his daughter was obvious.

Sarah had an idea on how to help. It was a long shot, but it couldn't hurt to call and ask, could it? Her teeth raked over her lower lip. She hadn't spoken with her brother in several months. After that last fiasco, she'd lost all faith in him. This job could be just what he needed to get his career back on course. She took a deep breath, mustered up some courage and dialed the number.

Chapter Two

The phone next to Beau's bed rang. He glanced over and had a moment of apprehension; his sister's cell phone number appeared on the caller ID. Why was she calling him? Their last conversation had ended on a sour note.

"Ginger, get me a cup of coffee will you, darlin'?"

Her lips set in a pout, the voluptuous auburn-haired beauty retrieved Beau's discarded t-shirt and reluctantly crawled off the bed. Taking a deep breath, he reached for the phone.

"Hello."

"Beau, it's Sarah."

Though her voice sounded pleasant, he was still skeptical. "Hey, Sarah, what's up?" He scooted to the side of the bed, swung his legs over the edge, and rested his elbows on his bare knees. "Everything all right?"

"Yes, everything's fine. I was just wondering if you've found a real job yet." *Here it comes.* In her eyes, being an apartment building superintendent wasn't a *real* job. And no, he hadn't found a position at one of the physical therapy clinics. "If not," she continued, "I might have something for you, but it's here in northern California".

What's she doing in northern California? "No. I haven't found anything long-term. What type of work is it?"

"Miller Electronics has been sold to a company in Monterey, and I've been sent to show the owner the sales promotion proposal for Fort Worth. When I met with him this morning he told me that his daughter had been in a serious car accident."

"How old is she?" he asked, all thoughts of past conflicts set aside.

17

"He didn't say, but he called her his 'little girl'—I'm guessing seven, maybe eight years old?"

"Where is she now?"

"She's home with her father and aunt. He said that besides not cooperating with her doctors and therapist she refuses to speak."

"I've heard of that happening sometimes. It really makes recovery that much harder on everyone involved."

"She's been treated at several hospitals, and her doctors say she has a chance at a substantial recovery. It sounds like she's had limited results. What do you think?"

"Have you mentioned me to him?"

"No, I wanted to talk to you first."

"I'm not sure, Sarah." Although the opportunity sounded challenging a thousand questions ran through his mind. He would do anything to be in his sister's good graces again, but he just wasn't sure this was the answer.

"Beau, what do you have to lose?"

He heard the slightest hint of frustration in her voice. He couldn't take the chance at disappointing her again though it seemed to be the one thing he was really good at. As a kid his grandmother encouraged him to become a classical pianist. He had disappointed her and his sister by choosing a career in football. That had only gotten him a body riddled with arthritis and a bum knee, which had put him on the injured list permanently. Disappointment was his middle name.

"Beau, I wouldn't put both of our careers on the line if I didn't think you could do this. This one little girl could open doors for you. Just e-mail me a couple references and a copy of your license. I'll present them to Mr. Pendergrass and see what he says."

"Sarah, it's been a while since I've worked with clients. I'm not sure if this case is the best way to get back into the game." He raked his fingers through his hair. His stomach twisted into knots every time the mess he made of his last job replayed in his mind.

"Beau, this job is a once-in-a-lifetime opportunity. If you help this girl you could regain your respect and re-establish your career. If anyone can get through to her you can."

"Thanks for the vote of confidence, but I'm not sure I'm ready to take on something like this." At his age, he couldn't afford any more mistakes. But she was right; this was a great opportunity for him, and he couldn't sit on the sidelines forever.

After she hung up, he listened to the silence, then whispered, "If he's willing to give me a chance you won't be sorry this time, Sarah. I promise."

His heart slammed against his ribs. This job could really kick off his career. He glanced around the empty undecorated bedroom. Besides, there was nothing holding him here in Texas. He was a free agent.

* * * *

George reclined behind the desk in his office and for the hundredth time mulled over his conversation from the day before with Sarah Winkelman, a very intriguing young woman. Had he only imagined the compassion in her voice? The concern in her eyes? Her image had kept him awake most of the night.

A soft knock sounded at his office door. "Come in."

It was Sarah. She wore a light blue sweater and skirt that flattered her slim figure. George's heart sped up. He smiled, stood and rounded the desk as she approached him.

"Good morning, Ms. Winkelman. How are you today?"

"Very well, thank you, but please call me Sarah."

"Please have a seat." He pulled back a chair in front of his desk. Did they have an appointment today? "I'm glad you stopped by." He glanced toward the door. "How did you ... I mean wasn't ... Never mind."

He glanced at the briefcase on her lap. "So what have you got for me today?"

Sarah offered a shy grin and handed him a folder. "After I left yesterday I couldn't help but think about your daughter. An idea came to me. I hope you don't mind, but I made a call to my brother in Texas. He's a physical therapist, and I mentioned her to him."

She fidgeted with the hem of her sweater.

George leafed through the information, and after several moments, he closed the folder. He laid it on his desk, leaned back in his chair and templed his fingers. Not only had she presented him with a great marketing plan, it appeared she brought him a miracle accompanied by a stack of references from some of the biggest names in the football industry.

He watched her as she took in her surroundings. She was fascinating.

"I've heard of your brother. He has quite a reputation in professional sports."

"Yes. Well, he hasn't played football in a few years."

"I followed his college career for some time. I have to admit I lost track of him after his injury."

She sighed. "He went through several surgeries and spent months in physical therapy, building his strength back up."

"He had quite the promising career ahead of him."

She nodded her head in agreement and relaxed into the chair.

George's mind wandered as he studied her. He would bet she was a country girl. He could picture her barefoot. *Why can't I stay focused?*

"After the injury he found his true calling. I mean, helping people recover from their own injuries." She squirmed in her seat and gave her hands a quick glance. "He's talked about opening his own clinic and specializing in treating professional athletes."

George leaned forward in his chair. "I'd think there'd be a need for that." He tapped the file on his desk. "His references are impressive. You really feel he can help my daughter?"

"Yes, I do." Her big brown eyes sparkled, and a sassy grin played across her lips. "Besides, what do you have to lose?"

He wanted to believe in this man as strongly as Sarah did. She was right. What did he have to lose?

"I've nearly lost my little girl. I'm afraid her time may be running out."

He stood, walked around the desk and then leaned back against it. "I'll take your brother into consideration," he said, folding his arms across his chest. "Let's get back to business for a moment. Last night I reviewed your proposal, and I like your concept. I also like what you've done in Fort Worth, and I think you'd be a great asset as Vice President of Marketing here at PTI. Of course, you'll oversee both Phoenix and Fort Worth. Congratulations."

"Oh!" He grinned at her surprise. "Thank you," she replied as her smile spread.

"You will also accompany me to Phoenix and Fort Worth." Her face paled, and he added, "It's just a formality ... a few meetings."

Before George could stop himself, he said, "Are you free to come by for dinner this evening? I have a couple of suggestions for your sales plan. And you can meet my sister Lily and my daughter Abigail."

Sarah nodded. "I'd like that." She stood and slid the briefcase strap up over her shoulder.

He jotted down his address and directions to his home then handed her the paper. "Do you think you'll have any problems finding it? I could send a car to pick you up."

Sarah glanced at the paper. "No, that won't be necessary. I'm pretty good with directions. What time?"

"Six o'clock?"

"That's fine."

He walked her to the door. Once she was gone his office felt empty, and it made him surprisingly lonely.

* * * *

Later as George climbed the stairs to his daughter's room, his enthusiastic mood faded. Now that he had decided to hire Beau, he worried about his daughter and how she would handle his hiring yet another therapist and the fact that he would soon be leaving on a business trip.

He paused outside her opened door. She lay on her back with her eyes closed. She looked so pale and fragile. "Abigail?" He eased closer to the bed. "Honey, are you asleep?"

She opened her eyes. He leaned forward and placed a kiss on her forehead then eased himself into the chair next to her bed. "Hi, princess. How are you feeling today?"

Eyes that looked too large for her thin face studied him. He hesitated, then cleared his throat. "I have some news. I've hired a new therapist." Abby closed her eyes and turned her face away. George's heart sunk to the pit of his stomach. This wasn't going to be easy on any of them.

"Abigail, listen to me." She didn't move. "Look at me, please," he commanded gently. She turned her head, her face masked in a blank stare. "Honey." He schooled his voice, scooted closer to the bed and reached for her hand. "Just meet..." She closed her eyes again.

George took a breath and prayed for patience. He would give all his money, everything he owned, to have time roll back to before that horrible day when so many lives had changed.

"There's more," he continued, knowing that what he had to say wasn't going to be accepted well. "The takeover of Miller Electronics has been successful. I'll be leaving in a few days." Her eyes shot open, and he saw panic in their depths. She knew the drill; these takeovers always took him away for weeks at a time. "I know this is the first time we'll be apart since you've been back home. I hate the idea of leaving you, but these meetings can't be rescheduled."

Her eyes filled with tears.

"Honey, everything will be all right."

Abby's eyes closed, and tears slid down her cheeks. George hung his head. He hated the idea of leaving her, but if truth-be-told, he needed to get away.

* * * *

Sarah felt relieved that Mr. Pendergrass was considering Beau. This job could really help him, but she was worried. This time it wasn't just his life and job on line but hers too. If he failed, George would blame her, and both of their careers would be over.

But everything was going to work out. Abigail was a young child; George's wife was gone. There wouldn't be anyone there to distract Beau or tempt him. He couldn't screw this one up.

She glanced down at her simply tailored tan dress and hoped she looked all right. She reminded herself that this wasn't anything other than a business dinner, though the idea of spending time alone with George outside of work had crossed her mind several times. He was quite charming.

Sarah stopped in front of a large marble entrance monument, which read Pendergrass. Monstrous black wrought iron gates hung open in welcome. Taking a deep breath, she proceeded up the winding drive passing large flowering bushes, tropical plants and a variety of trees. The trees thinned, and she saw an enormous modern style glass and metal two-story house, which resembled artwork more than a home. The structure was built on a ridgeline between the coastal highway and the cliffs overlooking the Pacific Ocean.

She let out a long breath and killed the engine. *I'm so far out of my league.*

She glanced around the gorgeous yard that could easily belong to an exclusive resort then exited her car and strolled toward the house. Once under the large glass overhang, she glanced back to her car and felt a sudden urge to run. Nervous, she tucked a lock of blond hair behind her ear and rang the doorbell. A moment later without making a sound the etched glass door opened.

"I like that," George said glancing at his watch. "You're right on time. Please come in."

She stood in awe of her surroundings. Rectangular crystals dangled from the gigantic chandelier that hung directly above a round glass-topped table. In the center of the table, a crystal vase held a lavish bouquet of fresh spring flowers. To her right a solid glass staircase rose out of the marble floor and ascended to the upper level. To her left double doors to the great room stood open. Full-length windows framed the lush landscape. A low backed sofa and Asian coffee table sat upon honey colored bamboo floors. Hoping George hadn't noticed her gawking, she turned her attention back to him. His slight grin told her he'd been watching her. She clutched her purse strap and said, "You have a beautiful home, Mr. Pendergrass."

"Please. I thought we were past that. Call me George."

Placing his hand on the curve of her back, he escorted her down the hall and into a brightly lit kitchen, which held a breathtaking view of the ocean. The walls were painted a light yellow, a strange but complimentary shade to the contemporary design. Gray-black Italian marble counter-tops housed stainless steel appliances.

A petite woman with short brown hair was busy at the counter preparing something that smelled wonderful. Sarah prayed her stomach wouldn't betray her by making a rude noise. Nervous about this evening, she had skipped lunch.

"Hi, you must be Sarah. Welcome," the woman replied as she moved about the room.

"We don't have many guests. It's only George and me, so we eat all of our meals family style. I hope you don't mind."

"Oh, no. That's perfectly fine with me." Lily stopped fussing long enough for George to make the introductions.

"Sarah, this bundle of energy is my sister, Lily Bendickson. She is an angel and a lifesaver. If I didn't have..."

"Oh, stop it, George. You're embarrassing me." Lily cut him off with a wave of her hand. "Truth be known, I have nowhere else to go, so he's stuck with me." She handed George a plate of chicken and pointed toward the grill out on the patio.

"I'm very happy to meet you, Lily. Is there anything I can do to help?" Sarah asked, looking around the large but well-organized kitchen. She noted a slight Asian influence in this room as well. A cobalt blue and white porcelain teapot with matching cups and a blue and white hand-painted porcelain bowl sat on one counter.

"If you'd like, you can fill those glasses with iced tea." Lily pointed toward the refrigerator.

Sarah retrieved a crystal pitcher and filled the glasses. She prayed her nervousness didn't show.

She sat at the table and sipped her cool drink as she glanced out the window. Beyond George, the tennis court and the pool lay a spectacular view of the ocean.

What a place!

"So, Sarah, are you married? Have you ever been married?" Lily asked, setting a dish of steaming mixed vegetables on the table. *He sure is surrounded by protective women.* The inquisitive little woman returned to the stove, removed the empty pans and placed them in the sink. She then turned and smiled, clearly expecting an answer.

Sarah cleared her throat; her cheeks turned warm. "No, I have never been married."

"I've been married three times! Loved them all, but they couldn't keep up." She winked. "You know what I mean?"

Sarah wasn't sure, but she didn't think anyone could have been able to keep up with this pint-sized dynamo. She smiled at the thought of this little live wire wearing out three husbands. "How long have you lived here with George and his daughter?"

"Let me see. Frank passed away four years ago. I lived alone for the first year, but our house was too large for just me. Then George asked me to come and stay with him and Abby until I knew where I wanted to live. Well, time has a way of running away if you don't keep an eye on it." She wiped her hands on her apron. Her voice wavered, and she added "And after Abby's accident..."

Sarah sensed the woman's frustration, and her heart went out to her.

Lily returned to her work at the counter. Sarah's gaze traveled around the room again. On the far wall hung four Asian symbol trivets, and she spied cookbooks from several different regions of the world.

Lily placed a garden salad in the middle of the table. "There! I haven't been able to fuss over a meal in a long time."

Sarah smiled in appreciation. "It all looks delicious. I feel like I should be doing more to help you."

"Oh, no. Everything is under control. We're just waiting on George and the chicken." Lily perched herself on the edge of a chair at the table.

"I don't mean to pry," Sarah hesitated. "But do you run this huge house all by yourself?"

"Land-sakes, no." Lily chuckled. "Once a week a team of people show up to clean the house from top to bottom and help with the gardening." She waved her hand through the air. "We even have a pool boy," she winked. "It gets pretty busy around here at times."

Sarah took another sip of her tea and asked, "But only the three of you live here—in the house?"

"Yes. Abigail isn't comfortable having strangers in the house."

Sarah wondered how Abigail was going to react to Beau living here. His size alone might be overwhelming to a small child.

"George tells me you're from Texas." Lily's question interrupted her thoughts. "Where did you grow up?"

"In Fort Worth." *In an old run down trailer court with my brother and grandmother.*

As if on cue, George returned, interrupting the inquisition. "I hope you're hungry." He set the plate on the table.

The food tasted wonderful, and the conversation was light and cheerful, but Sarah's nervous stomach wouldn't allow her to eat much. All through dinner, she thought about meeting George's daughter. First impressions were very important. Though her experience was somewhat limited when it came to children, she had always gotten along well with them. But small children were sometimes unpredictable. Soon enough she would know just what Daddy's "little girl" thought about her.

As Sarah and George followed Lily up the glass staircase Lily rattled off bits and pieces of the house's history. "This house was built by a retired film director in the late sixties. His wife hadn't cared for the seclusion." Lily turned and smiled. "So they moved back to Hollywood." Overwhelmed, Sarah could only nod in reply.

The evening sun streamed through extravagant, full-length windows that followed the curve of the staircase. On the landing of the second floor, George paused. "There are four suites, two on each side. Each suite contains a sitting area, bedroom with a balcony, an attached bath and a walk-in closet."

Sarah returned his smile and hoped her astonishment was masked.

Still chattering, Lilly hurried ahead of them into one of the suites. Sarah began to follow but was drawn back to the window and the magnificent view of the sunset on the ocean. It was like nothing she had ever seen before. She caught herself daydreaming and turned to find George watching her. "Sorry. The view is fantastic from up here." She knew she blushed.

"Yes, the view from here is amazing." Gazing out the window he added, "Abby and I used to sit here at night before I tucked her in. We'd talk about anything and everything. She's the light of my life."

Sarah smiled. Her heart ached for the man and the terrible situation he and his family was in.

"Are you ready to meet my little angel?"

* * * *

Abby glanced toward the door when her aunt rushed into the room and approached the bed.

"You'll like Ms. Winkelman. She's a very nice woman." She repositioned Abby's pillows.

Abby felt like an exhibit in a freak show. Earlier her aunt had washed, combed and fussed over her until she was poised like one of her porcelain dolls on display. She'd gone on and on about the new therapist her father hired.

Everyone is getting their hopes up for nothing. Why don't they realize nothing can change the facts? I'm never going to get better. I don't deserve to get better. They need to accept me as I am.

She glanced around the room. This was her life … this room and this hospital bed. They would only be disappointed again once this therapist got fed up and left. Maybe then, they would understand it had all been a waste of time and money. There wasn't anything anyone could do to change her life from what it had become.

Just then, her father and a woman entered her room. The woman appeared startled and confused.

"Abigail, this is Sarah Winkelman," her father said.

The woman stepped forward, and her features softened. "It's very nice to meet you," she said, her voice kind and gentle. Her soft brown eyes seemed to search the depths of Abby's soul. "You have a lovely room." Then she spied the china hutch that held the porcelain doll collection. "Very impressive collection," she said, stepping forward for a closer look.

Sarah's gaze swept across the room, coming to rest on the shelves of swimming and tennis trophies. "You must have been an excellent tennis player. I use to play myself, but I haven't been able to find the time..."

Realizing her mistake, she chewed on her lower lip. "I'm so sorry! I never meant ... Please forgive me."

"Don't worry about it," George replied. "Abby knows you didn't mean any harm."

Her father walked to the woman's side, put his arm around her shoulder and spoke softly to comfort her. Then he gently ushered her out of the room.

Abby frowned and turned her head toward the wall. Why wasn't he concerned with her feelings instead of those of a stranger? Why wasn't he upset about the woman's insensitive remark?

Well, that was just fine. She didn't want her father, or anyone for that matter, fussing over her.

Lily waited until Sarah and George were out of earshot before approaching her niece.

"You could have done something to reassure that nice young woman that she hadn't hurt your feelings." Lily waited for some kind of response.

"Look at me, young lady. I know you better than that. I know you wouldn't want her to leave here feeling guilty." Again, she waited, and then it dawned on her. "I get it. You thought if your father believed you were really hurt by her remark he'd make her leave."

Abby turned back, her face expressionless. *Does Abby think Sarah is the new therapist? If she does, the girl's in for a surprise.* Gently Lily reached over and pushed the short brown hair back from her niece's face.

"Don't concern yourself with Sarah Winkelman. She won't be around to bother you." *Was that a look of triumph in her niece's eyes?*

"No, she's not your new therapist, honey. Her brother is," Lily added with a smile. An expression that landed somewhere between horror and panic flashed across Abigail's face.

"You get some sleep, dear. I'll be back to check on you." Lily lowered the bed and pulled up the covers. Leaning over, she gently kissed the girl's forehead. She closed the window and then left the room.

Lily hurried to her own room and closed the door behind her. Quickly making the sign of the cross, she looked up. "I'm sorry, Lord. But that girl needed her cage rattled good and hard! I just hope this Mr. Winkelman has a tougher hide than his sister."

* * * *

Sitting on the patio by the pool Sarah rolled her glass of iced tea between her hands. She felt terrible. She couldn't believe what she had said to the poor girl. She had been stunned to find a woman lying in the bed instead of a young child, and the remark had just slipped out.

"Sarah," George hedged "What's the matter? You're not having second thoughts, are you? You don't think there's going to be a problem, do you?"

Problem? Yeah, this could definitely be a problem. It could also be the end of my career. All this time she thought Abby was a little girl. She even made Beau believe it. What was she going to do now? She didn't dare admit her fears to George. She hoped Abby was younger than she appeared or was that just wishful thinking on her part? Had she set Beau up to fail?

She glanced around the yard to the pool and tennis court; obviously, the girl hadn't gone without much in her life. If she was, just being bullheaded Sarah could see why George had a hard time finding someone to work with her.

Beau was definitely the right person to get through to her. There weren't too many people more stubborn or more determined than her brother. He could be pretty tough and demanding when he wanted to be. Sarah laughed at the thought of the two of them locking horns. Chihuahua vs. Great Dane.

Sarah turned to face George and saw concern in his eye. "There won't be a problem. I was just surprised. I thought your daughter was much younger, that's all. Just how old is she?"

"She'll be twenty-four this September."

"What was she like? Before her accident?" She raised her glass and sipped her tea.

George paused and glanced toward the house for a second. "I guess she was like every other girl." He sighed. "Of course, she was spoiled from the minute she was born. My wife had several miscarriages before and after Abigail's birth. As a matter of fact, Shirley died from complications after having a miscarriage."

He glanced toward the house once more. "Shirley was five months along when she started to hemorrhage. I rushed her to the hospital, and they did all they could, but they couldn't control the bleeding. She lost the baby then died later that same day. Abby was only five years old."

Sarah reached across the table and placed her hand over his. Her fingers curled into his palm, and she squeezed gently.

"That was a long time ago," he said. "As you can see, Abby hasn't wanted for anything."

"George, I know my brother will be able to get through to her. He has a way," she paused, "about him." She had almost said a way with women. She didn't know a woman that hadn't responded to him.

"I'm glad to hear it. How soon do you think he can get here?"

"He said he only needed two weeks to get his affairs in order." Why did she have to say *affairs*? She grimaced inside but offered him a sweet smile.

"That will be perfect. We'll leave for Phoenix after he gets settled." George gave her a quick smile. "Does that work for you?"

"That's fine. I'll call him tonight and find out exactly when he'll arrive. I'll call your office Monday morning to let you know." She stood up to leave. George walked her to the kitchen door. Lily was just coming out to join them.

"Are you leaving so soon?"

"Yes, I'm afraid so. I have so much to do before we leave town. Thank you so such for the delicious dinner. You're a wonderful cook."

"I'm glad you enjoyed it. It was nice to meet you, Sarah. I'm really looking forward to meeting your brother."

They both walked Sarah to the front door, but before they said their goodbyes, Lily asked Sarah, "How old did you say your brother was?"

Just a few more steps and she would have been home free. Would his age be a problem? Sarah pasted a confident smile on her face. "Beau is thirty."

"Oh," Lily replied dryly. Her expression told Sarah nothing of what the woman was thinking.

The air thickened with tension. "Well, thank you again. It was very nice to meet you." She reached out and shook Lily's hand then George's. She hurried to her car, turned and forced a smile and waved goodbye.

As soon as the door closed, Lily turned her full attention on her brother. "Did you know he was only thirty?"

George put his arm around her shoulder. "Now, sis, don't go worrying your beads. Everything is going to be just fine." He leaned down and kissed her cheek, but the gesture didn't pacify her one bit.

"And what's this about the two of you leaving town?" She folded her arms in front of her and waited for his reply. She liked Sarah, and it was quite obvious how George felt about the woman.

* * * *

Abby listened as Sarah's car drove down the driveway. It was funny how she could hear things she had never heard before. Her senses, especially her hearing, had been heightened since her accident.

She sighed and glanced around her room. She was frustrated and confused. Who was this man her aunt had talked about? The thought of some big ugly guy's hands touching her made her ill. She couldn't stop him from coming, but how long would he stay? *What will he do if I can't do the things he wants me to? Dr. Voight is the only one who truly understands my condition. He knows there is little hope for recovery. He knows therapy isn't helping me.*

She turned her head toward the window. A slight glow from the setting sun painted a streak of reddish-orange across the sky. Abby never had problems sleeping before, but since returning from the hospital, she felt isolated in her room. Sometimes her imagination wandered, and she envisioned someone walking around in the other rooms or coming up the stairs. She worried about someone breaking into the house at night especially when her father worked late. Her little aunt was no match for an intruder.

She glanced toward the dim lamp across the room that created shadows that danced on the ceiling and walls. Maybe having a man in the house at night while her father was gone wasn't such a bad idea after all.

Feeling more at ease Abby drifted off to sleep. It wasn't long before the nightmares crept back through the thin cracks in her subconscious.

* * * *

Beau sprawled on the sofa, reading over the contract his sister faxed him. The balmy evening breeze blew through the open sliding glass door. It was warm for May, which promised a hot and humid summer for Texas.

Setting the papers down, he rose and ambled into the kitchen. His six-foot-four frame filled the cramped space. Reaching into the refrigerator, he pulled out another Corona and twisted off the cap. Dropping a lime slice into it, he whirled the bottle a couple of times and took a long drink. Condensation dripped from the chilled bottle onto his bare chest and slid down, pooling at the waistband of his cut-off jeans.

Returning to the sofa, he picked up the papers and reread the contract and the attached paper that outlined additional terms—Sarah's *terms*. It was obvious she didn't want a repeat of his past.

This was his chance to make it up to her, to prove she could trust him again. He would do everything in his power to help this little girl make a substantial recovery and to make Sarah proud of him once more.

Later Beau reclined on the sofa, watching a college football game on the television. A soft knock sounded at his door. He opened the door to find Ginger standing in the hallway wearing a big smile and little else. One hand held a six-pack of Corona, the other played with the hem of her tight fitting tank top.

He treated her to one of his slow one-sided smiles that she loved and could never resist. His smile was all the invitation she needed. She giggled, and as she wiggled past him into his apartment as he reached out and grabbed one pert little cheek. He glanced down the hallway to see if anyone observed his "forward pass" of the "tight end" and laughed to himself. Football wasn't going to be the only thing he would miss when he moved away from Texas.

31

Chapter Three

Dr. William Voight exited Monterey Bay General Hospital. The graveyard shift in the emergency room had been long and quiet for a Friday night which gave him ample time to review the progress of his carefully calculated plan. He hurried to his old Buick sedan and hoped no one would see him get into the rust bucket, then headed for the nearest exit.

When he turned thirty-four a few months ago, he had taken a long look at his financial state and decided it was time to turn things around. He had made a few bad investments, but once his strategic plan as "solicitous and benevolent doctor" fell into place it wouldn't be long before he would have everything he had ever wanted. He would pay off his student loans and move from the run-down resident's apartment building that he'd been forced to live in to the grand house perched high on the cliffs of Big Sur. He smirked.

He may have grown up on the wrong side of town, but soon everyone would be looking at Dr. William Voight differently. *They will revere me as a hero.*

Will smiled as he drove down the highway. The cool fresh morning air revived him, and he tapped his fingers on the steering wheel, keeping time with the radio. By the time he arrived at his apartment, he had decided to take a quick shower and make a surprise visit to his favorite patient. It was time to activate the first phase of his plan.

He would stop and pick up some flowers for her along with a bottle of Dom Perignon for her father. If he were lucky, he would acquire an invitation to stay for the day. He envisioned a poolside lunch, a game of tennis, then a dip in the pool, followed by one of Lily's wonderful dinners. A perfect day.

He would be the doting doctor and prospective son-in-law. And although Abigail couldn't speak to him he would have the day to spend time with and visit with Mr. Pen ... George.

He grinned. Not only did the man own a successful company, he held shares in several multi-national companies around the world along with a position on the board of Monterey Bay General Hospital.

* * * *

Abby experienced another restless night. She hadn't fallen asleep until late, but once she did, the nightmares had taken over. By morning, she was exhausted. Her head pounded, and her body ached.

A noise from the hall drew her attention as her aunt waltzed through the door with a tray of food. Without making eye contact, Lily set the tray down and instinctively started fussing with Abby's pillows and bed.

"Did your father tell you about the business trip he has planned?" she said, shaking her head. "He and Ms. Winkelman are going to Phoenix and Fort Worth. They'll be gone for several weeks."

Abby heard the discontent in her aunt's voice.

"It's been a long time since your father has gone away on business. But don't worry. They won't leave until her brother, Mr. Beauregard Winkelman, arrives and is all settled in."

Beauregard? He sounds like a real prize. Abby rolled her eyes. *What did they call him as a kid? Bullwinkle?*

"Sarah is very fond of her brother, and she's confident that he'll be able to help you," Lily said as she fussed about the room. "She says he's quite capable."

With a name like that, he would have to be.

Lily rambled on as she fed Abby her breakfast.

The idea of her father and Ms. Winkelman leaving on a trip together left a sour taste in Abby's mouth. How long had he known her? She couldn't recall him ever mentioning the woman's name before. Were they just business associates? Friends? Or could it possibly be that her father had feelings for this person? The notion made her stomach turn. She didn't welcome change unless it was *her* idea. Her father would be off traveling, going to parties and entertaining guests over dinner, while she lay here, her arms and legs being manipulated by some loser with a funny name.

* * * *

George started up the stairs to check in on his daughter. The doorbell rang, and he glanced up the stairs and sighed. It wasn't like she was going to speak to him anyway. He answered the front door and was pleased to find Dr. William Voight standing across the threshold. The doctor held a large bouquet of flowers and a bottle of Dom Perignon.

"Hi, Will. Come on in." He motioned the young doctor into the foyer. "It's been a while since we've seen you." George patted him on the shoulder. "I've been getting good reports from the hospital about you."

Will smiled and handed George the champagne. "I've been putting in some long hours. But I have the rest of the day off, and I wanted to stop by and check on my favorite patient. How is she doing today?"

George shook his head and glanced toward the staircase. "Let's go into the great room. I have something I'd like to discuss with you." George led the way through the French doors. He gestured for Will to sit in one of the brown leather chairs before making himself comfortable in the other one.

He cleared his throat. "I'm going out of town on a business trip for a few weeks. I've hired a new physical therapist to work with Abigail. He'll be moving in before I leave."

Will leaned forward in his chair, his brow creased with apparent concern. George raised his hand before the doctor could speak. "Don't worry. This man comes highly recommended."

"Who is he? Is he from around here?"

"He's from Fort Worth, Texas."

"How old is this guy?"

"He's thirty." George knew that Will's foremost concerns centered on leaving Abigail virtually unsupervised with the man and the amount of close and physical contact they would be sharing. He had thought long and hard on these issues himself. He interrupted Will's next question. "Your thoughts have already crossed my mind, and I've been reassured that there won't be any problems."

"Good," Will said, settling into his chair. "I'm glad that you've outfitted your home with personal monitors. If there's a problem during the night or anytime—" He glanced at the bouquet. "I mean, your sister would know about it."

George agreed. He knew the young doctor had feelings for his daughter. He was relieved Will had taken the news of the man moving into the house better than he expected.

George stood. "You know I'm counting on you to stop by while I'm gone to check on my girls." He glanced at the bottle of wine and grinned. "I'll get a vase for those flowers then we'll go on up to see Abigail. I'll be right back."

Will smiled triumphantly. He didn't need a reason to stop by now. He would be the man of the house while George was gone. *I could get used to that role.* His gaze swept around the great room and landed on the grand piano. He didn't play, but he would keep the monstrosity as a token of his achievements. He didn't care for the strange wood grain on the piano. It would look snazzy painted black though.

He intended to get rid of the Asian hand painted eggs, the jade Fu Dogs and Buddha statues. He stood and walked to the bookcase. Next to a stack of travel guidebooks of Beijing, Shanghai, China sat a funny little ceramic figurine of an old man with an overly large forehead and long beard, holding a long staff and a peach. *Who liked this sort of stuff? It looks as if it all came from a flea market.* He did like the large ceramic planters that were planted with tall Coloradans and the cat palms nesting in the corners.

He loved the ocean front location, the enormous size of the house and property and what they symbolized—wealth privilege and prestige.

Strolling into the hall, he checked his appearance in the large gold leaf framed mirror. He liked George, and now he knew the feeling was mutual. He was elated that the old man had shared something important with him and valued his opinion. It proved his confidence in him.

His smile turned into a frown. He didn't like the idea of a strange man moving into the house. Fortunately, the timing fit well with the next stage of his plan.

The doorbell rang. He turned and pulled the door open. He was both surprised and pleased at what he discovered.

"How beautiful! Are those for me?" The woman smiled and nodded at the bouquet of flowers he still held.

Dumbfounded, Will stared into the biggest prettiest brown eyes he had ever seen. She was tall and slender, her blond hair framing her captivating face. Who was she? Before he had a chance to ask, George appeared at his side.

"Sarah? Hi! Please come in." A boyish grin flashed across the older man's face. "Dr. William Voight, let me introduce the new Vice President of Marketing at PTI, Sarah Winkelman."

Will smiled and held out his hand. "Very nice to meet you, Ms. Winkelman."

"Thank you, Dr. Voight. Are you Abigail's doctor?" Before he could answer, George interrupted.

"Yes, as a matter of fact, Will was in the emergency room the day of her accident. He pulled a triple shift that day to make sure my baby was given the best of care." He slapped Will on the back. "He never left her side."

"Surely, Dr. Voight, if George has his way, you'll be up for sainthood. I'm honored to meet you." There was a slight southern accent to her voice, and her eyes twinkled when she smiled. Turning her attention to George she said, "I was shopping for our trip and found something for Abby." She held up a gift bag. "Would you mind if I went up and gave it to her?"

"Well, this is Abby's lucky day—two visitors and both bearing gifts. We were just about to go up." George shoved the vase at Will, and several droplets of water splashed onto his shirt. George took Sarah's elbow and started up the stairs.

New Vice President of Marketing! Will had to hand it to him; the old man had good taste. When he reached the second floor landing, he found George and Sarah standing at the window, their heads together, whispering. George looked up, and Will winked at him. Not wanting to interrupt them, he knocked once then entered Abby's bedroom.

Lily noticed the beautiful bouquet of flowers. "Oh, look, honey," she said. Taking the vase, she held the flowers for Abby to see. "Aren't these beautiful?" She crossed the room and set the vase on a walnut desk. "I'll put them right here so you can always see them."

Will moved closer to the bed and smiled at Abby. There were dark shadows under her eyes. "How are you today?" He reached out and took her hand. "You look a little pale. It's a nice warm day. Would you like for me to carry you down stairs and out onto the patio for a while?" he asked, hoping he didn't sound overly anxious.

She blinked twice which meant no. She glanced toward the door and saw her father and Ms. Winkelman in the doorway. Abby's jaw muscles tensed; her mouth fixed into a thin line.

Sarah's smile faded as a look of uncertainty crossed her face.

This wasn't their first meeting. The interaction between the two women should be fascinating. Will smirked, but only to himself.

Cautiously Sarah walked up to the bed and gently placed the present next to Abby's leg. Multicolored tissue paper poked daintily out the top of the shiny silver gift bag.

"I saw this today, and it made me think of you. I hope you like it."

"Isn't that wonderful, dear?" Lily said as she eagerly reached into the gift bag. Lily lifted the peach colored bed-jacket out of the bag and held it against her chest. "Oh, this is beautiful! I think this color will look nice on you. Would you like to try it on?"

Abby's gaze stayed on Sarah. Her father reached out and took Sarah's hand. A sharp pain struck Abby's chest; she closed her eyes and turned her face away.

Lily reached over and picked up the bag. "Maybe later. I'm sure you're tired. We just finished a therapy session," Lily informed everyone.

Will glanced from Abby to Lily. "I hear you have a new therapist moving in soon."

"Yes," Lily said dryly, placing the bed jacket on an ivory colored cushioned hanger. "Did George tell you that the therapist was also Sarah's brother?" Her only expression was a slight pursing of her lips. For some reason, Lily wasn't in favor of this new therapist.

Surprised, Will's gaze traveled to George and Sarah and then back to Abby. Although her eyes were closed, the grim line of her mouth showed her displeasure. Was it the color of the bed jacket, the idea of a new therapist or the fact that her father was fawning all over the young woman? The woman who just happened to be the new Vice President of Marketing.

Sarah took a step backwards. "I think I'd better go. Nice to meet you, Dr. Voight. Nice to see you again, Miss Lily."

Abby's eyes flashed open. Her gaze shot to her father's hand then to Sarah's face. Will witnessed the quick exchange between the two women. A definite message passed between them. A warning? Sarah tugged her hand from George's grip and exited the room. George frowned and followed her.

What was going on here? Will understood George's attraction to the pretty blond. He understood her attraction to George and his money. He even understood Abby's adverse reaction toward her father with a young woman. What he couldn't understand was Lily's disapproval toward the new therapist. Just what was it about this guy that she didn't like?

Lily barged in front of Will, causing him to step back from the bed. She pulled Abby forward and roughly fluffed her pillow.

"You burn too many bridges, girl, and you'll end up stranded in a place you don't want to be. I'm going to my room." She turned to face Will. "You talk some sense into her. I'm getting too old for these kinds of games."

Will could still hear the little woman grumbling as she headed down the hall. With an ally like Lily on his side, he might only have to *slightly* shuffle his plans around.

He turned his attention back to Abby. A lone tear slowly slid down her cheek. He leaned over and using his thumb gently wiped it away.

Pulling a chair close to the bed, he sat down, reached for her hand and gently caressed the frail fragile appendage. She gazed up at him, her blue eyes reflecting pools of anguish and confusion.

"Don't worry about your father, Abigail. I doubt he has any real feelings for her. I assure you this will all blow over very soon. As for your new therapist, your father told me all about him. I'll stop by as often as I can while your father's away." He kissed the back of her hand. "I won't let him push you too hard. What's best for you is to take things slow and easy. There's no need to push yourself and cause any new injuries." He brushed the hair back from her forehead. "Don't you worry about anything, darling. I'll take care of everything."

Abby glanced up at Will. Had he been right about her father? Was this just an affair? As far as she knew, he'd never had one before. She admitted she'd pushed her father away, but had she pushed him too far?

Her heart ached at the thought that they would never be close again. She had had him to herself for so many years; would she be forced to give him up now?

She'd never been with a man, and it didn't look like she ever would. Yet she had a pretty good idea what her father had been missing in his life. He was still a youthful fifty-four. This woman could come between her and her father. Could Sarah make him forget her completely? A fist tightened around her heart. Her father was leaving her for another woman. It was imminent; everyone she had ever loved had left her. First her mother, then Carolyn, and now her father.

* * * *

"Here, drink this." George handed Sarah a tall glass of iced tea. "It will make you feel better." Sarah took a sip.

It had started out to be such a nice day. She had awakened early and made a list of what she needed for her trip. While shopping she had found the pretty bed jacket and thought Abby would like it. Yet Abby acted as if she despised it and Sarah. Abby's behavior puzzled her. Was the girl jealous of the time her father was going to spend with her, or was this just a game? Maybe she enjoyed making people uncomfortable. Maybe she wanted everyone to feel her unhappiness.

She couldn't tell George what she suspected. Her teeth bit her bottom lip. *He would never understand or believe his "little princess" could behave in such a manner.*

"I know it's hard to see her lying there," he said interrupting her thoughts. "You'll get used to it. Besides, I have high hopes that your brother will work his magic on her. Even though I'm still too young I had hoped one day I'd get to be a grandfather."

She wanted to comfort him. She couldn't imagine what this past year must have been like for him. "George, it will be okay," she said reaching for his hand. "Beau can work miracles. I guarantee it."

After only meeting Abby twice, she knew her brother had his work cut out for him. He would need nothing less than a miracle to get through to her especially if all of this was just a game to her.

* * * *

39

Hidden from view in the kitchen, Will studied the couple on the patio. He had taken George for a much smarter man. Why wasn't he realizing his preoccupation with this woman was hurting his daughter?

He couldn't help but wonder what Ms. Winkelman was really up to. His hands clinched into fists. It was one thing to entertain the boss in hopes of get a promotion. But if the woman set her sights on something more, that would definitely throw a wrench in his plans. Will wasn't about to let that happen. Too much was at stake to permit some *skirt* to waltz in and take it all away from him.

Lily entered the kitchen. "Oh, Dr. Voight, you're still here? It's so beautiful today. I had hoped you could've talked Abby into coming downstairs. The sun would have done wonders for her."

"Yes, that would have been nice. I'd never pass up the opportunity to hold a pretty girl in my arms." He winked and grinned at Lily, and she laughed.

"Can I offer you a glass of iced tea?" She pulled open the fridge door, retrieved the crystal pitcher of iced tea and poured herself a glass.

"Actually I was just going out to say goodbye."

"Oh. I'm so glad you stopped by. We all look forward to your visits, and the flowers were beautiful. You're so sweet."

He'd been hoping for a dinner invitation. Disappointed, he turned back toward the window. "Looks like they're discussing something important. I'll talk to George before he leaves town. It was nice to see you again." Lilly set her glass on the table and turned in the direction of the hallway, prepared to see the doctor out. Will waved a hand toward the table and said, "You sit. I can find my own way out." Heading for the foyer, he paused at the glass staircase leading to the second floor and glanced upward.

Yeah, he would keep a close eye on things while Daddy was off amusing himself with the help.

* * * *

Beau's landlord relinquished his lease and job without notice. With summer around the corner, he informed Beau he would have no trouble replacing him.

It hadn't taken Beau long to pack. Boxes of all sizes from the liquor store lined the bed of his red Ford pickup truck. He entertained the thought of checking out the local watering holes and some tanned beauties before he started his new job in California, but that wasn't an option. He needed to prove to his sister that he could be trusted and wouldn't screw everything up this time.

From the corner of his eye, Beau caught a glimpse of Ginger Gonzalez. She sashayed toward him, her auburn curls bounced playfully around her ample breasts. Three-inch heels clinked like castanets on the concrete; her hips swayed in perfect rhythm to the blood pounding through his veins.

"Did you get a hold of your sister?" Ginger asked, handing him a plastic container. He glanced at the container puzzled.

"Cookies. I made them this morning. I was hoping to catch you before you left." She stepped closer and moistened her lips with the tip of her tongue.

"Thanks." Beau placed the container on the seat of his truck. "I missed her again, but she knows I'm leaving today."

"You know," she said, red lips pouting as she cuddled in between Beau and the box of his truck. "I wish you weren't leaving." With practiced precision, she ran a long red fingernail down his chest. In a soft southern drawl she purred, "Do you know when you're coming back?"

Beau licked his lips. "It's hard to say." Ginger wasn't going to make his get-away easy. Lately she'd gotten a little too serious. Even mentioned moving in together. He didn't want to hurt her feelings, but there were more quarters to the game, and he wasn't ready to watch from the sidelines just yet.

"I won't be that far away. I'll call you when I get a chance." He pulled her tight against him and gave her one quick hard kiss. Then he set her aside, jumped into his truck and pulled the door shut. If she got a good hold on him, he might be forced to forfeit the game.

"Well, I better get started. You take care, sweet cheeks."

Putting the truck in gear Beau pulled away from the curb. He glanced in the mirror and returned her wave. He smiled and shook his head. *That went better than I thought it would.* He promised to call but knew he wouldn't. He quickly smothered an unfamiliar pang of regret. He had never been famous for keeping promises.

* * * *

Abby lay in her bed, trying to ignore the commotion going on around her. Her aunt had rushed in and announced that Mr. Winkelman would be arriving at the end of the week.

"Your father's a little nervous about leaving you, but I'm sure we will be just fine with Mr. Winkelman here. Did your father tell you Mr. Winkelman once played college football? Imagine that!" She went on. "He's six-foot-four and around two hundred pounds." Lily shook her head. "That's a big man!"

Placing her hands on her hips Lily frowned. "I had better make a trip to the market before he comes. He's likely to eat us out of house and home."

Panic started to bubble deep inside Abby at her aunt's vivid description of the man. What would he do when she couldn't do anything he asked of her?

Lily interrupted her silent trepidation. "I'm finished for now, but I'll come back up in an hour to check on you."

Lying on her back, her arms positioned neatly at her sides, Abby sighed. Unable to sleep, her thoughts wandered but quickly returned to the new therapist.

She wondered why he was no longer playing college ball. Maybe he was just a big oaf and couldn't run or catch a ball. Or maybe they couldn't fit his name on a jersey? That thought made Abby smile. Who names their kid *Beauregard Winkelman*? Bullwinkle. He probably got used to running as a kid. A sound similar to a snicker found its way up from the depths of her dormant sense of humor.

She drifted off to sleep with her aunt's description of the man running wild through her mind, flooding her dreams with horrifying images.

The house was dark and quiet. Abby heard the glass breaking, and then a giant stormed up the stairs to her room. His bulk filled the doorway. When she tried to yell for help, he tipped his head back and through chipped and broken teeth, he roared with laughter. Trudging forward, a big hairy hand shot out and ripped her from her bed. She hung like a rag doll as he dragged her down the stairs. The roar of laughter echoed in her ears. He shoved her lifeless crippled body into a car, strapped her in and pushed the car down the driveway. She tried to scream, but she couldn't make a sound. She was terrified.

Freeing Abigail

The car picked up speed. She struggled, but it was hopeless. There was no way Abby could free herself. Out of control, the car raced down the road. Hitting a stretch of loose gravel it launched over a cliff and plummeted to the ocean below.

Abby woke with a start, her heart slamming against her ribs. Her room was dark, and her blankets were pushed to one side of the bed. Drenched in sweat, her whole body ached as her left leg jerked and jumped uncontrollably with spasms. Exhausted and alone in her bed, trapped in her prison of a body, she cried soundless tears. Closing her eyes she pleaded with God to just let it end.

* * * *

Beau arrived at his sister's apartment. Sarah ordered a large pizza, and they stayed up the rest of the night getting reacquainted.

The next morning he awoke to find the apartment empty. A note taped to the refrigerator informed him, "I'll be back around three o'clock. We have been invited to the Pendergrass's for dinner. Please shave!"

Scratching his chin, he admitted he did feel a little scruffy. The clock on the stove read half past one. Opening the fridge, Beau grabbed a soda and headed for the shower. Hot water rushed over his body, and his mind replayed parts of the conversation with his sister from the night before.

Abigail wasn't a small child as they first assumed, but was a young woman. Without hesitation he'd reassured his sister that there wouldn't be any problems. Sarah shared her concerns about Abby's loss of speech, how she struggled with therapy and the lack of any improvement. She told him of her suspicions of this all being a game to Abby. Something didn't sound right about the girl not being able to speak. Whether this was a game or not, he would know soon enough.

* * * *

Sarah returned to find Beau lounging on her deck in a pair of cut-off jeans. Placing her packages on the table, she grabbed a soda and joined him. "You're up. I see you shaved. Thanks."

"I figured since I'm going to be meeting the Boss Man today I'd better. Besides, you did say 'please'." He flashed a one-sided grin, and his brown eyes twinkled. He raked his hand through his sun bleached blond hair and added, "I suppose I'd better get a haircut, too. What do you think?"

"That would be a good idea." Sarah settled into an empty lawn chair and took a drink of her soda. She hadn't realized just how much she'd missed her brother. It had been almost two years since she had last seen him. His affair with his last patient's mother almost cost him the only family he had left. It had taken a long time before she could forgive him. She hoped he'd grown up since then and understood what was at stake this time for both of them.

Even though she had misgivings about Beau and Abby being alone together she was going to have to trust him. "There is a barber shop just around the corner. We can stop on our way. I also picked up a few new shirts for you. I hope you have a nice pair of slacks to wear tonight."

"You mean I can't go like this?"

"No, you can't!" she playfully jabbed a finger at him, and they both laughed.

Sarah stifled a laugh as she watched Beau attempt to squeeze his broad shoulders and long legs into the little yellow Honda Civic. With the passenger's seat pushed back as far as it could go, he bent, twisted and painfully worked his way in. No matter what he did, it didn't look as if he was going to get his large frame into the compact car without messing up his hair and clothes. Several minutes later, he finally stopped fidgeting.

"I don't see what's so funny!" he growled, glancing at her.

Then he noticed several people standing on the sidewalk, laughing at his discomfort, and scowled.

Sarah couldn't hold back her laughter any longer. "I'm sorry, Beau, but you looked like the last clown pushing his way into a Volkswagen Beetle." Tears filled her eyes at the state of his hair standing straight up after all his hard work.

"Just how far is it from here? I don't know how long I can sit boxed-in like this." He reached between the seat and door for the seat lever. "Can this thing go back further?"

"I'll drive fast." Sarah giggled and avoided looking at him as she backed out of her parking spot. "Don't worry. You'll have lots of room to stretch out when we get there."

Forty-five minutes later Sarah turned off the main road onto the Pendergrass Estate. She drove through the open gates, wound her way through the trees and recalled her first reaction to the cliff side property.

"Holy ... My God, Sarah would you look at this place? It's right out of one of those flower-house magazines."

"Wait until you see the inside of the house. I just got a glimpse of the great room and dining room. It's like a museum in there. I'm counting on you to be on your best behavior tonight."

"I won't let you down, sis. I promise."

Sarah turned in Beau's direction in time to see his stern expression. Good. He was taking this job seriously. Patting his knee, which was wedged between his chest and the dash she couldn't help but giggle and smiled.

She pulled up in front of the house. She didn't think she could stand to see him crawl out of the car and then be expected to keep a straight face all evening. She quickly climbed out and closed the door behind her. She hurried along the crushed white rock path toward the house, leaving Beau to his own devices.

After a few minutes and several incoherent curse words, Beau lumbered to her side. He raked a hand through his still too-long hair, attempting to rectify it. Dressed in khaki slacks and a flowered shirt he looked more like a surfer than a Texas physical therapist.

* * * *

For as anxious as Lily was about meeting Mr. Winkelman, George was a nervous wreck. He acted as if he was meeting Sarah's parents instead of her younger brother. He had changed clothes three times, rechecked everything in the kitchen and dining room at least a half dozen times and was driving his sister crazy.

As George stalked through the kitchen again, Lily couldn't help but confront him. "George, please. Sit down! You're wearing out my rugs and making me nervous," she scolded.

"I'm sorry." He sank down into a chair. "I guess I just want this to work out for everyone. If I could reschedule this business trip and stay home I would."

Lily felt his frustration. Being away from his daughter for the first time since she'd returned home tied the poor man up in knots.

George rubbed the back of his neck. "I'm praying this therapist does the trick, and we get our Abigail back."

"From your lips to God's ears," Lily said, crossing herself. She prayed every night since her niece's accident for Abigail's recovery.

"Honestly, I'm feeling guilty about leaving her."

"Don't worry. Dr. Voight said he would stop by to check on us. If we have any trouble I'll let him know." She patted his hand. "Besides what could go wrong?"

Chapter Four

Beau took an instant liking to the man who opened the door.

"You must be Beau," he said and reached out to shake Beau's hand. "Please come in. This is my sister Lily Bendickson." A petite woman appeared from behind him.

"Very nice to meet you, ma'am," Beau said, offering his hand and his best smile.

"Please don't be so formal. You can call me Lily."

The older woman appeared friendly, yet her expression reflected disappointment in him for some reason. Not to worry. He would just pour on the old charm.

"Yes, ma'am." He nodded and moved into the large foyer. Glancing around, he marveled at the spectacular glass staircase and wondered if it led to the tower and Daddy's little princess.

Lily excused herself. George ushered Beau and Sarah into the great room where a massive white marble fireplace dominated the far wall. Beau stopped and gaped at a seven-and-one-half-foot Steinway grand piano in the corner. He played piano but never anything like this. His fingers itched to stroke the ivory keys. Did it sound as rich and elegant as it appeared?

As hard as he tried, he couldn't imagine what it must have been like to grow up in a huge place like this. It was a far cry from the trailer court in Texas. His thoughts were interrupted as the sober little woman approached with a tray of crystal glasses filled with wine.

"Would you like a glass of wine or would you prefer a cold beer?" she asked dryly.

Note to self: don't ever play poker with this one. "This is just fine, ma'am. Thank you." He reached for one of the glasses and hoped it was sweet, not dry.

"I have to tell you, Beau, I'm a huge football fan," George confessed. "Come and sit down. I have some questions I'd like to ask you."

George appeared fascinated with Beau, and it wasn't long before Beau had everyone laughing at his anecdotes about his days playing college ball. He kept his stories light and entertaining.

Lily announced dinner, and Beau followed George to a luxurious dining room. Expensive looking Chinese porcelain plates hung on the walls and assorted vases decorated the sideboard. He felt like a bull in a china shop. Dropping his hands to his sides he attempted to squeeze his shoulders together. Rounding the table he selected a chair where nothing hung on the wall behind it. He slid back a chair and settled himself at the table. During dinner, Beau continued to monopolize the conversation, and George hung on every word. Sarah seemed content to sit quietly and let him sell himself.

Lily had gone out of her way to make a real "man's" meal: T-bone steaks with sautéed mushrooms, baked potatoes, mixed vegetables, homemade bread and, to top it all off, chocolate cake. Beau had flattered her all through dinner. He poured on the charm and was on his best behavior. Even Sarah showed her approval by smiling and nodding at him. Yet Miss Lily still appeared to be disappointed in him. She seemed immune to his charms. He would have to come up with a different strategy.

When the meal was finished, Lily stood and started to clear off the table. Beau jumped to his feet. "Here, let me help you, Miss Lily."

Lily frowned. "I'm not the one you're here to help, Mr. Winkelman." She wasn't going to be taken in by him like her brother had. He would have to prove himself to her before she would put too much stock in him.

"Yes, ma'am," he replied and took a step back.

George stood; Beau and Sarah followed him out of the room.

Lily truly wanted to like Beau. He was tall, handsome and he knew just what to say, but there was something about the over-confident young man that didn't sit right with her. She stacked the plates and gathered the silverware. *He's too nonchalant. Too smooth. He has no idea what he's up against.*

Earlier she prayed to God to send someone that could help her niece. She promised to accept and go along with anyone he sent, and she wasn't about to go back on her promise, but now she wasn't quite sure she had made herself clear in her prayers. She glanced toward the ceiling. *I've heard of sending a boy to do a man's job but the Devil to do yours? I hope you know what you are doing!*

* * * *

George cleared his throat and said, "Well, I think the time has come to see just what you're made of, son." Good-naturedly he slapped the young man on the back.

"Yes, sir." Beau was quick to answer, and George grinned at his enthusiasm.

Sarah's gaze darted around the room, and she chewed on her lower lip. "I think I'll help Lily in the kitchen."

George saw the uncertainty in Sarah's eyes. He felt ashamed and embarrassed of the way Abby had treated her, and he didn't have the heart to put her through that again.

"I think it would be best if only Beau and I go up." He smiled at her obvious relief and then glanced toward Beau. "How much has your sister told you about Abigail's injuries?"

"Not very much I'm afraid."

George drew in a deep breath. Explaining his daughter's injury to someone was never enjoyable. "She has an incomplete spinal cord injury at her cervical seven disc at the base of her neck which has left her partially paralyzed. At first she responded well to physical therapy, but after a couple of months she quit cooperating with the therapist and refused to continue sessions with her psychologist." Beau frowned, and George wondered what the man concluded from his comments.

"When we first moved her home several therapists came to the house to work with her. Even her psychologist came here. But after a few weeks Abigail started to distance herself from us. When I suggested that she return to the rehabilitation center, she threw a fit." George rubbed the back of his neck. If this man couldn't get any response out of Abigail, he didn't know what he was going to do. The only other option was to return her to one of the facilities and leave her there. Though it would probably be for the best in the long run, he didn't think he could do that to his baby.

Beau had worked with patients with spinal cord injuries, and he was well aware that with any traumatic accident nine times out of ten there were psychiatric problems. George returned his gaze to Beau. His good humor had vanished; he appeared older. Beau flashed him a confident smile. The man's hands were literally tied where his daughter was concerned.

"Shall we go up so you can meet my little princess?"

Beau nodded and followed George up the staircase. Sarah hadn't been able to tell him much about the accident or the severity of the girl's injuries. Though she had mentioned she feared this was some sort of game to the girl. Well, as far as the resident princess was concerned, he had never had any problems getting women to do what he wanted before, and he doubted he had lost his touch.

* * * *

Abby confronted the giant that plagued her dreams, and in doing so, her nightmares had vanished.

What was the saying—picture your enemies in their underwear? Well, she had pictured the big dumb oaf, his big gut hanging out over his boxer shorts with an overly large forehead and a receding gray hairline, and he didn't look so scary, just a washed-up has-been.

Deep voices in the hallway signaled the arrival of her father and the renowned Mr. Beauregard Winkelman. Putting on her best poker face Abby braced herself for her first encounter with her nemesis.

No amount of preparation could have readied her for the vision that filled the doorway. He was incredibly handsome. Sun-bleached blond hair brushed the collar of his Hawaiian shirt. His chiseled features were set deep in a stern expression, and dark brooding eyes the color of cappuccino slightly dusted with cinnamon meticulously studied her.

He wore his arrogance like a gold medal that awoke a spark of defiance in her. Their eyes locked. Refusing to be the first to back down, she held his stare. Hoping to find a clue to what he was thinking she searched the depths of his mystifying orbs and saw a powerful force. He stepped closer. His height, broad shoulders and muscular chest filled the room. The man was a giant. Her nightmare had come to life.

Oblivious to the lethal standoff, George broke the silence, commanding everyone's attention.

"Hello, dear. Did you have a nice rest?" he asked, kissing her cheek. "Abby, this is Beauregard Winkelman. He's your new therapist."

Amused by his name and unable to let it slip by unnoticed, she raised one eyebrow and treated the man to a muffled snicker.

One point for me, thank you very much!

"Beau, may I present my little girl, Abigail Sue Pendergrass."

She glanced back, and one side of the handsome stranger's mouth curled up to form a lopsided grin. He winked and with a slow deep southern drawl remarked, "Nice to meet you, Miss Abigail Sue."

One point for him. Big deal. Turn-about is fair play.

His southern drawl dripped like sweet maple syrup. She hated being called Abigail Sue, let alone *Miss Abigail Sue*. If he was mocking her, she didn't care. But she could feel the heat rise up the back of her neck, and she knew her cheeks were burning a pretty shade of pink. She'd be damned if she would let his presence bother her.

Her father continued to praise her tennis playing, swimming and where she had gone to college.

Beau noted that George spoke to his daughter in a patient tone as if speaking to a young child. Her skin was pale and chalky, but this was no innocent child who stared back at him with such contempt. Beau could see why other therapists had been intimidated. Her hatred for him flashed in her large blue eyes.

Never being one to be easily intimidated, he walked closer to the bed, raised an eyebrow in question and received a glare that clearly stated the battle lines have been drawn—let the games begin.

George said something about his daughter's trophies. Beau turned, smiled and nodded. He continued to praise his daughter, his only child. Yet she never acknowledged her father's presence in the room. She just glared at Beau.

There was more going on here than any of them knew. Was this a game as Sarah predicted? This girl seemed to have everything. A dedicated family that loved her, a pool, tennis courts and by the dozens of trophies that lined one whole wall, it was clear that at one time she'd been very competitive. Why wouldn't she fight to have all of that back? It didn't make sense that she'd just give up and refuse to cooperate.

He would have done everything possible to get back into the game after his knee injury. Maybe her heart hadn't been in it before. Maybe she won the trophies because her father expected it of her. Whatever her reasons were now, he'd dig deep and find the answers.

* * * *

They descended the stairs in silence, each consumed by his own thoughts. George led the way to his study where he circled his desk and lowered himself into an old comfortable black leather chair. Beau settled into the only other chair in the room.

George assessed the young man seated before him. Earlier in his daughter's room, he noted the look of disappointment that crossed the man's face. He needed Beau's assurance that he could help his daughter. He was running out of options and feared this might be Abigail's last chance. The more time that passed without any signs of improvement the less chance she had for any kind of substantial recovery. He would pay the man any amount he asked if he would just try.

"I have some papers to show you." He reached into his desk, pulled out a thick file and pushed it across the desk to Beau. "Inside are letters from various doctors and institutions. Hopefully this information will help you to understand the extent of Abigail's injuries."

Beau opened the file. After a moment, he looked up. "There's quite a bit of information here, but I can't help but wonder if she wouldn't benefit more by seeing a psychologist first." He leafed through the pages. "I mean, get her mind healthy first and then have a physical therapist come and work with her."

George leaned forward on his elbows. He had been through this before. "We've been down that road already." He sighed. "As I'm sure you witnessed, Abigail can be very stubborn. Dr. Berkman had been making progress. Though minute, it was still progress. Then for reasons only Abigail knows she refused to see her or anyone else. We had hoped that eventually Abigail would open up to her aunt or me, but that hasn't happened. She lets Lily move her arms and legs around, yet she won't speak to us. I'm afraid she needs someone who can break down those barriers. She needs someone who's unaffected by her diminishing state.

Someone more stubborn than she."

Beau nodded, flipped the file shut and asked, "May I take this with me?"

George tapped his fingers on his desk. "Does this mean you're willing to work with her? You think you can get through to her?"

Beau rubbed the back of his neck. "Well, I'll admit I've never worked with anyone with this severe of an injury before, and I have a feeling she's going to fight me the whole time," he smiled. "But I like a good challenge." He stood up and thrust out his hand. "I'll do it."

Relieved, George rose from his chair and shook Beau's hand. He prayed this man would be the one to make a connection with his little girl.

* * * *

As Sarah drove back to her apartment she tossed a curious glance in Beau's direction. His lips were pulled tight. His jaw muscles bulged as he gnawed on his thoughts in silence. He hadn't shared what had happened in the girl's room. *Was this situation more than he could handle?*

"Beau?"

"Hmmm?"

"Are you having second thoughts?" She rested her teeth on her lower lip.

"No, I'm just trying to figure something out." He turned his head toward her, his brows pulled together in a frown. "I don't understand. If she played sports competitively, what drove her to succeed? To win? Why doesn't she still have that instinct to fight? What could she possibly gain by not trying or for that matter, not even wanting to get better?"

"I don't know," Sarah professed.

"Why would anyone want to just lie there day in and day out and not want to get better?" He rubbed his jaw and once again retreated into his own thoughts.

Sarah's heart went out to him. Once he got a good hold on something he wouldn't let it go until he dug to the bottom and found the answers he wanted. He would obsess over this all night.

As a kid, Beau loved nothing more than a good riddle or puzzle. He wouldn't—couldn't—stop until he solved it. That quality was what she was counting on now … what she'd staked both of their careers and futures on.

It was dark by the time they reached her apartment. Once inside Sarah set her keys on the small table in the entry. Beau dropped a file on the table then walked to the sliding glass door. He stood with his back to her. She felt helpless. She had no idea what she could do to help him.

"You know," he said abruptly, gazing out into the darkness, "If she hasn't spoken for six months she may need a speech pathologist." He turned back around. "They would teach her how to use various types of adaptive equipment that would help her communicate."

"Do you really think she can't talk at all?" Sarah swallowed a lump in her throat.

Beau shook his head "I don't know. The way she behaved tonight makes me think that there is something buried deep that's keeping her from speaking. It might be something she's not even aware of." He closed his eyes and ran his hands through his hair. "Maybe I should have taken more psychology classes."

His lips thinned into a straight line as he rambled around the apartment, digging in drawers. Once he found what he was looking for he headed for the table. Sarah watched with fascination as he opened the notebook and started writing. He made a list of questions for which he would demand answers. She watched for several minutes, knowing that by morning her brother would have an extensive game plan and would be ready to tackle the job with full force.

Walking to the refrigerator, Sarah pulled out a beer and opened it. Without speaking, she set it on the table next to Beau. He glanced up and smiled. She patted his shoulder. "Try to get some sleep."

Beau spent the next few hours at the table reading over the information George had given him. In the file he found a letter from Abby's psychologist, Dr. Nicole Berkman, one from a neurosurgeon Dr. Wendy Grace and a copy of the report from the emergency room doctor, Dr. William Voight. There was also a discharge letter from her medical doctor, Dr. Maxwell B. Hanson, who referred Paris Jenkins, an occupational therapist, to Abby.

The emergency room report listed the time the patient was brought to Monterey Bay General Hospital as 5:42 p.m. It stated that the patient was unconscious with suspected head and neck injury. Injuries were listed as an apparent concussion with internal and soft tissue injuries. Visual bruising and broken radius and ulna bones in right arm. A C-spine x-ray was ordered.

A trauma code team did the blood work, and a CAT scan was ordered. The radiologist's report indicated head and neck injuries. An MRI was ordered, and the neurosurgeon was called.

Patient regained consciousness at 8:04 p.m. and complained of headache, dizziness, loss of motion, swelling, stiffness and numbness. Additional injuries found were blurred vision and blood in the urine.

Doctors Voight and Grace reviewed the MRI. Dr. Grace ordered a myelogram that showed an incomplete spinal cord injury at cervical disc seven.

Beau checked the clock hanging on the kitchen wall. Eleven forty-five. He rubbed his temples. Getting up from his chair he walked to the refrigerator and got another beer. He twisted off the cap, returned to the table and continued to go through the file.

A letter from a spinal cord and traumatic brain injury physician, a physiatrist, caught Beau's eye. As he read, several things became very clear to him.

After an extensive stay in our facility, Abigail Pendergrass shows no improvement. She has actually regressed significantly. Abigail's father wishes to take her home. He feels she may respond better in familiar surroundings. Through dedication and hard work with a specialized therapist Abigail may expect to regain considerable mobility.

However, she lacks the initiative, desire, and the persistence needed for her to regain even the smallest amount of mobility. Strong emotional support to combat her depression and depersonalization will be required. It is imperative that she begins rehabilitation as soon as possible. I highly recommend a live-in physical therapist. Our office has a list of highly skilled professionals in this area from which to choose.

Abigail should have progressed much faster due to her age and good physical condition at the time of her accident. However, besides her state of mind at this time, I am very concerned about the amount of atrophy and disuse atrophy due to lack of use of her limbs. I fear that if she returns home in her current state the atrophy may increase due to her adverse behavior.

Family physician and longtime friend Dr. Max Hanson assures me that he'll keep close tabs on Miss Pendergrass' progress and have constant contact with the physical therapist.

Beau leaned back in his chair and drained his beer. Although the letter answered some of his questions, it left him with many more.

He worked late into the night, jotting down a list of what he was going to need. First, he would need to know if anyone started a baseline measurement of strength and sensitivity after Abigail returned home. He knew the sooner muscles started working again after a spinal cord injury the better the chances were of additional recovery, especially for walking. The longer you went without seeing improvement, the worse the odds were of improvement happening on its own. Though in this particular case there hadn't been any improvement.

With Abigail living at home, she'd missed out on many important in-patient programs, classes and a chance to interact with other people with the same types of injuries. And now she wasn't getting any kind of interaction other than with her father and aunt. It wasn't going to be easy making her understand that she would have to do as much as possible for herself—as soon as possible.

Beau's chair creaked in protest as he leaned back and closed his eyes. Not only did she need to think about her physical health but her emotional health as well. He rubbed his face with both hands. Somewhere he had a book explaining what functions were possible, according to where the spinal injury occurred.

Getting up from the table, he slid the glass doors open, stepped out onto the small deck and settled in a chair. Locking his hands behind his head he stared off into the distance and wondered what made Miss Abigail Sue Pendergrass tick.

The most important thing he needed to do was break down the barriers she'd erected to keep everyone at a distance. If his guess was right, she could speak. She just didn't want to. There was a chance she had somehow convinced herself that she couldn't speak.

He recalled the look of total defiance in her eyes and smiled. There was still a little fight left in her no matter how hard she tried to fool everyone. Then his smile faded. Why was she trying to fool everyone? Just what was it that she was trying to hide? What was she really afraid of?

Chapter Five

"Good morning. Did I wake you, dear?" Lily entered Abby's bedroom and hurried to the bedside stand, setting the breakfast tray down. "Did you sleep well?" She elevated the hospital bed to a sitting position.

Abby had been asleep. Her aunt woke her from a dream where she was Scarlet O'Hara and Mr. Beauregard Winkelman had been Rhett Butler. He had just taken her into his strong arms. His hands roamed roughly over her body as he kissed her senseless.

"You look like you got a good night's sleep. Your cheeks are even flushed a pretty pink."

Abby smiled. Thank goodness her aunt had no idea about her dream. Lily chatted on, but Abby was unable to shake the feeling of the man's strong arms wrapped around her. He looked so handsome in his tailored suit with long black tails. It had only been a dream, yet she could still hear the soothing southern drawl of his deep voice as he whispered mysterious words of love in her ear.

This is crazy. He's my enemy. She had no business dreaming about him in this way. Her thoughts were interrupted. Lily informed her they wouldn't be doing any therapy today.

"I need to clean and set up one of the rooms down stairs for Mr. Winkelman. Your father wants to see how you two get along before he leaves. Mr. Winkelman will be moving in bright and early tomorrow morning."

Abby recalled her father's business trip. Maybe if things didn't work out between her and this new therapist her father would stay home. What could she do that would keep her father from leaving? That thought occupied most of her day.

* * * *

Sarah spotted her brother on the sofa, his hair standing out on all sides. He was surrounded by a pile of reference books, some opened, the pages marked with green sticky notes. A notebook covered with scribbled notes lay open on the coffee table. She wondered if he had slept at all last night.

"Did you find what you were looking for?" she asked.

"What? Hi. Yeah, I had forgotten about some of these. This one," he said holding up an old tattered book, "has a graph that tells you which muscles still work and what you'll be able to accomplish, depending on where your spinal cord injury is. That's assuming the patient is motivated and has a positive attitude. Having all the right equipment helps a lot, too."

Sarah pushed the strap to her purse back over her shoulder and said, "George mentioned something to me about a room full of exercise equipment that he bought. You should ask him about it." He scratched something into his notebook.

So much was riding on him and his ability to help Abigail. She never realized how much medical information was involved. It was one thing to know what Abby should be able to do and what she would never be able to do. Getting her to even try to help herself was a different matter completely. Where would a person even start?

Although she was having second thoughts, she had to reassure Beau that she had confidence in his abilities.

"What's the matter?" Beau questioned, making eye contact. "Don't worry. I can handle this."

"It's not that, Beau. It's just that Abigail seems determined not to get better. It just doesn't make any sense to me."

"I have been thinking about that." He relaxed against the sofa and closed his eyes. "Her father hasn't done her any favors by letting her stay at home. He should have returned her to the hospital the instant she refused to continue her sessions with the therapist and psychologist."

Her heart ached for him. "What's done is done. I'm confident you'll be able to get through to her."

"Thanks." He opened his eyes and glanced toward her. "That means a lot to me." His easy grin reminded her of a time when they were much younger; a time when she had more often played the part of mother rather than sister.

"I'm going to run to the store and pick up a few things. Do you need anything?"

"No, I don't think so. I'm going to finish sorting through these books, then I'll put the ones I don't need in your garage. Is that going to be okay?"

"Yeah, I've got some stuff out there so just push it to the side, and you should have plenty of room."

"Thanks. I need to clean out my truck, too."

"I'll be back in an hour or two. See ya later," she called over her shoulder, closing the door behind her. *I hope I haven't made a huge mistake. He's just got to be able to get through to her.*

* * * *

George strolled to the doorway of one of the rooms down the hall from the kitchen. "Looks like you've been busy today," he exclaimed behind Lily.

"I just finished. I hope it's good enough for our houseguest." The room held a single bed, a dresser and a chair. "The windows and the curtains have been washed, and I put clean sheets on the bed. I washed the floor and shook out the rugs. The room is as ready as it's going to be."

George smiled at the slight edge in her voice. She wasn't thrilled with the fact that he was leaving town so soon after Beau moved in. He had spent a good part of the day on the phone trying to move meetings around to shorten up his trip. In the end, he'd been unsuccessful. "It looks great, but you should have waited until I was here to help you."

"This room was easy. I'm glad I didn't have to clean that one," she said pointing to the room across the hall which was filled with exercise equipment.

"What about the bathroom?" He nodded his head toward the room down the hall.

"That's cleaned, and I put more towels in the closet."

George grinned. His sister was incredible. "How about dinner? Did you start anything yet?" he asked, placing a hand on her shoulder.

Lily spun around. "You're pushing your luck, George," she responded with a frown.

"No, I mean, should we order something? Maybe Chinese? Or would you rather have pizza tonight?"

"Chinese is good. And it's easier for Abigail to eat." She patted his chest as she walked past him into the kitchen.

George walked to the phone. "You sit down and rest. I'll call in the order." He finished his call and turned. "I'm going up to see Abby. I don't think she likes the idea of me going on this trip."

Lily laughed. "Oh, your trip is only a small part of what "Miss" Abigail doesn't like."

George nodded in agreement, and they both chuckled.

* * * *

The next morning was one of those mornings Beau thought that you only read about in books. Anxious about his new job he awoke early, slipped into running shoes and shorts then snuck out of the apartment. Shades of pink and orange streaked across the sky of the oceanfront city. Heading south, he took the hiking trail his sister mentioned that skirted Monterey Bay Aquarium Lover's Point Park and Point Pinos Lighthouse. As he jogged he observed an old cannery building which now housed unique boutiques and an art gallery. Fisherman's Wharf and the pier offered colorful shops restaurants and a charter boat service.

Could he work in some time for fishing before he left California?

As he ran, a myriad of questions flooded his mind. He wondered about Abigail Pendergrass and what she'd been like before her accident. By the many swimming and tennis trophies he had seen in her room he knew she had the mind and body of a competitor yet what about her heart? What other things had she been interested in?

Was she the type of person who hung out with a large group and had a lot of friends, or did she only have a couple of close friends with whom she shared her most inner thoughts? Did she have a boyfriend? Beau shook his head.

Waves crashed against the rocky shoreline, and the crisp salty air filled his lungs. Several snowy white seagulls dove into the surf in search of their morning meal. Off in the distance a yacht sliced through the waves. But no matter how hard he tried, his thoughts always came back to the question of a boyfriend. It wasn't a stupid question. Was there a boyfriend? Was he going to have to put up with him hanging around and getting in the way? Then he remembered her indignant yet apprehensive blue eyes, eyes that revealed more about her than she probably realized. Despite the fact that she wore a mask to show the world she was tough and unaffected, her anguish, suffering and vulnerability were quite evident. There had to be more to the story, something that everyone else had overlooked.

He loved a good challenge and he would do whatever it took to piece this puzzle together and help Abby reach her actual potential. The one thing he loved more than winning was playing the game.

* * * *

Later Beau pulled up in front of the Pendergrass house where George strolled out and approached the truck.

"Did you see the first driveway before the big willow tree?" he asked, pointing behind the truck.

"Yeah?"

"That leads to the side of the house. Back up and drive around. I'll meet you there."

"Okay." Beau shifted the truck into reverse. He took the worn path and stopped by a small building he presumed to be a guesthouse.

George appeared at the rear of the truck. "Is this all of your stuff?"

"I don't need much. Some clothes and my books." Beau picked up a suitcase and handed it to George then picked up a box overflowing with books and turned.

George laughed and shook his head. "Follow me."

Beau wasn't sure what the older man found so amusing but trailed him around the house and into the kitchen.

Lily stood at the stove, removing cookie sheets from the oven. The heavenly smell of warm peanut butter cookies engulfed him. Closing his eyes Beau took a deep breath. It didn't make any difference. Peanut butter cookies smelled like heaven whether they were made in a trailer court in Texas or a mansion on the cliffs of California.

"Good morning, Mr. Winkelman," Lily said, her voice dry.

Her eyes matched the cool tone of her voice. For some reason the women in this particular house didn't fancy him. That was okay; that wasn't why he was here. But it was damned strange. Usually he made a great first impression.

"Ma'am." He tipped his head with respect. "It sure smells wonderful in here." He offered a slight grin and continued to trail George down the hallway.

"I hope this is acceptable for you," George said, placing the suitcase on the bed.

"Don't worry about me." Beau set the box down on the floor. He straightened, placed his hands on his hips and looked around. "This suits me fine. I've lived in smaller places."

"Good," George replied. "Lily said there's a television upstairs. If you want you can bring it down."

"Thanks, but I don't watch much TV unless there's a game on. I'm sure I'll have enough to keep me busy." He kicked the box on the floor. "How about the pool? It looks pretty tempting."

"By all means." George grinned. "It might be cold. It was just filled last week. The service man said he would stop by in a couple of days. Have him turn the temperature up to where you prefer."

"Thanks again, Mr. Pendergrass." Beau reached out to shake the man's hand.

"Now none of that. I insist you call me George." Ignoring the hand George patted Beau on the back. "I'll let you get settled. I'm going up to check on Abigail."

Abigail sounded too stuffy, Abby suited her better. It sounded sassy, like the girl he bet she once was. He recalled her expression when he'd called her "Miss Abigail Sue." That got her dander up. He grinned.

He put his clothes in the small dresser and neatly placed his research books and notebooks on the top.

"All settled?" Lily asked from the doorway with a sober expression.

"Yes, ma'am."

"I thought you might like some cookies." She held out a small plate.

Beau watched her warily as he reached for one. "Thank you, ma'am."

Her gaze policed the room as she placed the plate on a stack of books. Without another word, she disappeared back down the hallway.

The warm cookie dissolved in his mouth. Heaven. He closed his eyes, and at that moment he didn't care if she'd laced them with a dash of arsenic. He quickly popped another one in his mouth but restrained from eating them all.

"How's it going?"

Beau glanced up from the book he had been leafing through. George leaned against the doorframe, his arms folded across his chest.

"If you've got a minute I'll show you the exercise equipment I've purchased. I hope we've got everything you'll need to help my little girl—" His voice broke, and he turned away.

Beau tossed the book on the bed, snatched up his clipboard and followed George to a room across the hall. George opened the door and flicked the light switch. The light revealed a small room crammed full of equipment. A compressed wheelchair leaned against one wall. A folded walker lay on a rolled-up exercise mat. A full-sized massage table stood in one corner surrounded by a mountain of free weights.

Beau grinned as he weaved through the other equipment, making his way to a treadmill training system with partial body support, fully equipped with handrails and a wheelchair ramp. "I can't believe you have one of these. I haven't worked with one since my ambulation training at the VA hospital in Houston." He inspected every inch of the treadmill from its nylon harness to the safety stop on the speed display mechanism.

"You really went all out, didn't you?" He turned toward George, his voice charged with enthusiasm. "This is top of the line." His hand glided over the display box. "It's set up to operate at a very slow speed which can be increased in small increments to match the patient's recovery rate." He pointed to the display screen. "This shows the speed of the walking surface, and in case of emergency it's also equipped with a safety stop."

"It sounds like you know what you're talking about, but if you need one there's a box containing all sorts of manuals somewhere in this mess."

Beau poked around until he located the box in question. As he knelt beside it, he tossed over his shoulder "Good. I'll go through them to make sure everything's assembled correctly." Several minutes later he glanced up; he was alone.

His gaze swept around the cramped room. No way was it large enough to set up the equipment to maximize their function. He scratched his head. He would make it work. He would ask about the empty room at the end of the hall.

Beau returned to his room. After seeing the type of equipment he had to work with, he made a list of additional supplies he needed.

Glancing out the window, he spotted the swimming pool. A few laps in the sparkling water would loosen up his muscles and help clear his head. He set the clipboard aside, replaced his dirty clothes with his favorite cutoffs and headed out the door.

He still couldn't get over the place. It resembled a resort more than a home. He climbed the ladder to the diving board of the Olympic-sized pool. Taking two steps he stretched his arms over his head and dove into the water. The cold water brought back memories of swimming in the dark deep quarries in Texas.

Emptying his mind, Beau concentrated on his breathing. He reached the end of the pool, rolled, kicked off the side and continued back across the pool. Twenty or thirty laps would be a good warm-up.

* * * *

Will tugged on his collar and checked his shoes for dust. He wiped the toe of one shoe on the back of his tan slacks. Confident that he looked reliable and dependable he threw back his shoulders and rang the doorbell.

George pulled open the door. "Will! What a nice surprise! Come on in. You're just in time. There's someone here that I want you to meet."

Confused, Will followed George down the hall and into the empty kitchen.

"I'll be right back. He must be in his room."

Will inhaled the homey scent of homemade cookies and smiled. He turned and walked closer to the windows to bask in the ocean view, but something caught his eye. "There seems to be a man swimming in your pool," he said as George joined him at the window.

"Oh, that's where he went. That's the man I wanted you to meet." They both watched as Beau's fluent powerful arms sliced through the water.

"Hello, Dr. Voight," Lily said, walking up behind them. "I didn't know you were here. What are you two gaping at like a pair of fools?"

"Beau's in the pool," George stated. "I told him it was probably too cold, but it must not be for him."

"Who's Beau?" Will asked, surveying the tall muscular man as he pulled himself up out of the pool.

"He's Abigail's new physical therapist."

Will was immediately jealous.

The man shook his head and wiped his long wet hair back with his hands. He turned his face upward toward the sun.

Will couldn't hold back the snarl that crossed his face as he studied the man. He knew too well the type of man taking advantage of his surroundings. Also he didn't look like any therapist Will ever knew.

Lily raised an eyebrow and whispered, "The water must not be *that* cold!" She turned in time to see that Dr. Voight had noticed the same thing. She laughed to herself at the stunned look on the young doctor's face.

"He just moved in today." George said, slapping Will on the back. "He still looks like he could play college ball. Come on out, and I'll introduce you." George opened the kitchen door and strolled out to the patio.

Lily laughed again at the look on the doctor's face as Beau sauntered toward the house. It was obvious the poor man hadn't been expecting to see a blond Adonis emerged from their pool when he arrived.

She had always liked Dr. Voight. He followed Abigail's progress and had even stopped by to see her several times since she returned home. She suspected the young doctor might be sweet on her niece. She watched through the opened door and wondered if Will would step up to the plate and somehow mark his territory.

"How was your swim?" George asked, striding toward Beau.

"Refreshing." Beau reached for a towel and wiped his face and hands.

Will stood next to George, his shoulders back, his head slightly tilted up.

"Beau, I'd like you to meet Dr. William Voight."

Beau took a deep breath, his broad tan chest expanding to its full girth. One corner of his mouth hiked up in a lopsided grin as he extended his right hand toward the doctor. "Nice to meet you."

Will returned the gesture "And you."

"How many laps did you do?" George inquired.

"Honestly I lost count. Swimming clears my head. It helps me to relax."

Lily shook her head as she watched the two men discreetly size each other up. She smiled to herself. *The next few weeks should prove to be very interesting.*

* * * *

Abby waited until her father was halfway down the stairs before she opened her eyes. That athletic over-achiever had moved in on the main floor, and she didn't want to hear about it. It wouldn't be long before he would be coming up and bothering her.

Her nightmares of him had taken a slight twist. No longer did an overweight balding eight-foot monster plague her. He had transformed into a knight in shining armor with beautiful blond hair, rich chocolate brown eyes and a sexy southern drawl.

She even fantasized about running her fingers through his hair, but her fantasy vanished as she realized that was never going to happen. She was never going to get the chance to do a lot of things she foolishly dreamt about.

She sighed and glanced out the window. Her life was over, and she'd accepted it. The hope of getting married and having children could never be anything other than a dream—a dream best abandoned. Not having children had been the part that bothered her the most. Growing up as an only child she'd always planned on a house full of children. Her major had even been set in elementary education. Then in a heartbeat everything changed. Due to Abby's selfishness, she had caused the car crash that killed Carolyn, leaving her damned and condemned to suffer a life of loneliness.

The stabbing pain came on fast, causing Abby's left leg to jump uncontrollably. Within seconds the pain increased past discomfort to unbearable. She needed her medication. Turning her head she searched for the clock. How much longer before her aunt showed up with her pills? She wanted to scream. Damn, she hated this. At one time during the night the spasms were so severe she thought for sure she was going to fall right out of the bed.

They were downstairs, entertaining that big lummox, while she was lying up here in pain. What the hell was taking so long? The spasm subsided, but the pain lingered. She turned her head in search for the clock again and saw Dr. Voight standing in the doorway.

"I wasn't sure if you were awake or not." He entered the room. "How are you today?"

She closed her eyes and then opened them again.

"Sorry. Are you in a lot of pain? Do you need your medication?"

Finally!

"I'll get your aunt. I'll be right back." He hurried out of the room and returned with her father, her aunt and her nightmare following close behind.

Lily set the tray down next to her bed and raised the bed to a sitting position. She administered the medication and apologized for not being there earlier.

Her father and Will stood off to the side speaking in low tones. Beau glanced at his watch and wrote something on his clipboard before approaching the bed. He was dressed in faded jeans and an equally faded T-shirt. His wavy sun bleached hair was combed back and appeared wet as if he had stepped out of the shower recently. His presence filled the room.

Now that everyone was in her room Abby wanted them all to disappear. The walls and ceiling seemed to close in around her; she wanted to scream. She closed her eyes, willing the pain in her heart, soul and body to stop.

Lily rubbed lotion on Abby's slim arms. Arms with very little muscle left, Beau noted. Lily pushed the covers aside and started on her niece's right leg. George ushered Will toward the door.

"Beau, are you coming?"

"No." He turned toward George "I'll stay."

George nodded, and he and Will left the room.

Beau stepped closer to the bed. He ignored the dagger-stares Abby hurled his way. He questioned the medications she was given and who prescribed them.

After a few minutes of massage Abby noticeably relaxed. Beau checked his watch, jotted down the time and a note that the medication had apparently started to relieve some of her discomfort.

Lily straightened and sighed. Like a magician she pulled a tissue from her sleeve and wiped her brow.

"Would you like me to continue for you?"

A certain look flashed across Abby's face, a familiar look close to the one he'd once seen across the line of scrimmage when nose tackle Bubba Johnson took the set position beside him.

"I think that's enough for tonight," Lily replied wearily.

Not wanting to offend the woman, Beau nodded.

Lily offered Abby a sip of water before repositioning the bed for the night. "I'll be back later when it's time for more medication." She leaned over and kissed her niece's brow. "Get some sleep, dear."

Beau finished his scribbling, said goodnight and headed downstairs to his room. A small portion of the puzzle was becoming very clear. Although her father and aunt loved her and wished to see her well they only saw Abby as what she was right now, not for what she could be again. But Beau had glimpsed a slight flicker from the fire that still burned deep within the young woman. He stopped, turned and glanced up the stairs behind him.

I've got just the fuel to ignite those coals.

* * * *

George was pleased and hopeful after dealing with Beau's enthusiasm. The young man had impressed him with his knowledge base. His careful examination of each piece of equipment and the way he tested each piece with hands-on attention to make sure it was sturdy and functional. He even mentioned a couple pieces of equipment that George hadn't heard of.

Though Lily entertained doubts about Beau's capabilities, George liked him, and he hadn't missed the look of opposition on his daughter's face when she first laid eyes on him. No one had been able to get any kind of response from her in quite a while. He had a feeling this brawny young man had no problems drawing attention from women, but his daughter wasn't just any woman. In her prime she would have given Beau a run for his money.

George smiled. At her best she had been an accomplished athlete; her countless trophies had proven that. She had had the determination of a long distant runner, the agility of a world-class ballerina and the

68

stamina of a prizefighter.

He rubbed the back of his neck. As much as he hadn't wanted to admit it, Abigail wasn't a little girl any more. She had turned into a woman when he hadn't been looking. *A woman yes, but would she ever be strong again?* He studied the videotape he had removed from his desk drawer. The hand written label read *Carolyn*. Would Abigail ever be strong enough to face the largest hurdle she would ever come up against?

George saw Beau walk past his office door. "Beau? Will you come in here, please?" Beau entered, and George gestured with one hand. "Please have a seat."

Beau settled into the chair in front of the desk. The older man studied a videotape, his brows furrowed with deep lines. After several seconds he shook his head, set the tape inside his center desk draw and closed it.

"Did Lily go to her room to lie down?" His voice lacked its normal conviction.

"Yeah, she looked pretty tuckered out."

George leaned back in his chair and rubbed his temples. "You'll be a big help to my sister. I haven't been here to assist her, and I'm afraid this has all been a heavy burden on her."

Beau shifted in his chair. "If what was just done is the extent of your daughter's therapy I think I know what her main problem is, if you don't mind me saying, sir?"

"No." George raised one hand. "I know what you mean. I've known for a long time that Abigail needs much more than we've been able to give her. We've tried. When the first therapist came to the house she declined to cooperate and brow beat the poor woman. The next therapist was a man, and we moved him into the spare room down the hall from hers, thinking that would be better. Well, the brow beating soon turned into all-out verbal abuse. That's when Lily said since she was already feeding and washing Abigail it wouldn't be that much more to work in a little therapy. She said after having three husbands she could take whatever abuse Abigail dished out." Knowing Lily was probably right, both men grinned.

"I wish I didn't have to go away on this trip right now, but it can't be helped. I just hope everything goes smoothly while I'm gone."

Beau stood. "One way or another I'll break through her barriers and get her to respond. Don't worry about Miss Lily or Miss Abigail. I'll take good care of both of them."

"It's not them I'm worried about, son. It's you."

Chapter Six

With her keen sense of hearing Abby heard his footfalls on the stairs long before he actually entered her room. He came alone and from her position on the bed his overwhelming size seemed to fill the room. He wore a snug fitting gray T-shirt and faded blue jeans that hugged his muscular thighs. His shoulder length wavy blond hair hung loose around his shoulders. The smell of soap, fresh air, and sandalwood floated in the air around him.

He walked around the room and casually perused her private and personal belongings. At first he seemed to ignore her which made Abby edgy, and she fought to mask her nervousness with an air of annoyance. She might be trapped in this body, and this bed, but she wasn't his prey, and she would be damned if she would let him intimidate her. She watched as he cased her room like a low-class detective.

After a few seconds he stopped, turned and his gaze locked with hers. Today his eyes appeared darker, like black coffee, no cream and no sugar.

"Your therapy is going to be longer and more difficult than what you've been used to." His deep authoritative voice echoed through the room and vibrated in her chest. "You'll get sore and tired. Spinal cord injuries like yours can affect motor nerves more than sensory nerves or vice versa. In time you will learn to deal with the residual deficits. Do you have any questions?"

She stared in response.

"Good," he replied. "First we'll start with baseline measurements of strength and sensation to compare to later. Then range of motion, rolling and sitting." He walked across the room, and she strained, pushing her cheek into the pillow to follow him.

"We need to establish the amount of atrophy and disuse atrophy you have. I also noticed a standing frame and wheelchair downstairs. We will be utilizing them."

She wasn't impressed by this "Therapist of the Year" wannabe. At the mention of using the wheelchair she puffed air through her nostrils. The man was dreaming if he expected her to submit to his wishes.

"After reading your file and the letters from doctors and past therapists I'm setting your goals high. With all the data I've read, you should be able to achieve a fifty to seventy-five percent recovery. That is, with the help of leg braces.

"I would also like to see you have an independent ADL." Abby frowned, and he quickly added, "Adaptive Driver's License. They evaluate and train people with disabilities to drive a car or van by themselves."

Abby couldn't believe what she was hearing. Couldn't he see the condition she was in? Didn't he realize that everything he said was impossible?

He's an idiot to even think I would ever get back into an automobile again!

* * * *

Beau sensed her doubts about what he was telling her. That was okay for now. He'd gambled his little speech would get a verbal response out of her, but no such luck. What was it going to take to get through to her? What was she hiding?

Deep in thought he walked across the room and opened the antique china cabinet that held a porcelain doll collection. After several seconds his curiosity got the best of him. He picked one up, turned it over and peeked under its dress.

A sound similar to a gasp came from the bed. Turning, he was treated with the fuming red face of his infuriated patient. He laid the doll on the bed next to Abby's right hand then wandered across the room.

George entered the room, and Beau welcomed the interruption. He was convinced she could speak and move her arms. She was just being stubborn. Maybe she would take this opportunity and tell her father just what he planned for her.

"Good morning, darling." George leaned over and kissed her cheek. "Did you have a good night? What's the matter, dear? Your face is all flushed!" He then turned his attention to Beau.

"I was explaining the style of therapy I've selected." Beau peered around George and winked at Abby. His heart skipped a beat when he noticed the fingers of her right hand entwined in the doll's hair. *That-a-girl.*

"Oh. Good. The sooner you get started the sooner our little girl will come back to us." George patted his daughter's hand. "I wanted to say good morning before I drive into town to pick up a few things for my trip. I'll come up when I return." He kissed her again and headed for the door.

"We'll be here," Beau affirmed as he cast a quick glance toward the bed. He turned away to hide his amusement at the indignant expression on Abby's face.

"Now where was I?" He reached over and picked up a tennis ball from a shelf filled with tennis trophies. He held the ball up and studied it then bounced it on the floor a couple of times. No response. He admired her self-control.

"You played tennis. I used to play myself. I prefer to swim though. As a matter of fact, I did a few laps last night in your pool." Her brows puckered; her lips pursed. "That's a real nice pool y'all have there," he drawled. Then he noticed a photo on the nightstand next to her bed. The picture was of Abby and a friend posing in matching swimsuits, each girl holding trophies. He studied the snapshot, grinned and said, "You know what? I think I'll work swimming into your training program later this summer."

Casually he placed the tennis ball on the bed next to her left hand and wondered if it would hit him in the back of the head before he reached the door.

"Your aunt will be up soon with your lunch. Make sure you eat all of it. You'll need your strength."

He paused at the door. "I'll be back later, and we'll get started."

Half way down the hall he heard the ball drop and roll across the floor. He snickered. The morning session had gone pretty much as he had thought it would, though it was promising to know she could move her fingers. He chuckled and wished he could have seen her expression when she realized she could actually move her hand. So anger was the key to the first layer of locks. Breaking through the remaining locks wasn't going to be so easy.

* * * *

The afternoon therapy session had been a bust. Beau stretched out his long legs under the kitchen table and raked his fingers through his hair. He had failed everyone he had ever loved one way or another, but there was no way he was going to fail now. He couldn't afford to fail; there was too much riding on him. Too many people depending on him to make a difference.

Abby hated him, but he didn't care. She had refused to cooperate, and Lily didn't have a clue what he was trying to achieve. He had explained each exercise and what he hoped to accomplish, yet neither understood the purpose behind the treatments. He shook his head.

His therapy consisted of various stretching exercises, muscle manipulation and abdominal control. He positioned Abby in a sitting position on her bed. Holding her by the shoulders and supporting her weight, he sat directly behind her. Then he asked her to try and balance herself by using only her stomach muscles.

The exercise had gone pretty much as he predicted. Her body went limp as a rag doll, and she slumped back against his chest right into his arms. His chest tightened as he remembered how small and frail she felt. Leaning forward he nodded toward a picture of her holding a trophy and whispered, "I'm surprised. I would have thought the girl in that picture wouldn't have given up so easily. She looks like a fighter—no, a winner to me." She still wouldn't respond. Her eyes just held a vacant stare.

Beau rubbed his temples. The throbbing behind his eyes intensified as he sorted through the similarities between Abby's attitude and that of Joel Jurday's—a friend he couldn't save.

"There you are." George's voice interrupted his thoughts. He entered the kitchen, strolled to the fridge and retrieved two beers before settling in a chair across the table from Beau. "I guess by your expression the afternoon therapy didn't go as you planned."

Beau shook his head and reached for the cold bottle. After a long satisfying drink he set the bottle down and relaxed into his chair. How was he ever going to explain his suspicions to the man across from him?

After several silent moments Beau spoke, hoping he could relate the tale without embarrassing himself. "I had this friend once. Joel Jurday." He cleared his throat and began again. "He was from Corpus Christi, Texas. He had a little place right on the Gulf." A lump rose in the back of his throat. "Joel was a good guy. We played ball together for two years. When Joel's brother Shawn turned twenty, Joel bought two brand new jet skis. His brother was so excited." Beau paused and took another swallow of cold beer.

"They fired them up, and Shawn shot across the open water at full throttle like he had ridden one every day of his life. Joel raced to catch up to him, but Shawn whipped around some rocks and was out of sight. Joel rounded the reef just as Shawn's jet ski shot through a swell, crashing head on into some rocks. Shawn broke his neck and died." Beau paused and pinched the bridge of his nose.

"Joel blamed himself. He blamed himself because he'd bought the jet skis. He never forgave himself." He glanced out the window. George never moved.

"He suffered nightmares, flashbacks and eventually turned to alcohol for any kind of relief. At first he swung in and out of a deep depression. One day he was fine, and you could talk to him, then the next day it was as if he changed into someone else. Other times he wouldn't even remember you spoke the day before. Eventually he shut all of his friends and family out of his life. An old guy walking the beach with a metal detector found him."

"I'm sorry, Beau…" George murmured.

"At the time I didn't know what I could do, but since then I've learned that although the accident wasn't Joel's fault he believed it was. He had what is called 'Post-Traumatic Stress Disorder'." He placed a hand over his chin and rubbed his jaw. Just the thought of how his friend suffered tightened his chest. He cleared his throat. "It affects people who have experienced severe trauma, assault, rape and sometimes military combat. It comes with a host of complications. To mention a few, nightmares, flashbacks, panic attacks, claustrophobia and more often than not substance abuse."

George rubbed his hand on the back of his neck. "And you think Abigail may have this 'Post-Traumatic Stress Disorder'?"

Beau nodded. "She sure could. She seems to have reason enough. And even though I haven't spent much time with her, besides her obvious depression I've identified several of the signs of PTSD. She may also feel guilty about the accident and the fact that she lived, and Carolyn died."

"Why would Abigail feel guilty? My baby wasn't driving!"

"That's a nasty little bonus called survivor guilt. The survivor is troubled because they were unable to control the situation, preventing it from happening. Her unwillingness to participate in her recovery or life itself is her mind's way of punishing herself. Her unresolved guilt has caused her negative response, adding to her trauma recovery."

George stood and gazed out the window toward the ocean. "Soon after the accident something like this was mentioned, but at the time my only concern was that Abigail would live."

"I'm not claiming to be a psychologist," Beau said, coming to his feet, "but if she spoke to one it wouldn't take very long to make a diagnosis."

"Dr. Berkman." George turned, and his eyes reflected his sadness. "She saw Dr. Berkman a couple of times. I don't think their sessions went very well, but I'll contact her and see if she's willing to come by the house and try again."

"I'll write up a report on what I've observed over the short time that I've been here and have it ready for her."

They both returned to their seats. Beau placed his forearms on the edge of the table and leaned forward. "I'd like to utilize some of the exercise equipment you bought—set up a training room."

"If you think you can use some of it, help yourself." George pushed his unfinished beer away. "I just wish I didn't have to leave."

Beau sensed his hopelessness. It must be killing him to see his only child crippled and to know she didn't want to get better. And that she thought she didn't have anything to live for. "There's no physical reason why she can't talk or have limited movement of her arms. I guarantee I'll do whatever it takes to help your daughter get her life back."

George nodded, stood and walked away. Beau reclined in his chair, folded his arms across his chest and closed his eyes. He needed answers.

His mind reeled as he pieced his thoughts together.

Was Post-Traumatic Stress Disorder and clinical depression the real problem, or was it something entirely different? Was she hiding the true reason from herself and her family? He needed to break down her barriers and get her to communicate. To do that, everything as she knew it would have to change.

* * * *

Abby woke the next morning suffering more than she thought possible. Piercing pain hovered behind her eyes. Every muscle in her body screamed with agony.

Aunt Lily, come soon!

She twisted and strained to see the clock. Damn, her aunt wouldn't be up for another forty-five minutes. She should scream. No, she wouldn't. She wasn't even sure she still could.

Her legs jerked and jumped with spasms. The pain increased to an excruciating level until she feared she might pass out.

Free of her sheets her body propelled dangerously close to the edge of the bed. *Please make this end. I can't take much more.*

Her teeth chattered as she fought to hold back the tears. Inching closer to the edge, Abby closed her eyes and mentally braced herself for the inevitable.

* * * *

"Oh, my God! Abigail!" George ran to his daughter's side. He lifted her and gently placed her back in the middle of the bed. Turning toward Beau, he ordered, "Get Lily, and tell her to bring Abby's medication right away."

Beau turned and ran for the stairs. He found Lily in the kitchen, the pill bottle in her hand. She gave him the pills, and he ran back up the stairs, taking several steps at a time.

George gently cradled his daughter with one arm. His free hand placed the pills in her mouth and held a glass of water to her lips. Her leg continued to spasm, and tears ran down her cheeks. Although she avoided eye contact with Beau, she blushed with embarrassment.

George's ashen face was stricken with fear as he struggled to speak. "Are you all right, dear? Do you want me to go get Lily?" She nodded her head. He positioned her against a stack of pillows and moved toward the door. "I'll be right back."

The anguished man exited the room. Beau turned to find Abby's tears had subsided, and her face was once again set in stone. Her expression of defiance set Beau's teeth on edge.

"You're a fool. Why didn't you yell out if you were in so much pain? That's what the monitor's for." He pointed toward her side table. "What if you'd fallen and hit your head on the edge of the table or something?

"Can't you see what your behavior is doing to your father and your aunt? Can't you see how much they love you? It would kill them both if you fell and hurt yourself. They would hold themselves responsible.

"I know you think you don't have anything to live for, but you're wrong! Look around you," he said, waving his arms in the air. "And what about those two people downstairs? Have you ever stopped to think what this is doing to them? How this is affecting their lives?"

She glanced up at him, her eyes glazed with anger, her right hand clenched in a fist. She was furious with him. Good! She blinked, and one tear slid down her cheek.

"Save the tears for your father, Princess," Beau growled. "They won't work on me."

* * * *

George found his sister sitting at the kitchen table. Her hands neatly folded on her lap, she stared out the window as if in a trance, her face as white as a sheet. "Lily? Are you okay?" The room was quiet. He had never seen her in such a state before. He leaned closer and questioned? "Lily? Are you sick?"

She drew in a deep breath. "No, George, I'm fine." She offered a slight smile and added, "As a matter of fact, I think everything is going to be just fine now."

George reached for her hand. "Abigail needs you. I gave her medication, but she needs you to come up."

Lily slowly pulled herself to her feet. Her smile contained hope, something George hadn't seen for a long time. "All right," was her only response.

As they walked together to the stairs George wondered what had happened to cause such a change in his sister. He thought maybe he should reconsider his business trip.

* * * *

Beau debated leaving Abby alone yet he needed to get out of there before he did or said something he would regret. Turning, he stormed out of the room and met George and Lily at the top of the landing. Although George hurried the little woman along, she stopped and laid her hand on Beau's arm. She smiled, and it dawned on him that she had heard every word he said over the monitor in the kitchen.

Beau jogged down the stairs to his room. He changed and headed for the pool. He could be fired for that speech, but at the moment he didn't care. He wanted to yank her out of the bed and shake her until she screamed at him to stop.

Maybe he had been wrong to think he could handle this job. What if he had been mistaken about Abby? What if there were more wrong with her than they knew. What if he had made matters worse?

* * * *

Surfacing from the pool Beau found George standing at the edge waiting for him. Had Lily told him what she had overheard? Would he be able to get his old job and apartment back?

"You looked pretty intense," George remarked with a chuckle. "I wasn't sure you were ever going to come up for air."

"Sorry. I get a little carried away sometimes." He pulled himself up and out of the pool. "Is everything alright?"

"I hope I'm not making a big mistake." George said rubbing the back of his neck. "I have mixed feelings about going on this business trip, but Lily assures me that everything is going to be just fine."

Beau sighed. The sweet little darling hadn't told her brother what she overheard in the kitchen. "Getting away for a while may do both you and your daughter a world of good."

George nodded his head in agreement.

Just then Sarah and Lily walked out onto the patio, smiling and holding hands like old friends.

"Looks like your sister and the taxi are both here. I've said my goodbyes to Abigail. I wanted to wish you luck. And if you need to call me, Lily has my cell phone number."

Beau reached out and shook George's hand. They said goodbye, and

George and Sarah headed back into the house, leaving him alone with Miss Lily. He anticipated a good tongue-lashing for speaking to her niece the way that he had. He glanced back toward the pool.

"As much as it hurt me to hear what you said to my niece, you're right. She's spoiled and selfish."

Beau opened his mouth to interrupt, but she cut him off with a wave of her hand. "No. No. You were right. You were also right about her having a lot to live for. That's more important than her ever walking again. As much as I hate to admit it, I'm convinced that you're the one who can make her understand that. Thank you." Reaching out, she patted his arm and smiled, turned and headed toward the house, leaving him standing there stunned.

Beau collapsed into one of the patio chairs. It couldn't have been easy for her to confront him and admit he had been right. When he first met her, Lily hadn't liked him for some reason, and she hadn't hidden her feelings. He had somehow offended her. Just how, he didn't know. Now after hearing him yell at her niece when she *should* have been offended, she suddenly approved of him.

"Women!" *What was the old saying? You couldn't live with them, and you couldn't live without them.* He shook his head. He wasn't too sure about living with them, but he sure as heck couldn't live without them.

Chapter Seven

Beau spent the morning setting up the exercise equipment in the dining room. He moved the buffet out into the foyer and planned to use the large dining room table as his desk. He positioned the table at the far end of the room to take advantage of the view through the French doors that led out onto the terrace.

After Lily fed and massaged Abby, she had boxed up the hand painted porcelain plates that hung on the walls and the ginger jar and the European porcelain vase which sat on the dining room buffet. The four-foot tall potted Mass cane and bamboo plants were moved into the great room.

Beau arranged the exercise equipment to match the drawings he worked on half the night. Charts of the skeletal system, muscular system and nervous system lined one wall. A variety of weights lay scattered across the exercise mat. Lily walked by the doorway and glanced in. "Oh my, you've been busy," she said, glancing around the room.

"This room is perfect," he proclaimed with a big grin. "The marble floors will make it much easier for Abby to get around in the wheelchair and later when she gets her leg braces. There are a few more pieces of equipment left to bring in here."

Placing his hands on his hips, he continued "Then I'm going to clean that room out and move her downstairs. That room is big enough to hold her bed and a dresser. It will be more convenient for everyone if she's nearby."

Lily didn't respond but gave him a skeptical look.

"Plus," Beau continued "It's time she gets reacquainted with people and her life."

"Well, I can't argue with that. It makes perfect sense, but I don't know. What's Abigail going to say about it?"

"She can *say* as much as she likes," he replied with a devilish grin. She wasn't going to like anything he planned for her.

* * * *

As Abby wondered when Beau would be up he walked right in without knocking. Didn't say anything, only nodded his head then moseyed around her room. He took stock of her bedroom set, assessed her hospital bed side table and dresser. He even ran his hand across the aged oak finish then picked up a picture frame, inspected it and returned it to its former place.

What was he up to? Whether he was in the room or not, it was like waiting for the other shoe to drop. She never knew what to expect from him. And she was sure that that's just the way he wanted it.

Why wasn't her aunt with him? Was he going to work her over by himself today? She couldn't help but be concerned. He walked back and closed the bedroom door. When he spoke his strong voice broke through the silence and sounded louder than usual. Abby flinched and almost rose off the bed. Her heart sped up, and the pulsation echoed in her ears.

"Today I'm going to test your arms and legs." Walking toward the bed, he reached down and picked up her right hand, lacing her fingers with his. Using his right hand, he started to slowly massage her hand. He smiled when he saw her expression change from uncertainty to fear.

"Since you refuse to cooperate and do your therapy like you're supposed to, today we are going to do things my way. I need to know how much strength and movement you possess in your arms and legs.

"First I'm going to massage your hand then move up your arm. Since you refuse to speak," he raised his eyebrows in silent challenge, "When you want me to stop moving my hand up your arm, push against my hand, and I'll stop. If you don't push against my hand, I'll continue to move my hand until you do. Do you understand?" She didn't respond. "Good."

He watched her swallow; her eyes never wavered from his. How far would she let him get before she gave in and pushed against him. How far was he willing to go to get her to respond? If his gut feeling and everything he had read were true, she should be able to do quite a bit more than she was letting on. Besides he had seen her make a fist with her right hand the other day. And before that she had pushed the tennis ball onto the floor. She could move, and she could speak. Just how long it would take before she did either he didn't know, but he had all day.

Earlier Beau explained to Lily his plan to get Abby to speak. He had thought about it long and hard and was convinced it was the only way. They sat for hours and talked. He showed Lily the research and the letters from the different specialists. Finally she gave him permission to go ahead with his plan. She also agreed to sit by the monitor and listen.

It was time to see what these Pendergrass girls were made of.

Slow and easy Beau glided his hand over Abby's palm and wrist. He massaged her flesh, inching his hand further past the elbow and along the soft underside of her arm. He moved on, all the while willing her to push against his hand. She held her ground.

Stubborn bullheaded spoiled brat. He ventured on. Her skin felt like silk. Reaching her armpit, Beau glanced to her breasts and then back to her eyes, challenging her, daring her to let him continue.

At the last second before his fingers brushed against her breast, she tightened her fingers around his and pushed his hand. Beau stopped, released her hand and gently placed it back on the bed. "Good," was all he could say.

His heart pounded in his head. Obstinate little witch. Crossing to the other side of the bed, he picked up her left hand. Lacing her fingers with his, he started again. "Same as before. Push against my hand when you want me to stop."

Although it appeared to take quite a bit more effort on her part, Abby's hand moved slightly against his when his hand slid past her elbow. Just as he expected, the incomplete spinal cord damage had affected her left side more than her right.

"Good girl. I knew you could do it."

Beau threw back the covers, exposing her bare legs. Her eyes opened wide, and she drew in a large breath.

He swallowed hard. "Now we'll try your legs. Same thing. Push against me, and I'll stop. Okay?"

He gently lifted her right foot and rotated it in small circles. Her foot felt so small and feminine in his large hand. *Stay focused, Beau.*

"Are you ready?"

Abby closed her eyes, but Beau wanted her full attention. "Keep your eyes open, Miss Abigail Sue." He wanted her to see that he meant business. That he would go all the way. Well, no, not all the way. But she didn't know that. If he couldn't scare her into speaking he would make her mad enough to speak.

This little exercise was meant to break the ice, to get her to say something. Anything. And he would do whatever it took to push her to the breaking point, and the sooner the better. If he could get her to talk again then her recovery would be that much quicker.

Starting up her leg, he explored and massaged the muscles. With one hand on each side of her leg, he let her foot rest against his lower abdomen. Her toes curled somewhat as he massaged her foot.

Her long leg was just as silky smooth as her arms; no doubt due to Miss Lily's loving care and special lotions.

He continued on. Their eyes stayed locked, neither intending to back down first. His hand gently moved across the top of her calf, around the sides and along the back to the tender underside of her knee. Her eyes rounded with shock, or was it sensation? Not willing to break his rhythm, he roamed over her knee and proceeded up her thigh. She was good, he thought. She was going to hold out until the very end. The only problem was, just where was that going to be? Then she lightly pushed her foot against his abdomen. He stopped and placed her leg carefully on the bed.

Shaken and unable to speak, he proceeded to the other side of the bed. Lifting up her left foot, he gently started his ascent. This time there was no curling of the toes; she held her foot perfectly still which confirmed his suspicions. She had little to no feeling on her left side. The fact that her left arm responded at all was a good sign. Beau slid his hands over her knee and up her thigh, kneading the muscles as he went.

Her expression changed. She had no feeling, and the fear in her eyes begged him to stop. If he continued, she would think he was after something else completely. He planned on using that to his advantage. It was now truth or dare time. Which one of them would give in first? He prayed it would be her.

Why isn't he stopping? He knows by now that I have no feeling in that leg. What does he think he's going to prove by continuing? Abby swallowed hard. *I can't move my foot to make him stop.* Panic rose deep inside. Her heart pounded at her temples. He was planning on taking advantage of the situation!

Abby remembered that he had closed the door. She turned her head toward the monitor. Was her aunt listening? Was she even home? Was there anyone out there who could stop him if she cried out? If this was a game, she didn't want to play anymore.

He could read her thoughts, and she was helpless to do anything to stop him. With each stroke, his face came closer and closer to hers. His hands rode higher and higher up her thigh.

She watched as her leg moved of its own accord in his hand and felt nothing. His hand moved higher, almost reaching the hem of her nightgown, only inches from slipping underneath.

Then she remembered she had nothing on under her nightgown. She panicked. Opening her mouth to protest, nothing came out. She swallowed and tried again.

Come on, baby. You can do it. Beau held her gaze and willed her to try harder. He watched tears fill her eyes as they pleaded for him to stop. He couldn't. If he backed down now he would lose more than just this point. He would lose the whole game. Hell, they would all lose. But Abby would lose the most, and she didn't even realize it.

The fear he witnessed in her eyes almost did him in. *Come on, baby. Try harder,* he coaxed silently. *You can do it.* Why wasn't she giving in? One word—that's all he wanted. He fought his conscience, knowing deep down in his heart that what he was doing was best for her.

He ventured on, the tips of his fingers disappearing under her nightgown. He didn't know how much more of this he could take. A lump rose up and lodged in his throat. The pounding of his heart echoed in his head. Would he pass out before she gave in? He licked his dry lips.

"STOP!" Abby's response wasn't much more than a whisper, but Beau heard her loud and clear. Relieved, he gathered her into his arms and rocked her back and forth. Her tears soaked through the front of his shirt.

"That's my girl. I knew you could do it. I'm so sorry I had to put you through that, sweetheart, but it was the only way."

The ice was finally broken. She was on her way to recovery. He had gotten through to her, and now they could communicate like two adults. The battle was over.

"You dirty rotten son of a bit…"

"Now there's no need to get hostile, Abby darlin'. It was for your own good." He set her back against the pillows and backed toward the door.

"You! I hate you!" She reached for the glass on the bedside table.

Beau opened the door and quickly slipped out, closing it as the glass hit and shattered against the other side.

Shirt and hair disheveled, out of breath and with a sheepish smile on his face, Beau came face to face with Lily. Curse words any sailor would have been proud of followed close behind him.

"What on earth happened?" Lily exclaimed.

"Well, she's talking and moving," Beau said but added, "Now might not be a good time to go in there though." He glanced over his shoulder at the door. Another crash sounded.

"I sure could use a cold beer. How about you? Care to join me, Miss Lily?"

* * * *

"That dirty rotten... He tricked me! Abby's heart slammed against her ribs. Her throat hurt, and her voice sounded hoarse. She swallowed again and watched the water from the glass drip down her bedroom door.

Damn him! This was all just a game to him. He was just pushing her buttons, trying to get a rise out of her. She had convinced herself that she was the one in control. Then his breathing changed, and the thought that he might be enjoying himself a little too much crossed her mind.

I can't believe he did that to me. Wait till my father hears about this … what he tried to do to me. No one had ever taken such liberties with her before. She had looked deep into his eyes and saw an emotion she hadn't recognized, and it had sent icy fingers up her spine. She wiped her damp palms across the sheets.

Abby's gaze swept around the room. Where was her aunt? She shouldn't have left him alone with her. He had tricked her. She hated him. Every time his rough hands roamed over her skin little waves of sensation washed over her. He knew all along that she could speak. But now she reached up to touch her throat. *She* didn't believe she would ever speak again.

Abby sighed. Her heart felt heavy, and her head throbbed. Now what? She closed her eyes and tried to collect her scattered emotions and place them back under control. What would happen to her now? She massaged her sore throat, and tears slid down her cheeks.

"He tricked me once," her voice cracked. "He won this battle, but he's in for a long war!"

* * * *

Lily hadn't been sure Beau's plan would work, but he had expressed the importance of not putting it off any longer.

She had sat on the edge of her bed, and when she heard Abby cry out, she jerked off the bed and staggered to her feet. Darting out of her room she saw Beau exit her niece's room. She couldn't describe his expression. He appeared shaken and relieved.

Twenty minutes later, Lily eased open her niece's door, pushing broken glass across the floor and entered the room. Abby reclined against several pillows, her face pinched as if she had been sucking on lemons. When Abby noticed her standing by the door, she appeared disappointed. Had she been expecting Beau?

"Well, I hear congratulations are in order," she said, watching her niece as she approached the bed and set down the tray of food.

"Did he tell you what he did to me?" Abby responded in a sarcastic tone. Her face was flushed, and her eyes sparked with anger. Oh, yes, the old Abigail Pendergrass was back and fixing for a fight.

"I want you to call Daddy right now and have him come home." Her voice wasn't strong, but her right hand was fisted in the blankets. "I want that man out of this house today! How dare he..."

"That's quite enough, Abigail. I know what he did, and I gave him my permission. Furthermore..." She raised her hands to ward off any further tirade. "I will call your father so you may speak to him, but you *will not* have him leave his meetings and rush home. And you *will* do whatever Mr. Winkelman tells you to do. Understand?"

"What? You can't be serious!" Her eyes flashed with indignation.

Lily placed her hands on her hips. "Oh. I assure you I am quite serious. And you will do as you're told. Do I make myself clear?" With a rigid spin, she peered down at her niece, hoping to appear intimidating.

"You're treating me like a child!" Abby huffed and turned her face away.

"That's because you've been acting like one. You be a good girl and do as you're told, and you just might end up with a real life when this is all over."

Lily fed Abby her lunch. She drew her niece into conversation and marveled at how wonderful it was to hear the sound of her voice again. *George will be so relieved. Thank you, Lord.*

* * * *

After dinner, Beau thanked Lily and headed off to the exercise room. He dug through a stack of papers, searching for Dr. Maxwell Hanson's number and then phoned him.

The family physician was pleased with Beau's report, yet surprised at the unexpected progress he had made. They discussed Beau's treatment plan along with his decision to move Abby down to the main floor.

"I agree whole heartedly," Dr. Hanson remarked. "She'll recover much quicker if she's in the middle of things again."

"It just makes sense," Beau said. "Everything is on the main floor. She can eat her meals with us and workout in the exercise room I set up."

"What exercise room?"

"I took all the equipment out of storage and turned the formal dining room into an exercise room." He leaned back in his chair and glanced around the room. "It's perfect! There's plenty of room, and the marble floors will make it easier for Miss Abigail to get around."

"You're a wonder, boy. I have to admit at first I had my doubts. George was right. You're the right man for the job."

"Thank you, sir. I appreciate that, but to tell you the truth, I don't believe her paralysis is what's keeping her from recovering. I think her state of mind is what's really holding her back." Beau rubbed the back of his neck.

"Her psychological reasoning plays a large part in allowing her body to heal," Dr. Hanson stated.

"George and I talked about the chance that Abby may have Post Traumatic Stress Disorder and/or Survivor Guilt." He leaned forward and placed his forearms on the desk. "He called Dr. Berkman to set up an

88

appointment before he left on his trip. She'll be dropping by next week sometime."

"Talking with Dr. Berkman again is a great idea."

"I appreciate your support," Beau replied.

"I will be expecting a written weekly report on Abigail's progress," Dr. Hanson added.

"That won't be a problem, I assure you."

Pleased with all that he had accomplished, Beau changed into his cutoffs and headed to the pool for a well-deserved relaxing workout.

* * * *

Abby didn't need to see who was in the pool to know it was Beau. Through her open window she heard the diving board vibrate from his weight. Were there no limits to what this guy thought he could touch of hers? He had touched her doll, her tennis trophies and ball, then *her*, and now he was back in her pool again! This guy had a lot of nerve. She pictured his strong body slicing through the water. Did he wear revealing trunks like the guys on her swim team at school? She smiled; she would like to see that.

Earlier Beau mentioned extending her therapy to the pool. Once she had loved to swim, but now the idea terrified her. Leaving the safe haven of her room was alarming. Here she was protected, sheltered from the outside. She ran her right hand across her bedspread as she gazed around her room. She was safe in this room, and she was never going to leave it.

Lily entered Abby's room, the telephone to her ear. "She's right here." She held the phone to Abby's ear. "It's your father," she said, smiling, her eyes filled with happy tears.

"Daddy?" She had so much she wanted to tell him, but at the moment her mind drew a blank, and tears filled her throat.

"Princess? Is that really you?" She heard his voice crack with emotion. Damn her stubbornness.

"Yes, Daddy, it's me. I miss you."

"Oh, Princess, you don't know how wonderful it is to hear your sweet voice again."

"I love you, Daddy, and I'm so sorry that I've caused you so much pain." Reaching up, she wiped away hot tears.

"That's all behind us now, dear. You just concentrate on getting better."

"How's your business trip going?" Abby asked, ignoring the look of warning her aunt was giving her. What she really wanted to ask him was why he had taken that Sarah what's-her-name with him and had his assistant Paula accompany them.

"I'll be home in a few weeks. I'll take some time off, and we'll have all the time in the world to get reacquainted."

"All right." She paused. "Daddy, have a safe trip."

"You rest and get your strength back. I'll call again real soon. I love you, baby. Take care."

"I will, Daddy. Don't worry about me."

* * * *

Lily reclined on the patio furniture in the shade and watched Beau's strong arms slice through the water as he swam across the pool. *To be young and have that much stamina.* She stared off into the distance, into a time when she was much younger.

"Miss Lily? Are you all right, ma'am?" Beau reached for his towel that lay on the empty chair.

"I'm fine, dear. I was just admiring the scenery." She smiled. "I brought you a beer. My husband Frank and I used to sit outside at night like this. He liked his beer, too." She saluted him.

Beau picked up the bottle and downed a good portion. "Thank you, ma'am."

"Sit down, Beau. I need to talk to you about something."

He sat, resting his arms on the table.

"Abby is a very special girl. She once had a strong and competitive spirit. Today I saw that spirit again for the first time in a long time. To tell you the truth, I never expected to ever see it again." She took a sip of her beer. "I would hate to see that spirit crushed or broken."

"I understand. That's not my intent. Miss Abby's like a young filly that's been hurt or spooked. She's skittish! Overly cautious, wary of what people want from her. Once she learns she can trust me she will come to me of her own free will." He leaned back in the chair. The look on his face wasn't arrogant; it was confident. He knew what he was talking about, and that reassured her.

Droplets of water fell from his long hair onto his bare chest. He wiped them away and continued, "Once a wounded animal understands you're only trying to help them they stop fighting you. There's a living, breathing woman inside of her that wants out. She's afraid of what life has in store for her so she's holding herself prisoner."

Lily understood what he meant, but she couldn't help but worry about how her niece would respond to him after her anger wore off.

"That young woman in there is also very innocent." She wasn't telling him anything he didn't already know, yet it needed to be said out loud. "I may be sixty-eight years old, nevertheless I know an attractive man when I see one. You're very handsome, Mr. Winkelman. And I'm sure once my niece gets past her anger, she'll come to the same conclusion. She's very vulnerable right now."

Beau leaned forward to speak. But Lily raised a hand in warning and pinned him with a well-seasoned stare. "Don't make her any promises you don't intend to keep."

"No, ma'am. I won't."

Chapter Eight

"Don't do this! Put me down! You're asking for it if you don't put me down right this minute!"

Beau held Abby in his arms, determined to carry her down the stairs. Why was she being so bullheaded? He searched her angry eyes for an answer.

They had been over this several times already. He explained how much easier it would be on Lily if she moved downstairs. Whenever she wanted she could use the wheelchair and go outside and sit on the patio in the sun. And it would be much more convenient to do her therapy. Most of all, it was time for her to leave her comfort zone and rejoin the living.

"I'll make a deal with you," he said sitting down on the edge of her bed with her still in his arms. "Try it until your father comes home. Then if you don't like it downstairs I'll move everything back up here. All right?" Her eyes filled with tears as she looked away. "What's the matter, sweetheart?"

"Please don't make me do this."

"What are you afraid of?" He reached up and placed a strand of loose hair behind her ear. "I'll be right across the hall. I won't let anything happen to you. I promise. Come on! Miss Lily is waiting downstairs with your wheelchair, and I think she has a surprise in store for you!"

Her fragile body felt so small in his arms.

He placed a finger under her chin, tilting her face toward his. "You have to trust me."

She studied his face, and after several seconds she rested her head against his shoulder, surrendering. It couldn't have been easy for her.

"That's my girl." Beau stood, pulling her tight to his chest. He started down the stairs. She stiffened in his arms, and he stopped.

"Wait! I'm dizzy!" She closed her eyes, and her weight shifted in his arms. Beau tightened his hold on her, and she placed her head back on his shoulder.

"The dizziness is normal and will soon pass, sweetheart. You're all right. You're safe in my arms."

If Abby hadn't been so terrified she would have laughed out loud. She doubted any woman was safe in this man's arms—for long. He had scooped her up as though she weighed nothing at all, which proved how defenseless she really was against him.

The thought of leaving the shelter and security of her room sent her into a panic. Beau surprised her. He hadn't bullied her into doing what he wanted—instead he had made a point of reassuring her that everything would be all right. Nothing would ever be *all right* again.

He exited her room, her safe haven. He started down the stairs, and the sensation of falling hit her. Her eyes filled with tears, and she swallowed hard. It would serve him right if she threw up all over him. Trying to calm herself, she inhaled a ragged breath. The light musky scent of Beau tickled her senses. Closing her eyes she relaxed against him.

They reached the main floor in a matter of minutes though it seemed much longer. They found Lily pacing the foyer, wringing her hands. From Beau's arms Lily appeared small and somehow a little older. The foyer appeared smaller, too. Bending down and with great care, Beau deposited her in the wheelchair.

"There. That wasn't so bad, was it?" He grinned.

The room spun like a slow motion merry-go-round, and Abby's body veered to the right. She had been downstairs two minutes, and now she was going to end up face down on the imported Italian marble.

"Oh, no, you don't!" Beau reached for the safety straps and secured them across her chest.

The room came to a stop. Strapped into the wheelchair, Abby realized that she only traded the prison of her bed for one on wheels.

Beau kneeled in front of her chair and positioned her feet on the metal footrests. He placed a hand on her knee and treated her to one of his lopsided sexy grins. "You're doing great, sweetheart."

"If I could, I'd kick you right in the teeth, *sweetheart*."

He countered with a triumphant grin that lit up his whole face.

"I have a surprise for you, Abigail dear." Her aunt rushed forward, taking control of the wheelchair and pushing Abby through the hall and into the kitchen. The walls tilted and spun in a circle as Abby was propelled through the house.

"It's such a beautiful day. We're going to have our lunch out on the patio, just the two of us," Lily chirped from behind her.

Abby's stomach lurched, and she clenched her teeth together. Lunch? Great. Maybe she could throw up in the pool.

* * * *

Beau wrestled with Abby's furniture while the two women enjoyed their lunch in the sun on the patio. He brought down her small dresser and placed it in the corner of her new room, then placed the small combination TV-VCR on it. The biggest challenge had been the hospital bed, though disassembling and reassembling it had proved more time-consuming than difficult.

He made up the bed with a set of pink-flowered sheets Miss Lily had given him. Tossing the sheets at him she told him once he got the bed put together he could make it. Then the wicked little woman had the nerve to laugh at his stunned expression.

"After lunch," she added "While Abby's resting, we'll pack up a few of her clothes and belongings and carry them downstairs for her."

Beau shook his head. "I liked it better when neither one of you were speaking to me. I'm starting to feel like a hired hand instead of a high-paid professional." Lily's eyes had twinkled with a bright youthfulness as she waved away his comment playfully.

Beau glanced around the sparse but adequate room. He stretched the tight sore muscles in his back. He accomplished a lot today. He was tired and sweaty. He felt wonderful. *I could use a cold beer with a steak chaser then a cool shower and a hot woman.*

* * * *

Dr. Voight knocked again, though again no one answered the door. Heated voices echoed through the open windows. He instinctively became alert and listened.

"You're mean. I hate you!"

"Quit being such a baby."

"I'm not a baby. I just can't do any more."

"Any more? You've only done two!"

"I don't care. That's enough."

"I don't think so! Listen, sweetheart, you're going to do as many as I say you're going to do!"

What's going on? Will reached for the large brass door handle and let himself in. He followed the sound of raised voices to the dining room. "What the devil's going on in here?"

"Good! Dr. Voight is here. Now you can't make me do anything I don't want to!" Abby spat out the dare.

Beau's fists settled on his hips. "You know what you need? A good spanking! And you just might get one before the day's over."

"Did you hear that, Dr. Voight? He threatened to spank me!"

Shocked, Will stared at Abigail. He couldn't believe what he was seeing—or hearing. "Abigail! You-you-you talked! You can talk!"

"Of course I can talk," she snapped, rolling her eyes. She raised her right arm and pointed toward Beau. "He's being mean to me!"

"Oh, shut up." Beau glared at his verbal opponent.

"You shut up. You've been picking on me all day!"

"Have not!"

"Have, too!"

"That's enough!" Will placed his hands up in to the air. He had been caught between two squabbling four year olds. "Has everyone gone crazy? What's going on here?"

"He dragged me down here against my will..."

"Did not."

"Did so!"

"Hi, Dr. Voight." Lily appeared out of nowhere and offered him a greeting as she passed with an armload of groceries. "I see they haven't murdered each other yet."

Will glanced back at the standoff in the dining room and hoping for someone sane to talk to, he trailed Lily into the kitchen. "What's going on around here?"

Lily flashed him a grin over her shoulder. "Mr. Winkelman is wonderful."

"Wonderful?" he echoed with a snort.

"He got through to Abigail and *persuaded* her to talk." She laughed, tilting her head toward the hall. "Although I think he liked it better when she refused to speak. Would you like something cold to drink, dear?"

Will watched as Lily poured him a tall glass of iced tea. He didn't care for *Mr. Winkelman*. And he didn't care for Abigail's quick recovery either. This could mess up his plans. The plans he carefully fabricated over the past few months. He would get to the bottom of this.

"Just when did all this take place? Her speech, I mean? Does George know? How did that guy move her down here?"

"Two days ago and only one question at a time please. This house has gone from peace and quiet to a full-blown riot."

"I'm sorry, Ms. Bendickson. It's just all so sudden."

"I know! Isn't it wonderful?" Lily's voice had a joyous lilt he had never heard before.

"Yeah, wonderful. How well do you know this guy? I mean, who recommended him?"

"Beau came with several glowing references, and George is very impressed with what he has accomplished in such a short time."

"I'd like to see his credentials. I'm not comfortable with the way he's handling Abigail." He glanced toward the hall. "He's pushing her too hard."

Lily peeked over the top of the grocery bag she had set down. "You'll have to speak to George. He's handling everything."

He planned on doing just that. "Do you know anything about him? Like where he went to school?"

"I'm not sure. I guess I really don't know much about him." Lily's hands stilled, her expression puzzled. She appeared to be searching his eyes for answers as if he suddenly turned into a raving lunatic.

"I don't like this, and I don't trust him." He closed the distance between them and lowered his voice. "You shouldn't be here alone with this guy."

"You're overreacting, Will. Beau is a very nice man." She continued to pull items from her grocery bag. "I have to admit I had my doubts about him at first, but he's done wonders with Abigail."

Will turned and proceeded to pace the floor. He didn't like this guy, and he sure as hell didn't trust him. "Ms. Bendickson, how much time does he spend alone with Abigail? I mean, do you observe them at all times?"

"Well, no. They are alone a great deal of the time, while I'm cleaning, gardening, or when I go to the store like today."

This guy had moved in and made himself right at home. He crossed to the counter and reached for one of her hands. He needed her to understand what was at stake here. "It's very important that you keep an eye on him. Abigail's in a very vulnerable state right now. This guy could easily take advantage of her physically and mentally."

"Oh, I don't think he'd do anything like that." Lily patted his hand affectionately.

She wasn't taking him seriously. He squeezed her hand for effect. "Just promise me you'll keep an eye on him. We can't afford to be too careful. Abby's too valuable—I mean important. If you have any concerns day or night, anytime, call me. I'll come right over. All right?"

"I promise, Dr. Will." She smiled sweetly and returned to her chores.

Will took his glass and walked toward the sliding glass door. His mind was too clouded with questions to appreciate the view. Questions he wanted answered before he left.

* * * *

"Just one more. Good girl. That's it. Great job!" Beau placed a strong hand on her shoulder and squeezed gently. "I knew you could do it."

"Can I stop now?" Abby pleaded. She felt too exhausted to fight any longer. She just wanted to go to her room and lie down. It seemed like they had been at it for hours.

"Yeah, that's okay. You did a great job. I'm afraid it's going to get harder before it gets easier. But I'm sure you'll be able to handle it." He moved around to stand in front of her and placed his hands on his hips. His dark brown eyes held a hint of mischief. The front of his sleeveless shirt was damp, and his spicy scent tickled her nose. Even sweaty the man was sexy.

"I'll help you to your room." Beau turned Abby's wheelchair around and pushed her out of the dining room, down the hall and into the kitchen. Ignoring the two standing in the kitchen, they turned and started down the hall. Teasing, he asked "Did you want help changing your clothes?"

Abby shook her head. This guy was unreal. "Don't you think you've touched me enough for one day," she spat over one shoulder. "Don't you ever get tired?"

She ached all over; her muscles trembled from exhaustion. She didn't care if she changed her clothes; she just wanted to fall into a deep sleep. She thought for sure his plan was to work her to death before her father returned from his business trip.

"I'll send Miss Lily in to help you change. I'll be back to rub you down." He winked and grinned.

"Lucky me!" she snorted, and he laughed.

* * * *

Beau walked in to the kitchen and helped himself to a cold bottle of water. "I'm finished for now." He glanced toward Lily. "I'll be back to rub her down."

Dr. Voight's voice followed him as he headed out of the room. "I need to talk to you, Winkelman."

"Terrific!" Beau replied, without stopping or turning his head.

Will followed him into the dining room. "Just what type of therapy are you using with Abigail? She's very fragile, and I don't want you pushing her too hard."

There was a pause. Beau didn't turn, hoping the man had rethought his play and left quietly.

"Plus," Will continued, invading his peace and quiet. "Show me your credentials!"

Beau wasn't going to stand there and debate his qualifications or abilities with this cocky second-string doctor.

Fighting for control he gently set his water bottle on the desk, turned and glared down at the shorter man.

The doctor stood poised in the doorway with his arms crossed, a massive frown creasing his brow. If he hadn't been so annoyed Beau would have laughed.

"I have a few questions of my own, Doctor!" Beau said leaning against the desk, copying the other man's stance. "First, are you Abby's husband or fiancé? Are you her psychiatrist or even her general medical doctor?"

Will made no reply. Raising one eyebrow, Beau added, "I didn't think so. I plan to continue as I see fit. If you don't like it, tough."

Beau's long legs closed the distance between them in seconds, bringing them face-to-face. "You're out of bounds, Doc," he whispered between clinched teeth. "I'll tell you what. I won't come to your office and tell you how to treat your patients. Don't come back and tell me how to treat mine."

Red faced, Will turned on his heel and headed for the door.

Beau rubbed his hand on the back of his neck. He had enough to deal with; he didn't need some know-it-all doctor hanging around and getting underfoot. This job was turning out to be more stressful than he had anticipated.

* * * *

Will sped down the driveway. "The nerve of that guy! Winkelman and his sister will be sorry they ever came to California."

Will's poor excuse for a car skidded out onto the highway, spraying gravel into the air behind him. "Nobody dismisses me like some delivery boy!" Winkelman couldn't get rid of him that easily. He had come too far to let some washed-up jock get in his way and spoil his plans.

They've all gone mad. George has run off with the little blond fortune hunter, and Lily has been taken in by the guy's charm, causing her to turn a deaf ear and blind eye to the whole situation.

What about Abby? He snorted and shook his head; she had been transformed from a frail invalid back to shades of her former self. "The little fool actually thinks she can recover from this!" That was something he couldn't afford to let happen.

How had the situation gotten so far out of his control? After a moment the cloud of despair lifted; he had connections. "I'd bet with a little investigating I'd find some dirt on either the wonderful Mr. Winkelman or his pretty sister." Catching his reflection in the rearview mirror he smirked.

"Then what would George think of them?"

* * * *

The next few days between therapy sessions Beau installed handrails

99

down both sides of the hallway and in the small bathroom next to his and Abby's rooms. He added a transfer bench to the inside of the tub and a raised toilet seat with attached arm rests. Lastly he installed a hand-held shower sprayer with massager. Abby wasn't ready for these things quite yet, but at the rate she was improving it wouldn't be long.

As a reward for how rapidly she responded to therapy, Beau installed a couple of shelves in her new room and brought down several of her dolls and some framed photos.

He entered her room and set a box on the end of her bed.

"You had no right to touch any of my things," Abby snapped. "I told you I didn't want those things down here." Abby sat in the hospital bed, her arms crossed in a defiant position, one she had mastered quite quickly.

"Since I couldn't bring your whole bedroom set down, I thought these might make this room homier for you." Beau unwrapped one of the dolls and paused at her frown.

"I'm sorry." She sighed. "I guess I'm just tired." Perched up against a stack of pillows, she flattened the blanket next to her leg and replied, "Since you went through all this trouble, let me see what you brought down." Encouraged, he unwrapped each item for her approval and placed several picture frames around the room.

He felt proud of the progress she made, not only physically but also mentally. He enjoyed rewarding her, even if it was a small token. But was it enough? There must be something more he could do. Sitting on the edge of her bed, he smiled. He had the perfect answer. "How about I take you and Miss Lily to town for ice cream? It's a nice day. We could take a drive up the coast."

Abby's body stiffened. Her eyes widened with alarm, and the color in her cheeks faded to an ashen hue.

"No!" Her response sounded strained, and her hands started to fidget with her doll's skirt.

"Why not? Don't you like ice cream?"

"I'm not going to town!" She turned away and glanced out the window.

"Come on. It will be fun. I'll even let you sit in the cab of my pick-up," he teased with an impish grin.

"Gee, thanks."

"It'll do us both good to get out of here for a while."

She turned and pinned him with her stare. "No."

"Why? Give me one good reason," he asked, hoping she would confide in him.

She flung the doll at the box. "I don't have to give you any reasons if I don't want to. Get out of my room." She held his gaze for a second before turning away, dismissing him. Beau watched as the barriers he had worked so hard to tear down blocked him once more. She retreated back into her own world—shutting him out.

Stunned, he sat for several more seconds, sighed, stood then shoved his hands in his pockets and walked out.

* * * *

Strolling into the kitchen Beau found Lily making a pot of coffee. She turned and studied his expression. "I heard shouting. What's happened now?"

"I don't understand." He leaned his forehead against the end of the upper cabinets. "Everything seemed to be going well, and then I said that I'd like to take you both to town for ice cream, and she froze up and ordered me out." He sighed and closed his eyes. "What did I do?"

"Dear, you didn't do anything wrong." Lily patted him on the back. "She's terrified of getting into a car. I wish that she would continue her sessions with Dr. Berkman. Maybe she'd be able to get over her fear."

Beau backed away from the cabinets. "Does she really believe that she'll never have to get back into a car?"

Lily sighed. "In order to bring her home from the hospital she had to be sedated."

"I'm sorry she suffered so much." He shook his head. "But this is ridiculous. This needs to be addressed right now."

Lily patted Beau's arm. "Sit down, Beau. There is something else you should know." Beau lowered himself into the chair. By her tone he knew he wasn't going to like whatever she had to tell him.

"Months ago, before Abigail stopped talking, she cried all the time. All day and all night." Lily rubbed her forehead. "We knew the accident had been horrible, but losing Carolyn, I'm afraid, was too much for her to deal with. They'd been friends since they were children." A lone tear slid down her face.

"They went to Europe for the French Open together, took ski trips to Colorado and spent spring break in Mexico." She wiped the tear away. "They made plans neither one of them ever dreamt they wouldn't be able to keep."

Beau's heart ached to see Lily upset.

"One day I heard her crying. She'd said she wished she'd died in the accident, too." Lily's tears slid freely down both cheeks. "I don't think she can live without Carolyn. I don't think she wants to live without her." Lily blew her nose. "I know what it's like to lose someone you love. Part of you dies with them." She gazed out the window and continued. "It takes a very special person to fill that void. It's hard to let yourself love again. To give your heart away again." She turned and smiled. "Then someone comes along, and your heart opens up like a rose that's just been waiting for the sun to come out from behind the clouds."

Beau stood and pulled her into his embrace. Lily chuckled. "I've been blessed several times in my life. God sent two more wonderful men to love me after my first husband died."

Holding her close, Beau whispered, "You're an easy person to love, Miss Lily."

He could make a list of what he thought Abby's problems were, but which one of them was the root of her condition? Was it reliving the crash in her nightmares each night? Losing her best friend? Or being left crippled? Or was it as simple as being afraid of getting back into a car again? He couldn't help her progress any further until he knew the answer.

* * * *

Later that day, Beau entered Abby's room without knocking and plunked himself down on the edge of her bed. She avoided his stare and ignored him. He had more time than money so biding his time, he sat and waited.

Her breathing increased. She was working herself up to a full head of steam. Glancing toward the bedside table he wondered if the picture frames he had brought down earlier were going to soon grow wings and fly through the air.

"What?" She turned to face him. "What do you want now? Can't you find anyone else to bother?"

"Nope. Besides I'm getting paid to bother you," he teased. He placed a hand leisurely on her leg. "It's all right, Abby. I understand."

"What do you think you understand?" Her voice raised a few octaves, and he was sure her agitation was conveyed all the way down the hall and into the kitchen. He didn't mind her yelling; he was getting used to it, but he wondered if it upset Lily.

"Tell me what's going on. What's really bothering you?"

She pinned him with her piercing gaze. "At the moment the only thing bothering me is you!"

"You know perfectly well what I'm talking about." He folded his arms across his chest. "I'm not leaving until we discuss this."

"No! You're here to help me physically, not psychoanalyze me!" Abby fired back.

"Abby, I can't help you if you won't let me."

"I don't want your help. Damn it—get out!"

Beau remembered a picture he brought down of Abby and another girl in matching tennis outfits. He stood and crossed to where the picture sat. Picking it up, he turned and asked, "Is this Carolyn?" He turned the picture toward Abby, and she looked away.

He was determined to get this out in the open.

"She's pretty." She didn't reply. "How old were you here?" Still no reply. He returned to the bed and sat beside her.

"Tell me about her. What was she like?" She still ignored him. He changed his game plan. "I bet you two were the kind of girls that did everything together." He held up the picture. "You dressed alike. You ate the same foods. Even wore your hair in the same style. I bet you couldn't bear to spend one day apart from each other."

Abby's flushed face turned an ashen gray, and the spark in her eyes disappeared like candlelight being snuffed out. He had seen grown men collapse in pain, but he'd never seen a person fold up and crawl inside themself before. Damn, what had he done?

"Sweetheart? I'm sorry." He pulled her into his arms and held her close. Her limp body shook softly as her soundless tears soaked his shirt. "I'm so sorry," he breathed into her hair. "Let me help you."

"She didn't want to spend any more time with me," she whispered softly.

Setting her back, Beau brushed the hair from her face. "I don't understand."

"Neither do I." She frowned. "I thought we were going to be together forever." She looked like a child who'd been punished for something they hadn't done. "Why did this happen?"

"I can't answer that." He pulled her close and kissed her brow.

"It should have been me that day, not her. Why didn't I die instead of Carolyn?"

"It wasn't your time." His protectiveness kicked in, and he gently rocked from side to side, hoping to comfort her.

"It was my fault," she sobbed.

"It wasn't your fault. Accidents just happen."

She pulled away and looked up through her tears. "But it was. We argued, and I made her turn her attention away from the road."

"Listen to me." Beau searched for a way to get through to her. "People argue all the time in cars. It wasn't your fault."

Abby struggled to meet his gaze. "You don't understand!" Her voice teetered on hysteria. "She told me she was going to switch to the same school as her new boyfriend, Josh. I made a big fuss and argued with her. It was all my fault." She collapsed against his chest, and he held her trembling body as her heart-wrenching sobs tackled his heart.

Rocking her gently in his arms, he kissed her brow and rubbed her back. He wasn't sure what else to do.

"Abby, what's done is done. You can't go back and change the past." He leaned back and gazed into her tear-stained eyes. "But you can change the future—your future." Her blue eyes gazed up into his, searching for answers.

"You need to rest now. We can talk about this tomorrow." He leaned her back against the pillow and pulled the blankets up. "Do you need your aunt for anything?" She shook her head. Beau walked to the door and whispered, "Goodnight, Miss Abigail Sue. Sweet dreams."

Beau stretched out on his bed, his ankles and feet hanging out over the end. He'd tried to read but couldn't concentrate and tossed the book on the floor.

Placing his arm over his face he sighed. She'd jumped a major hurdle today, and he was proud of her. He didn't want to admit it, but she was starting to get under his skin.

Why did she have to feel so good in his arms? His urge to protect her, fight all her battles and make her world right again was so strong that it scared him. The rude reminder that he was there to help her, literally, to get back on her feet and not coddle her shook him mentally.

Throwing the covers aside, he stood, stretched and walked to the window. He braced his hands on the windowsill and stared out at the starlit night.

He couldn't fail this time. He'd run out of chances. He couldn't afford to make any more mistakes. He needed to be tough with Abby. Push her back into the game. Force her to take a good hard look at her life as it was now and what it could be with a lot of hard work. He drew in a deep breath. But could he do all of this and still control his powerful attraction for her?

Chapter Nine

George and Sarah sat in one of the hotel's five star restaurants. Unable to concentrate, George pushed his food around on his plate. He couldn't believe he'd left his daughter alone with a stranger. She must hate him. He hated himself.

"What's the matter?"

He glanced up. "What? Oh I'm sorry, Sarah."

Sarah leaned back in her chair and folded her hands in her lap. "Is it really that bad?"

"What?" He asked confused.

"Your food. It is really that bad?" she asked again.

"Oh, no!" He glanced down. "I guess I'm not hungry." He sighed and placed his fork on the edge of his plate.

"What's the matter then? You haven't eaten any of your food or spoken a word in over ten minutes."

"I'm a terrible father."

"Why would you say that?" She leaned forward, placed her elbows on the table and casually rested her chin on her hands.

"Because I've left my daughter with someone she doesn't even know." *And I feel guilty because I'm spending time with a beautiful woman.* A pounding headache was closing in on him.

"George. You are not a terrible father. And she's not a little girl. Your sister is there to see to all of her needs, and Beau will take good care of both of them." The warmth of her words went clean through to his bones. The candlelight flickered in her whiskey colored eyes, and he caught the slight fragrance of jasmine. He was definitely a bad father. He

106

closed his eyes and rubbed at his temples.

Sarah placed her napkin on the table. "Would you mind if I just went back to my room? I'm a little tired—I'd like to lie down for a while," she stated as she reached for her purse.

He stood and said, "No, that's quite all right. I'll come with you. I have a few calls to make."

They reached the entrance. Sarah laid an understanding hand on his sleeve and whispered, "Say hi to everyone for me."

He couldn't help but smile as she walked away. Although he didn't want her to go, at least he was given the reward of watching her leave.

* * * *

Abby gazed out over the ocean as she sat in her wheelchair on the patio in the sun. The past few days replayed in her head like the rerun of a bad sitcom. Just when she thought she understood Beau, he did something to confuse her all over again. Yesterday he'd been gentle and understanding, then this morning he'd come on like a drill sergeant. He'd pushed her hard. He'd set his expectations too high—too high for her ever to meet.

Today at dinner he insisted she sit at the kitchen table and eat with them. He never laughed when her spoon didn't make it all the way to her mouth. Instead he'd encouraged her to try harder. Feeding herself proved difficult, but she could control her right hand better than her left.

When she threatened to give up, his attitude never wavered. The guy was made of ice. He had no feelings. He wasn't human. She could scream, throw things and he'd only look mildly disappointed. He expected too much from her.

Then she'd spilled a full glass of milk at the table; the cold liquid ran off the edge and over his lap. She'd laughed when he'd jumped to his feet, and the milk streamed down his bare legs. He'd just grimaced and left the room to clean up. How and why he put up with her seemed beyond reason.

Her aunt, however, hadn't been so understanding or forgiving. After Beau left the room Lily outright accused her of spilling the milk on purpose. Abby didn't feel bad about Beau getting the worst of it, but she felt guilty as her aunt got down on her hands and knees to clean up the spill.

They expected too much too soon. Just how much movement and feeling would return? Then what? What did they envision she'd do with the rest of her life? What if she couldn't live up to their expectations? What was she supposed to do? Go back to college? Out of the question! Marriage and children were dreams of the past like becoming a teacher.

Her life and all her dreams were out of reach, dead and buried like Carolyn. Like she should have been.

* * * *

Lily glanced through the kitchen window at her niece on the patio. Their lives had been altered drastically since Beau's arrival—she hoped in the end it would all been worth it. The phone rang and interrupted her thoughts. "Hello?"

"Hi! How are my girls?"

"George, hello. Everything's fine. How's the business trip going?" Lily sank down at the table.

"We have a board meeting tomorrow morning, then we're going to enjoy a little sightseeing."

"That sounds wonderful. I'm glad you're making time to have some fun."

"Speaking of fun, how is everyone getting along?"

Lily glanced through the window again and sighed.

* * * *

Lost in thought, Abby didn't hear her aunt approach her until the phone appeared under her nose. With a look of warning Lily handed Abby the telephone. "It's your father."

Abby took the phone and placed it to her ear. "Hello, Daddy?"

"Oh, honey, it's so wonderful to talk to you."

"How are your meetings going?"

"There are too many of them, but it's been productive, and the transitioning has gone well."

Listening to him, Abby realized how much she missed talking with him about his business. "That's wonderful."

"I didn't call to talk business, Princess. I want to know how you're doing. Your voice sounds stronger. How are you getting along without me?"

Abby glanced up toward her aunt and smiled. "I'm fine, Daddy. I'm getting stronger every day. I miss you."

"I miss you, too. You don't know how it makes me feel to hear your voice. I thought I would never hear it again."

"I'm sorry, Daddy. I don't know what made me act the way I did." She idly picked at the hem of her shirt with her weak hand.

"That doesn't matter now. You just work on getting stronger, and I'll be home soon."

"Anything you say, Daddy."

"Princess, is Lily close by?"

"She's right here. Would you like to speak with her?"

"Just for a second. I need her to go into my study and get my personal address book. I've got a college friend in the area, and I want to see if he and his wife are free to go out dinner while we're here."

"Of course, just a moment." Abby handed the phone to Lily. "He wants to talk to you again."

"Yes, George? I'll be right back. Here's Abigail again." She handed back the phone and trotted off toward the house.

"You're stuck talking to me again," she said and giggled.

"I wish I was there with you. How are your therapy sessions working out?"

She paused. "They're going well. I've gained a lot of strength back on my right side. I'm afraid we no longer have a dining room though. Beau set it up as a gym."

"That's great. I can't believe how fortunate we are to have him. I couldn't be happier!"

Lily hurried toward her with the address book. "Here's Aunt Lily. I love you."

"I'm so proud of you, Princess. I love you, too. Goodbye."

Abby handed the phone to her aunt. Hearing the joy and pride in her father's voice kept her from expressing her true feelings and misgivings. She loved her father. Once they'd been close. For him she'd try harder.

"Goodbye, George." Lily sighed and switched off the phone. She smiled down at Abby.

"You sit down and rest," Abby said. "I'll take that back in for you. I'm going in anyway. If I stay out in the sun much longer I'm bound to burn."

"Thank you, dear. I think I will sit for a minute. Are you sure you can make it all right?" Lily handed her the worn address book.

Setting it on her lap she remarked, "I think I can. If I have any problems I'll yell."

Abby made it to the patio door without incident. Getting over the threshold was another matter. On her third try Beau appeared and helped her.

"Thank you." At his confused expression, she giggled and went on her way, leaving him to stare after her.

She made her way across the kitchen, down the hall and into her father's study. She circled the large desk and pulled the center drawer open over her lap. As she placed the address book in the drawer she saw a videotape peeking out from under some papers. Curious as to why there would be a videotape in her father's desk and not on the shelf with all the others Abby reached in and pulled it out.

She read the label, and her heart jumped in her chest. Why did her father have a tape labeled 'Carolyn' in his desk? What was on the tape? Had he ever planned on showing it to her? Abby's mind whirled. She glanced around, tucked the videotape next to her leg in the wheelchair and hurried off to her room.

* * * *

Lily stood by her niece's door; she appeared to be daydreaming, her expression blanketed in sadness. How could one so young and beautiful look so depressed? Beau had been pushing her, but he knew what she was capable of. If she would only put a little more effort into it, Abby could accomplish anything.

Abigail had come so far in such a short time. Why she hadn't cooperated in the past, Lily still didn't understand despite Beau's explanation about Post Traumatic Stress Disorder. The guy had worked wonders with her niece, and Lily now felt confident that everything would work out fine. God had truly answered her prayers. She only wished Abigail could be happier and for her to realize she had so much to live for. God had a plan for Abigail, though what that entailed remained a mystery.

"Oh, Aunt Lily, I didn't hear you come in." With her right arm Abby reached for the wheel and turned the wheelchair around.

"Dr. Hanson is here to see you. He's in the great room with Beau."

With a teasing grin Abby replied, "It's been a while since he's been by to see me. But I'm not sure it's me he really comes to see."

"Oh, go on. Don't be silly." Lily felt the heat as it covered her cheeks. She turned away to hide her embarrassment then glanced back. Abby grinned and added, "I don't know. He could be number four. Besides it might be nice to have a doctor in the family!"

Shocked at the insinuation, Lily reached out and pretended to pinch Abby's arm. "Don't be brash!" Both women smiled. "You seem happier after visiting with your father on the phone," Lily stated. "I'm sure he's very pleased with how your recovery is coming along."

Abby reached out and took Lily's hand in hers. "It was so nice to talk to him again. I wish he were here though." Lily saw softness in her niece's eyes that she hadn't seen in a long time.

"I know you do, dear." Lily patted her hand. "He'll be back soon, and then you can show him all the things that you can do now. You've worked hard, and we're all very proud of your achievements." Lily leaned over and kissed Abby's cheek.

* * * *

Dr. Hanson reached for his coffee cup. "I have to hand it to you, Beau. You've accomplished more than anyone else has been able to do. However I must admit your tactics seem a little unorthodox."

"Yes, I know, sir. But after all the research I did, I realized that something wasn't adding up right. I found no reason for her not to be able to speak. I believed if I did something to shock her she'd snap out of her frame of mind and respond verbally. I wouldn't have gotten anywhere with her therapy unless she communicated with me. Besides I believed she was running out of time."

"You're right. Had this gone on much longer I'm afraid she would have had too much disuse atrophy to regain any strength or movement. And that might have affected her speech permanently."

Beau's brow furrowed with concern. "I explained to Miss Lily just what I planned to do. She also listened to the monitor in her room during that session."

"Well, we're fortunate Abigail has you for her therapist and Mrs. Bendickson for her aunt!" the doctor remarked.

Beau nodded. "I agree with you. Miss Lily is quite the treasure. Miss

Abigail and Mr. Pendergrass are lucky to have her."

Leaning forward he handed the doctor a file he'd compiled. "Here are the notes I have so far. Dr. Berkman also called and lined up a session with Abigail."

"That's what I like about you, young man. You're on the ball. It will be interesting to see how that turns out. She tried talking with Abigail while she was hospitalized. It didn't go over very well. But now that she's responding to your therapy hopefully she'll talk with the doctor."

"I'd like to get her a wheelchair work table for board games, a marker board and eventually a laptop computer. I've seen some people achieve great results from using them."

"I'll have one of the occupational therapists contact you."

Beau liked Dr. Hanson. He truly had Abby's best interest at heart, unlike another doctor he'd unfortunately met.

With a concerned expression Dr. Hanson leaned forward in his chair "How are you getting along with Abigail and Mrs. Bendickson? I know Abigail can be a handful."

"Handful? That's not the word I'd use to describe her," Beau replied with a smirk. His eyes were drawn to the doorway as Abby and Lily appeared. "Here they are now!" He rose as they entered the room. Although it took him a little longer, Dr. Hanson struggled to his feet.

Beau was happy for the interruption. He'd been having mixed feelings about Abby. One minute she acted like a spoiled brat that needed a spanking, the next a vulnerable young woman who just needed love and understanding. Ironically he was the man for both jobs.

"I have to tell you, Doc, it's not hard living in the same house with these two beautiful women."

"I'm well aware of what you mean." The older gentlemen winked. "Very nice to see you again, Miss Abigail, Miss Lily." Using his best southern drawl the doctor mimicked Beau's earlier endearments.

Lily smiled, flushing a faint rose pink at the doctor's comment. Abby chuckled. "It's nice to see you again, Dr. Hanson. I'm sure my drill sergeant here," motioning in Beau's direction, "has filled you in on his form of torture and my slow progress."

"On the contrary, my dear. He's told me what a great job you're doing. How hard you have been trying and how fast you're recovering. You should be proud of yourself. You've come a long way."

Both men waited for Lily to sit down before they returned to their seats. Lily blushed again and quickly found a seat.

"Thank you, sir. I can't take all the credit though. I do get a lot of *encouragement*." She glanced in Beau's direction.

"Well, I am very impressed, not only with your progress but with your equipment. I've been through your weight room, and I'm glad to see that you're utilizing all the equipment your father purchased. You've got everything. A massage treatment table, recumbent cycle free-standing pulley system and the daddy of them all, the body weight support treadmill trainer!" He laughed. "You're lucky to have such a large room to accommodate everything."

"Dr. Hanson and I talked about a treatment called NeuroMove therapy." Beau leaned forward in his chair, resting his arms on his thighs.

"Yes, let me check into that a little more and I'll get back to you," the doctor replied.

Beau turned toward the doctor. "I also wanted to get your opinion on a portable pool lift. I'd like to start Abby on some hydrotherapy with arm and head floats, of course."

The doctor chuckled and shook his head. "At this rate you should make quite a substantial recovery, my dear," he said, smiling at Abby.

"So tell me, Abigail," the doctor continued, "What do you think about all of this? Is there anything that you'd like to discuss with me?"

Abby's gaze traveled from the doctor to her aunt then to Beau. He smiled. He knew what she wanted to discuss. Winking, he dared her to say something.

Abby would have loved nothing more than to tell Dr. Hanson just how mean Beau had treated her these past weeks. She should ask him to call her father and inform him that his Mr. Winkelman was really a pervert!

"No, not really. I'm tired and sore, that's all. Maybe more leg spasms than before. It seems like the more exercise I do the more they jump."

"That's a very normal reaction. I suggest more massages. It wouldn't be a bad idea to start some hydrotherapy. When your father returns, I'll speak to him about purchasing a hydro tub for you." He turned toward Beau and added, "As far as the pool goes, you'll need to wait until the weather warms up. The pool will have to be kept fairly warm."

Beau nodded. "I'll call the pool company this afternoon."

Abby glanced toward Beau and frowned. He was crazy if he thought she was going anywhere near that pool.

"I also understand Dr. Berkman is going to be stopping by to see you. I think you're very wise in seeing her again." He patted Abby's hand. "Well, I guess I'll leave you in these capable hands, my dear." He stood. "I'll be back in a week or so to check on you." Nodding toward her aunt he added, "Don't hesitate to call me if you need anything."

Her aunt stood, and before Abby could comment, Lily had turned the wheelchair around and was following the doctor to the door.

* * * *

Beau followed the procession. He hadn't missed the meaning behind the doctor's statement. It was cute to see the older woman blush.

They said their goodbyes, and Beau closed the door. Amused, he turned toward the two women.

"What are you grinning at?" Abby scowled. "If he knew what you did he'd be on the phone to my father right now."

"Don't worry your pretty little head, Miss Abby." He stuffed his hands into his pockets. "I told him what I did."

"You're a liar! You wouldn't have."

"I did, and he thought it was quite ingenious!"

"Almost as ingenious as your pool therapy plan," she snarled.

Beau raised a brow. So that's what her frown had been about. It wasn't going to be easy getting her into the pool. He wasn't worried; once the heat of August came she'd be begging to get into the cool water.

Leaning toward Lily he teased, "You sure do look pretty in pink, ma'am."

"Oh! Go on with you," Lily replied playfully, swatting his arm. Beau heard Lily giggle as she pushed the wheelchair into the other room.

Pleased with how the meeting with Dr. Hanson went and that the doctor appeared impressed with his progress Beau stepped out into the late afternoon sun. The warm breeze rustled the branches of the stately trees that stood guard on the back lawn.

He walked across the lawn, hunkered down under a large tree and stretched his long legs out in front of him. The billowing sails of a lone sailboat appeared on the horizon, and a flock of sassy seagulls squawked overhead.

Beau's mind wandered to Abby. Why hadn't she made a big fuss in front of Dr. Hanson about him tricking her into speaking? She had no way of knowing that he'd already told the doctor what he had done.

Picking up a lone stick he broke off a piece, examined it and then threw it aside. Maybe she really wasn't as angry as she wanted him to believe.

* * * *

Abby's hands shook as she held the videotape. She rubbed her fingers across the label as if that would reveal the tape's mysterious contents. Suspicious but apprehensive she slipped the tape into the VCR. Fear at what she might see twisted her guts into knots. She wiped her sweaty hands on her slacks and debated whether to push Play.

The remote felt heavy in her hand. Her teeth raked over her lower lip. She wondered why her father had never mentioned the tape to her. Gathering her courage, she took a deep breath and pushed the Play button. Time ceased, and her world faded. The sound of her heartbeat drummed loudly in her ears as she stared at the snow-covered screen. Her fingers found the end of her shirt and made quick work of distorting the hem.

Soothing tones of an organ playing a peaceful hymn engulfed her. Abby watched as people filed into a large church and took their seats. The camera scanned toward the altar which had been adorned with rows of elaborate flower arrangements and plants in an array of colors and sizes. A myriad of giant white candles flickered in the background.

Then she saw it. In front of the flowers, plants and candles lay a closed white casket. Abby drew in a sharp breath as her stomach contracted with nausea. "Oh, my God, Carolyn!" Her stomach twisted. Her hand flew to her lips, and tears streamed down her cheeks. She wanted to stop the tape, but she couldn't move—she sat frozen in place.

The music faded. Muffled voices and sobs could be heard as a handsome young man stepped to the pulpit. He wiped his nose with a white handkerchief and cleared his throat. "My name is Joshua." His voice shook as he spoke, and he fidgeted with a piece of paper.

Abby gasped. *Carolyn's boyfriend*!

"Although most of you don't know me, you all know two very special women who shared a binding love and a lifelong friendship." The camera zoomed in closer until Abby could see a deep sadness in his eyes.

"Today we not only pray for Carolyn but for Abigail who is fighting for her life." The room grew warm, and Abby swayed slightly.

"Carolyn loved Abby more than just a friend. She loved her as a sister." He cleared his throat. "Carolyn had a big heart. I feel blessed that she had room in it for me if only for a short while. Although she's no longer with us on earth a part of her will stay with us in our hearts," he paused. "Forever."

The realization of Carolyn's love for her and permanency of her death struck Abby like a sucker-punch. Josh continued to speak, but his voice was drowned out by Abby's thoughts. She recalled the day her father walked into her hospital room and through his own pain told her Carolyn hadn't survived the accident. Instead of facing her feeling of guilt and grief she'd only hurt herself and others by withdrawing from her family and friends when she needed them the most. She'd only wanted to be left alone to die. How selfish it seemed to her now.

She clutched the arms of her wheelchair. Her chest ached as everything she'd worked so hard to bury deep down inside of herself clawed its way up to the surface. The back of her throat burned with acid.

She made herself focus on the small television screen. With a downcast head Josh stepped down from the pulpit. Her heart ached. She hadn't been the only one who'd lost Carolyn. For the first time she felt someone else's pain. Sniffling, muffled whimpers and sobs erupted from the congregation. Her own hand flew to her mouth to stifle her sob.

Weighted, she remained transfixed as the camera focused in on the casket draped with white roses. In the background a choir sang a hymn. The camera shifted from the casket to an easel holding a large portrait of Carolyn's and Abby's beaming faces on their graduation day.

Another sob caught in Abby's throat. Tears blurred her vision. She thought of her last words to Carolyn. Her selfishness had caused their accident, an accident that should have never happened. An accident that was all her fault.

Suddenly from the corner of her eye Abby glimpsed Beau in the doorway, watching her, his face a solemn mask. She flinched, and a convulsive sob escaped her throat. "It's Carolyn," she cried out.

Rushing to her side, he knelt and pulled her into a gentle comforting embrace.

"What are you watching?" his voice whispered close to her ear.

"It's a videotape ... a tape of Carolyn's funeral. I found it in my father's desk," she turned her head and smothered her sobs against his chest. "Please, please just turn it off."

Beau took the remote and switched off the VCR. He pulled the chair from the corner next to her, sat down and handed her a box of tissues.

"Do you want to talk about it?"

His low deep voice soothed her raw nerves, and she blew her nose. His brown eyes were filled with concern as he patiently waited for her reply.

"It was all my fault. I argued with her about changing schools." She watched for his reaction and wondered if he would be appalled at her confession.

"Sweetheart..."

"I told her to pull over. To stop at one of the cafés along the road but she was in such a hurry to get home to see her new boyfriend Josh." Ashamed she glanced down to her hands on her lap.

"Abby, did you feel she was driving recklessly?" He lifted her chin up with two fingers and gazed into her eyes.

Abby hiccupped. "I told her to slow down, but she wouldn't. The curve came up too fast. I'm so sorry. I didn't mean to distract her." Her tears returned.

"It wasn't your fault."

"Why did this happen, Beau? Why did she die and not me?" She searched the depths of his eyes, praying he'd have the answers.

Beau sighed and shook his head. "I guess that's something only the Lord knows."

"But why her and not me?"

"Maybe you still have things to do, to experience and to learn." He reached out, and his rough hands engulfed hers. "You need to go on." She shook her head, and Beau tightened his hold on her.

"I can't. What am I supposed to do?"

"Listen to me. What would Carolyn say about the way your life has been this past year?"

Abby swallowed the large lump in her throat.

"You need to move on. You can't hide any longer." She started to protest, but Beau turned the VCR back on. "It's time to say goodbye. To make peace with Carolyn. She knows that the accident wasn't your fault."

Abby glanced at the television. The camera scanned the room as more hymns were sung, and several people took turns at the podium. Minutes later it appeared to be over. Pallbearers were wheeling the casket down the center aisle of the church. Josh and Carolyn's family followed, weeping and clutching each other for support.

Beau leaned forward and spoke softly. "She wouldn't want you to sit on the sidelines. She'd want you to go out into the world and live your life. To be happy."

They watched in silence as the casket was loaded into a long white hearse. Organ music played in the background as people filed into the long line of waiting cars. Abby sighed in relief that it had ended, but the next scene that appeared showed the mourners and the cemetery. Abby stiffened in her seat, but Beau's strong arm wrapped around her shoulder in support.

When the casket and the family were in place another prayer was said. The words were incoherent as they bounced around in Abby's head.

The magnitude of the event hit Abby when Carolyn's mother removed a single long stemmed white rose from the top of the casket. She leaned against her husband and clutched the front of his dark suit coat.

Carolyn's last words echoed in her head. *"Someday you'll meet someone, and you'll want to spend every minute with him. Then you'll understand how I feel about Josh."*

* * * *

Abby turned and collapsed against Beau's chest in heart-wrenching sobs. Had he done the right thing? He'd stepped out of his realm of expertise. Had he gone too far?

Had he screwed things up worse than they already were? Unsure of what to do for her, Beau held her tight and let her cry. She'd been hiding; now it was time to face the past. Get on with her future. He assured himself that she would feel better. He hoped he was right.

The tape ended, and Abby's sobs subsided into exhaustion. Without a word Beau slid his hands under her knees and lifted her up. She settled against his chest as he carried her to her bed. He gently laid her down and covered her with the quilt that was folded at the end of the bed.

From the doorway he glanced back at the small fragile figure who at one time had been a strong independent woman. Had he helped her today or only enabled her to retreat back into her former state of mind? He prayed that his worse fear—that she'd regress and shut everyone out again—wouldn't become reality.

Chapter Ten

"I can't! I can't do anymore." Abby heard and hated the whine in her voice, but she couldn't help it—not today. She'd had nightmares all night long about Carolyn and the crash, and now a jackhammer pounded nonstop in her head. All she wanted to do was go back to bed and be left alone. The whole morning Beau had been pushing her to do just "one more."

"Yes, you can!" he said with a slight edge in his tone.

Abby glanced up at the contraption that she hung from. He'd called it a body weight supported training treadmill or something. He'd strapped her into a harness then hoisted her up into a standing position, her feet resting on the walking belt. He'd then moved her wheelchair away. She was literally a prisoner hanging from two cables in a giant slingshot.

"You can, Abby. Where's your athletic competitiveness?"

"Go to *hell*!" she spat. He walked out of the room, leaving her hanging in his strange sadistic contraption. Hysteria started to boil deep down in the pit of her stomach. She wouldn't scream. Her right hand gripped one of the bars that ran parallel to the treadmill, hoping to steady her frazzling nerves.

Was he going to come back, or was she doomed to hang here all day like a side of beef.

Several moments later Beau returned to the makeshift gym with an armload of trophies. Bemused she watched as he lined them up side by side along the front of his desk.

He pinned her with his dark walnut eyes and gestured toward her trophies. "Which ones did you win for giving up and backing down?"

She held his contemptible stare but didn't react. He'd have to do better than that.

"Or did you receive them because you're cute?" He took a couple of prowling steps toward her, and her pulse leaped.

"Or was it because your daddy's on the school board?"

He deliberately taunted her. The cords in his neck tightened, and he placed his clenched fist on his hips.

How cruel could he be, bringing her trophies down and then rubbing her face into them? Her eyes filled with tears.

He'd drawn the line, challenging her. She knew Beau well enough to know he wanted to make her mad so she'd fight back. Except her head ached and every muscle screamed in protest.

"I won those trophies because I was strong and good at what I did! Not for being cute or because of who my father is!" she yelled as she fought to hold her tears back.

"You can be strong again. Win again. All you need to do is dig deep inside yourself and pull up some of that fight that I know you have locked inside."

She closed her eyes and willed him to disappear.

"I know you're tired and hurting, sweetheart, but you can't give up now."

She saw his features soften. "Go to hell, *sweetheart*! Everything was fine before you got here!" She wiggled in her restraints. "I wish you'd never come here!"

"It was fine? Lying in bed and letting your aunt run herself ragged waiting on you? Making your father age ten years every twelve months because he worried about you?" Beau's hands dropped to his sides. "So you're ready to cash in your chips? Give up?"

Abby's breath caught as Beau walked to where she hung still strapped in the ridiculous harness. Placing one hand on each side of her he peered deep into her eyes. She saw an emotion she couldn't name. The heat from his body and his distinct scent engulfed her ... made her lightheaded.

In a whisper he asked, "Are you ready to stay like *this* for the rest of your life? To give up before you've even had a chance to play the biggest game of them all?"

He stood too close. He made her feel things she didn't understand, feelings she didn't know how to explore. She didn't have much left to fight with. She felt utterly defenseless. "Why not? What do I have to live for anyway?" A lone tear slid down her cheek as a sob tore from her lips. "How much torment are you going to put me through before you give up?"

"I'll never give up on you, Abby. I'll stay as long as you need me." He wiped away her tears with his thumb. He wanted to lean forward and kiss her soft pouted lips. To take her into his arms and show her just what she had to live for … what she was missing. He peered deep into her innocent eyes and wondered what she would do if he kissed her. As if reading his mind, her small tongue darted out and moistened her lips.

Beau leaned forward, her lips only a breath away. Then his conscience reared its ugly head, and words of warning filled his mind, pulling him back to reality. He released the straps that confined Abby and stepped away, leaving her swaying slightly.

The doorbell rang.

Now who the hell was here?

He raked his hands through his hair. His head was pounding. Although a cool breeze flowed through the opened windows his body felt overly warm, and the room felt crowded.

The bell rang again, and Lily hurried past the dining room to answer it. Their gazes locked for just a second before he averted his attention to unbuckling Abby. Neither spoke as he lowered her into the wheelchair, then began to free her from the harness.

"Dr. Berkman, please come in," Lily said, offering a big friendly smile. She wondered how long Dr. Berkman stood outside the door and if she had overheard Beau and Abigail arguing. She really should nail those front windows shut.

"Thank you, Mrs. Bendickson. I'm afraid that I might be a little early, but I was anxious to speak with Abigail again. Is she ready for me?"

"I think they are just finishing up. Please follow me." She led the way to the dining room. "Abby, Dr. Berkman is here to see you. Are you two finished?" Lily asked hopefully.

Beau turned and forced a slight smile for the woman. She stood by the dining room entrance with one eyebrow hiked; implying she'd just caught him with his fingers in the cookie jar. So she overheard them. He didn't care. He continued to remove Abby's harness. Finished, he turned and pushed her wheelchair toward the young psychologist.

"I'd like to freshen up a bit. May I?" Abby asked, her voice trembling.

"Yes, of course. That will give me a chance to speak with Mr. Winkelman for a few minutes."

Lily glanced in his direction. Her lips were pursed, and her brows were drawn together which was a look his grandmother often expressed. A look that clearly stated behave yourself or else. She then wheeled Abby out of the room.

Beau turned and walked to his desk. He pretended to go through a stack of papers. What had he almost done? If he'd kissed Abby that would have been the end of his career. He couldn't afford to repeat past mistakes. He must be going crazy. No, Abby was driving him crazy. The more she fought and argued with him the more beautiful she became. He had to remember to think of her as only a patient, not a beautiful desirable woman.

Closing his eyes he took a deep cleansing breath. Once he felt more in control he turned his attention to the shapely woman in the coral business suit. She had long curly blond hair which begged to be fondled. Sea green eyes any man could get lost in and luscious full lips, pouting lips. Abby's face flashed in his head. Damn it! Just when he thought he'd found a suitable distraction.

Dr. Nicole Berkman prided herself on her professionalism, but as she stood in the same room with Beau she was very aware of being a woman—first and foremost.

He appeared to be well over six feet tall. His shoulders and muscular arms bulged out of the sleeveless T-shirt he wore. She liked how his wavy blond hair hung loose around his shoulders and how the whole package was supported by tan muscular legs clad in faded cut-offs. He could have just walked out of a surfer movie.

She observed him closely, watching as he moved about the room. Turning to face her, he studied her from head to toe. One corner of his mouth rose in a sexy grin. Oh, yes, he was pleased at what he saw. Then a frown creased his brow. Something happened that she wasn't aware of. In a flash he'd gone from inviting to unapproachable. How peculiar.

Then he spoke, and his southern drawl caught her off guard. "You must be Miss Nicole. Sorry, I mean Dr. Berkman." His deep voice vibrated through the air and up Nicole's back.

"I'm Beau." He was all business as he closed the distance between them and reached out his hand. "Very nice to meet you, ma'am. Please have a seat." He gestured to the closest chair.

"Thank you," was all she could manage as she sat down.

"What was it you wanted to speak to me about?"

He had the prettiest brown eyes she'd ever seen on a man and then reminded herself that she was there to help Abigail, Ms. Bendickson and Mr. Pendergrass deal with and manage their stress levels. Also she was there to help Abigail plan for when she returned to school and to life itself.

"Well!" She mentally shook herself and commanded her voice not to tremble. "I couldn't help but overhear the two of you arguing when I first walked up." She crossed her legs, tugged on her skirt and strived to control the conversation. "I'm impressed that you've been able to pull down Abby's barriers and get through to her. And I realize that there is a lot at stake here." She paused and watched as his lips pursed slightly, and his beautiful brown eyes darkened to ebony.

"So what's your point?"

She shifted in her chair. "Do you think that maybe you're pushing her a little too hard?"

"I don't, but obviously you do." He perched on the edge of his desk, crossed his arms over his chest and waited for her response.

This guy was something; he had the whole package and the arrogance to back it up. Where'd they say he came from? Texas? Collecting her thoughts, Nicole ventured on. "I'm only saying that maybe you should back off a little. Go easy on her—at first anyway."

"Your opinion..." he began but stopped when Lily walked into the room. Nicole entertained a sneaking suspicion he'd been about to tell her what she could do with her opinion. He didn't strike her as the type of man to take constructive criticism too well.

"She's all ready for you, Dr. Berkman. I'll show you to her room.

You'll have more privacy there."

"Oh, thank you."

"Would you like some tea? Do you prefer it hot or iced?" The older woman grabbed Nicole by the arm and pulled out of her chair, across the hall and into the kitchen. For such a small woman Mrs. Bendickson was stronger than she looked. It was clear she didn't want her conversation with Mr. Winkelman to continue.

As she was hustled down the hall Nicole recalled her last session with Abigail. It hadn't gone that well. Perhaps today would go better. They reached Abigail's room. Lily motioned toward the lone chair. She offered a nervous smile, then turned and disappeared.

Abby sat nestled in her bed, staring out the window. Nicole took a cleansing breath and willed herself to relax. The exchange with Mr. Winkelman and the few times she'd tried to have a conversation with Abigail mingled together in her mind as she meditated in silence. Then an idea came to her; she'd try approaching Abigail woman to woman—it couldn't hurt.

"So does he always dress like that?" she asked with a grin.

Abby turned toward her and smiled, nodding toward the window "Sometimes he doesn't even wear a shirt!"

Puzzled, Nicole stood and walked to the window next to the bed and looked out. "Oh! My God!"

Beau stood by a table, stripped off his shirt and marched toward the diving board. Climbing the ladder, he strolled to the end and, with more grace then a man his size ought to possess, dove into the pool. He swam the length of the pool in seconds. Then emerged from the pool in one fluid motion, shaking the water from his hair. He returned to the diving board and repeated his actions.

The fantasies Nicole's imagination conjured up were interrupted by Abby's voice.

"At first when he put my bed in here I made a fuss. I was afraid to leave my room. But after watching him swim, without him knowing, of course," she added glancing down at her lap. "I didn't really mind so much."

"I guess not," Nicole chuckled. "How often does he swim?"

"Only when he's mad," she added with a snicker.

Nicole turned to study the young woman in the bed. "So let me guess. When you're tired, you make him mad so he'll stop with your therapy and go work off his frustrations in the pool. Then you sit here and enjoy the view."

"Yeah, something like that," Abby answered with a slight grin.

"You're a girl after my own heart, Abby." Nicole allowed herself one quick glance out the window then returned to her chair and sat back down.

"Is it difficult having such a gorgeous man living under the same roof?" Since the ice was broken she'd use the direct approach.

"He doesn't think of me *that* way," Abby answered. Her smile slipped away, and she glanced down at her hands cradled on her lap again.

"But what do *you* think? How do *you* feel about it?"

"What? Knowing he's right across the hall and doesn't think of me as a real woman?"

"He's actually said that to you?"

"Well, no. But he's made his feelings quite clear. He has no desire for me. Why would he? I haven't been a real woman since the accident."

"Give him more credit than that. He has eyes." *Beautiful brown eyes that when angered turn almost black.*

"Whatever. Men are out of my life anyway. Along with college and everything else."

"You can't be serious! Surely you plan on going back to college?"

"Why should I go back to school? My future is what you see." She raised her arms up a couple of inches off the mattress.

Disturbed by what she was hearing, Nicole worried that Abby had already given up on herself and her future.

They sat in silence for several moments before Abby continued. "I know my father and my aunt love me, and they think they're doing the right thing by having him here, but they're only going to be disappointed in the end."

"You're right that they both love you, but I don't think they could be disappointed in you. No matter how far you go with your recovery, they'll be supportive. They're happy you're here at all."

Abby's eyes brightened, and Nicole was pleased with how their session was going, but she didn't want to wear out her welcome.

"Well, I can see that you're tired. It is nice to see you again. I'm very pleased to see that you're at least willing to try. But do yourself a favor. Don't give up on your future so quickly. There's no reason that you can't go back to college and get a degree."

Abby's body hunched defensively; it was obvious that she was unwilling to discuss the subject anymore.

Nicole walked toward the bed and laid a gentle hand on Abby's arm. "At least think about what I said. Okay?"

"I will. Thanks for coming."

"Would it be alright with you if I came back in a week or two?"

Abby hesitated. Nicole smiled and then leaned forward to sneak a peek out the window. "You know, I heard it was going to be a long hot summer."

* * * *

Sarah paced across the ever-shrinking hotel room. She'd finally worked up the courage to tell George about Beau's last case. Since they'd become close she wanted to be totally honest with George—she wanted nothing standing between them.

Two quick raps sounded at the door. Sarah took a deep breath. "Come in."

George strolled in. His light gray summer suit was adorned with a steel blue tie that matched his eyes. Unlike most businessmen George Pendergrass wasn't the type to wear the traditional red power tie to flaunt his success.

He was so handsome. She felt the corners of her mouth turn up.

"What are you smiling about?" he questioned as he approached her.

"You." She reached up and dusted away a speck of imaginary lint from his shoulders. "You look nice in this suit."

His gazed traveled over her, and a slight shiver ran up her back.

He reached out and engulfed her hands in his. "You look beautiful today."

"Thank you." She glanced away, and her face heated up.

"I should be thanking you," George replied. "Your brother has worked miracles and given me back my daughter. I thought she was lost to me forever. I'm so blessed that *you* came into my life."

"George, I need—"

He leaned forward and kissed her lips. His lips were soft and warm, the kiss tender and sweet. Surprised and delighted by his kiss, Sarah wound her arms around his neck and melted into him. His arms tightened around her back, pressing her even closer. He took the kiss deeper.

Raising his head he said, "I've wanted to do that ever since the first time you strolled into my office."

Puzzled, she blinked several times. "You have?"

He still held her close. "I haven't felt this way about someone in a long time."

She didn't want to let go of him; she wasn't sure she could stand if she did. She wanted him to kiss her again. He read her mind, leaned forward and kissed her again.

Moments later, George's chuckle pulled Sarah from the spell. His eyes twinkled with mischief.

"What did you want to tell me?"

"What? I don't remember." Her gaze focused on the bedside clock. "Oh! We'd better get going, or we'll be late for the meeting."

* * * *

Abby stirred something in Beau not even several laps in the cold pool could subside. It was late, and he needed to find some kind of outlet.

The house surrounded him, dark and quiet. A soft rain fell. The cool breeze and fresh air were a welcome balm to his heated flesh. He recalled rainy days as a kid in the small trailer park in Texas. His grandmother said that the rain and thunder were God's music and that God made rainy days so little boys would practice their piano. She'd insisted that he take lessons and learn to play classical piano. He'd put up quite the fuss, but in the end he'd enjoyed it just as she said he would.

He loved to play on nights like this. He remembered the beautiful grand piano in the great room, and his fingers itched to play it. Lily and Abby would both be asleep by now. They wouldn't mind if he played.

Barefoot, he crept out of his room and found his way to the great room in the dark. He opened the French doors to the terrace, and the freshness of the spring rain filled the room. A cool breeze softly blew the curtains, giving the room an eerie but romantic setting.

His heart pounded with excitement as he sat down on the piano bench. Although it had been years since he'd last played he was confident he still could. He cracked his knuckles, grinned and began.

His first choice was Beethoven's "Moonlight Sonata." The tempo was slow, the style dignified; it was a good review piece. A hypnotic arrangement performed on a magnificent instrument.

Beau's large hands spanned the ebony and ivory keys. He rocked from side to side with the rhythm and let his mind clear—wanting to forget everything. Mostly he wanted to forget Abby and how much he longed to hold her close and kiss her. He poured his heart and soul into the arrangement which gradually alleviated his stress and frustration. His hands seemed to belong to someone else; they never wavered or missed a note.

The sheer lacy curtains billowed around him as his fingers caressed the keys. The fragrance of exotic flowers filled the room with intoxicating fumes. His eyes drifted shut, and his heart and soul soared.

Then he played Beethoven's "Füur Elise." He'd always loved this piece and all the changes and the feelings it inspired in him. Soon peace and tranquility like he hadn't felt in years washed over him, taking him to a place he never knew existed.

Beau played as if he had never been away from the piano. His long fingers glided over the keys, the sound gentle and seductive. Losing himself in the melodies, he played long into the night.

Beautiful music flowed up the stairs, and Lily wasn't sure what she was listening to at first. Reaching for a shawl, she walked to the stairs. Someone was playing the grand piano. It couldn't have been Abigail. She played, but never with such passion. Halfway down the stairs in the darkness she settled on a step and listened. The hypnotic music reached deep inside her, tugging at her heartstrings, bringing tears to her eyes.

The house was chilly; goose bumps covered her body, and Lily pulled her shawl tighter. Every window in the house must have been open though he played in total darkness.

She sat still and marveled at his talent. What would this imposing man look like as his large fingers fluttered like butterflies over the keys? How she wanted to sneak down the rest of the way and watch him as he played. She didn't dare. He sounded so captivated; she wouldn't risk breaking the spell.

Abby thought she woke to thunder. As she listened she realized someone was playing her grand piano. Powerful music filled the air, music that held her captive. Who was it? Lily couldn't play a note. Beau?

The storm raged outside, and it was hard to tell if the music was mimicking the rain or if the rain was echoing the music. Two tempos harmonized harder and louder as if the storm raged within the musician's soul. The music reached deep down inside her and awoke something. Something she couldn't name, like a rose opening for the first time.

Abby recognized the arrangements. She too loved Beethoven. Where had Beau ever learned to play like that? He was wonderful. It was obvious that he loved to play and been committed to his lessons.

Tears filled her eyes; she wanted so much to watch him play, to witness his concentrated emotion. She let her imagination wander, and she pictured Beau in long black tails. His white shirt left open at the top revealing his smooth suntanned chest. His long blond hair tied back with a simple strip of leather, befitting his wild independent spirit.

His long strong fingers floated over the keys. A large silver candelabra placed strategically to one side of the piano glowed, filling the room with romantic shadows. His audience consisted of only one person. Her. If only she was whole and could stir Beau's adoration like the music did.

As Abby lay absorbing the music she thought how much her father would have enjoyed Beau's playing. He loved going to the theater and concerts, but classical piano remained his favorite. He had purchased the piano in hopes that one day she'd play like Beau was playing now. Except she never did, and now she'd never play again.

After several minutes, she pulled the blankets tight around her neck, closed her eyes and drifted off to sleep. The combination of the beautiful music and the rain hitting the window made for a perfect lullaby. That night Abby dreamt of being in Beau's arms and her first taste of passion.

Beau headed for his room but paused at Abby's opened door. From the doorway she looked like an angel, a beautiful young woman. Yet she was more than that. She was a woman he couldn't have, and the more he reminded himself of that, the stronger he burned with the urge to have her.

He stumbled off to bed, his head light from his workout at the piano, his heart over-flowing with emotions. He had hoped to fall right to sleep, but the vision of Abby asleep just across the hall haunted him for several hours before he found peace.

Lily waited until she was sure Beau had returned to his room, then made her way back up the stairs. She'd been shaken by the powerful passion in his playing, and she had an idea where that passion had come from. Although she'd only heard arguing between the two, she'd felt the sexual tension and wondered how much longer Beau would be able to control his feelings.

As she crawled back in bed and curled deep under the covers, she recalled Beau's trips to the cold pool.

"Lord, I know my first opinion of Beau was a little off, but after what I just heard, the level of his compassion plus the great progress he has made with Abigail, I have to admit, You made a good choice. Thank You. I know he's only being hard on her because that's what works with her. Abigail has some emotional hurdles to get over, and You know she can be pretty stubborn at times. Yet, I can't help but feel that Beau has a few demons of his own."

Lily settled in and closed her eyes. Suddenly Dr. Voight's warning about Beau came back. Was it warranted? When Beau first arrived, she'd pegged him as a womanizing cowboy, but he hadn't done anything to make her keep that impression. He'd done wonders with Abby, and she'd responded to him.

His passion blazed just under the surface, merely hidden by his charming Texas drawl. Tonight he'd come close to losing control of his desires. How long before he lost control completely?

Chapter Eleven

"Get up!" Beau ordered. He stood in the doorway, hands braced on his hips. The glint in his eyes matched the challenge in his voice.

Abby's chin raised a notch as she glared at him. If he wanted a fight she was game. "I don't want to get up."

Beau stepped into the room.

Abby's gaze dropped to her hands, and she smoothed imaginary wrinkles from the bed.

"I said it's time for you to get up. You're going to transfer into the wheelchair today by yourself."

"If I have to do it by myself, I'm not going to get up. I'll just sit here all day," she snarled up at him. If he wanted her in the wheelchair, he could just pick her up and put her in the chair himself.

"We both know you can do this. You're just being stubborn," he growled, towering over her bed. She attempted to cross her arms over her chest, but the left one slipped through and dropped to her lap.

"You're going to have to do this sooner or later. I won't be here forever. You're going to have to start doing more things for yourself." He held her gaze and crossed his arms over his chest.

Abby made no attempt to move.

"Fine. I'm too tired to fight with you today." He sighed, shook his head, walked out and slammed the door.

It was wrong to want his arms around her, but damn it, she did. She'd never admit it to anyone else, but she savored the feeling of security that engulfed her when he held her in his arms. She liked the heat of his bare skin where his arms brushed against hers. Besides, once she could move without his help, he would leave. And she didn't want to think about the emptiness his leaving would bring. They may fight, but if he left she would be alone again. She wasn't sure she would be able to handle the loneliness again.

Lily stood just outside of the door, her face pinched with concern. "Do you think I should go in there and help her?" she asked. He knew she'd been hovering in the hall, just in case she was needed.

"No." Beau rubbed the back of his neck with one hand. "Leave her be. She's just being difficult this morning." Difficult ha! The girl was blatantly defying him.

"You look tired, dear. Didn't you sleep well last night?" Lily placed a sympathetic hand on Beau's arm.

"No, not really." No, his night had been filled with visions of Abby. Her face tilted up, begging to be kissed. Her pouty lips when he scolded her—begging to be kissed.

The closeness of her just across the hall was driving him crazy.

They entered the kitchen, and Beau dropped into one of the small kitchen chairs.

"Are you hungry?"

"I'm always hungry." He gave her one of his best-crooked grins.

"What would you like?" Lily returned his smile, but the concern in her voice didn't go unnoticed.

"Anything's all right, Miss Lily, as long as it doesn't bite back." Placing both elbows on the table, he slumped forward, placing his aching head in his hands.

"Do you want to talk about it?" Lily asked, opening the refrigerator.

"No. I've got too much on my mind, that's all. A few things I need to work out."

"I thought you worked them out very nicely last night." He turned and glanced up at her. She offered him a knowing smile.

"I'm sorry. Did I wake you?"

"No, I wasn't asleep. How did you ever learn to play like that? You're wonderful!"

"My grandmother would be pleased to hear you say that." An image of the sweet little woman who raised him filled his thoughts. "She made me take lessons and practice all the time when I was a kid." He chuckled. "The funny thing is I really enjoyed playing."

"Well, you're exceptionally good. You can play anytime you want. I enjoyed listening to you very much."

"Thanks. I haven't played in years. I wasn't sure I still could. I played in college when I had a lot on my mind or before a big game. I've never played on a grand piano before. I have to admit it felt pretty good."

"*Someone come and help me!*" Abby yelled from down the hall.

"Oh!" Lily wiped her hands one a dishtowel. "I'll go?"

"No, just leave her be. She needs to do it by herself." Lily glanced from him to the hallway. "She'll be all right," Beau added. "She can do it on her own."

"I don't want her to fall and get hurt."

"I'm not saying that she'll never fall or get hurt. I'm saying she needs to try to do it for herself."

There was a loud crash. Something hit the floor and broke. *"You son of a bitch! Get in here!"*

Lily wrung her hands. Her anxiety played across her face as she fought the instinct to rush to her niece's aid. He knew it was difficult for her to hold back, but she knew Abigail needed to start doing things for herself.

He could handle listening to Abby's tantrums, but the tears that were quickly filling Lily's eyes broke his heart. He stood and walked toward her, wrapping his arms around her.

He hugged her tight. "There's one thing two year olds and spoiled brats have in common. Eventually they learn to stop screaming and crying and ask for what they want nicely, or they learn to do it for themselves."

"You're right. It's just hard for me to not go to her," she sniffled against his shirt.

"I know." He rubbed a hand over her back. It was hard on him, too. He would feel terrible if she fell and got hurt.

"Would you please come in here and help me? Pleeease?" Abby's sarcastic tone drifted down the hall.

"See? What did I tell you?" Beau said, kissing Lily on top of her head. They both smiled. Beau gave her a quick hug before walking away.

Abby could hear them talking, but she couldn't make out what they were saying. Why was he being so mean? Why didn't he just pick her up and put her in the chair in the first place? Why did he have to close the damn door? He'd only made the tiny room feel smaller.

She glanced around the room and spied a water glass sitting on the nightstand next to her bed. Reaching over, she knocked it on the floor. No one came to investigate. Now what was she going to do? She was being left out of something, and she didn't like it. The pounding of her heart filled her ears, and she gathered the blankets in her fists. Why was her aunt letting him do this to her?

Taking a deep breath, she closed her eyes and gathered her wits. "Would you please come in here and help me? *Pleeease?*"

The door swung open, and Abby glanced up in surprise. Beau's broad shoulders filled the space. He stood with his arms crossed, feet slightly apart. The wavy blond hair that brushed his collar didn't hide his clenched jaw or mask his demanding brown eyes. *My God, he's gorgeous!*

"I'm sorry I yelled." Uncertain of his next move, she watched him with great caution. She gulped several staggered breaths. "I'm sorry."

She tossed the covers aside then struggled to scoot to the edge of the bed which caused her nightgown to hike up to her thighs. With great concentration she chewed her lower lip and attempted to lower her legs over the side. Beau battled with his conscience to stand his ground and not offer to help her. Every muscle in his body flexed simultaneously. He was going to explode. He glanced to the floor where a broken glass lay then gazed back up at Abby.

"I said I was sorry." Her eyes pleaded for forgiveness. She swallowed hard and continued, "I'll try now if you'll stand close enough in case I fall." He moved forward, pushing the broken glass aside with his shoe.

With slow calculated moves Abby maneuvered herself to the edge of the bed. Once her feet touched the floor she gripped Beau's arm with one hand and pulled herself to a standing position.

Beau stood ready to catch her if she started to fall. A new sense of admiration filled him as he witnessed the fighter in her surface and conquer.

Concentrating, Abby's teeth raked over her lower lip. After several intense seconds she turned and lowered herself in to the wheelchair.

She had done it. She'd gotten into the chair by herself without any help from him. He wanted to tell her that her father was going to be so proud of her, but the words stuck in the back of his throat. If she only knew what a big step this was in her recovery. She had validated his unconventional methods...

"I did it!" Her grin spread from ear to ear. Throwing her arms around his waist, Abby hugged him tight. "Thank you. I know you were only trying to make me do it by myself, and I did!"

Her cheek rested so innocently against his abdomen. Beau froze. If she had any idea of what he longed to do to her at this very moment she wouldn't have touched him.

His emotions were in total turmoil. He opened his mouth to speak, but nothing audible came out. Then Abby's weak arm started to slide down over his hip and backside. *I can't take much more of this torture. What the hell is wrong with me? Do I only want her because I can't have her?* He had never lusted over a woman like her before. She wasn't his type. He had always liked a little meat on the bones and someone who didn't challenge every word he said. A woman who knew what a man wanted ... needed.

Clearing his throat, he took a deep breath and removed Abby's arm from his hip, glancing at Lily who stood in the doorway. He looked away then, careful not to make eye contact with either woman, he turned and walked out of the room.

Abby looked dejected. She glanced up at her aunt. "What did I do? Did I do something wrong?" Her eyes welled up with tears.

"No, dear. You didn't do anything wrong. As a matter of fact you did everything perfectly." Lily placed her hand on her niece's shoulder. "I'm so proud of you."

"But Beau..."

"Don't you worry about Beau, dear. I'm sure he was very pleased with your performance. You just caught him off guard, that's all. He just wasn't sure how to respond. The right words seem to escape most men when they need them the most."

"I don't think I'll ever understand men." Abby slumped back into her chair. "I never seem to say or do the right thing."

"You're fine, dear." Lily said with a reassuring grin. Within minutes

Lily heard a splash and tried to swallow her amusement. *Seventy-five laps should extinguish the flame that's burning a hole in the poor man's self-control.*

Beau's reaction to the hug had been priceless. Lily didn't know whether to laugh or cry. She wondered if he had any idea what his true feelings were for Abby. What would happen when it dawned on him? Would he continue to fight his feelings, or would he act on them? If she'd read him correctly and he didn't think he could control his feelings they would wake up one morning and find he had left. He'd had ample opportunities but had never taken advantage of them. No matter what anyone ever said or how hard he fought against it, in her book Beauregard Winkelman was a true southern gentleman.

* * * *

The afternoon session went well. After tapping into Abby's competitive nature she seemed eager to try anything. She pushed herself hard, trying to give him more than he asked for. All morning she worked without putting up the smallest fuss. An emotion he could only name as pride swelled in his chest. Abigail Pendergrass would walk again even if it killed him.

Abby was seated in her wheelchair. Beau could tell there was something on her mind by the way she fidgeted with the hem of her shorts. "Can I ask you a personal question?"

What could she possibly want to know about him? "I guess." He crouched down in front of her.

Reaching out and running her fingers gently over his knee, she asked, "Tell me how you got this scar."

"Well," he replied, shocked at how her fingers burned his flesh. "Didn't your father tell you I used to played college ball? Football, I mean."

"Yes, he said something to that effect," she replied. Beau stood and lifted her out of the chair and placed her on the massage table.

"Just before the end of the season I caught an interception. I got hit broadside by two overly-enthusiastic tackles. My knee separated. I had several surgeries. They repaired the damage, and I went through a lot of therapy. But in the end I couldn't return to the game. I had to give it up completely." He applied lotion and massaged her right hand and arm as she lay on her back on the table.

"That must have been awful!" She appeared genuinely concerned.

He chuckled. "There was a time I lived only to play ball. I never thought about doing anything else."

"How did you get started as a therapist?"

"One day I watched this guy struggle with his therapy. We talked a little … sort of connected you could say. When I finished my sessions, I coached him through his sessions."

"Was he a ball player, too?" she asked.

"Yep!" Beau said, turning his attention to her left foot. He applied the lotion and started the massage.

"Beau?"

"Hum?"

"That guy ... did he ever play again?"

"Yes. Even though I couldn't get back in the game, I was determined that he would." Her eyes were round with curiosity and concern. It was strange to see this side of her. He didn't want her to feel sorry for him. He didn't want her to have any feelings toward him at all. He preferred she fight with him, not look at him with those big brown cow eyes.

"I learned something about myself that day," he said pulling his gaze from hers. She was trying to peer into his soul. He was a little afraid of just what she might find there. "I learned that I could have more than one dream. I had always wanted to play football, but that dream was gone—so I found a new dream." He moved up her leg and applied more lotion. "I like working with people, helping them. It's challenging and very rewarding." He stopped, and their gazes locked. "My point is, my life changed, and I couldn't have what I once wanted so I made new dreams."

"But don't you feel bad that you will never be able to play again? That you can't do the one thing you loved most in life?" she asked, her eyes filling with tears.

"Things change," he said. "Sometimes you have to change, too. My new life is very gratifying. I've learned things about myself that I never knew existed."

Abby's wistful expression changed as she glanced around the room, the room that at one time had been a dining room but now served as her personal gym and therapy center. The sadness in her eyes reached deep into his soul despite his resistance. She had dreams that were now lost forever; he wondered what they might have been.

"What was your college major?" he asked. She turned her face toward him, and her wounded spirit reflected in her eyes.

His chest tightened.

"I wanted to be a teacher—an elementary school teacher." Her voice cracked, and she swallowed.

"Are you planning on going back to school?"

She said, "What for?" and turned away once again.

"To get your teaching degree. You still want to be a teacher, don't you?"

"What kind of a teacher could I be?" she snapped.

"A good one if you wanted to," he replied as Abby huffed sarcastically and laughed.

Miss Lily had been right, he thought. This all boiled down to her being too afraid to go back to her life. She didn't believe there was anything waiting for her there. "What makes you so sure you wouldn't make a good teacher?"

"Like this? Yeah right!" She lifted her left arm and tried to make a dramatic gesture, but it flopped like a broken wing.

She held back tears. She looked so young, so vulnerable. He wanted to take her into his arms and hold her and push away all her doubts and misgivings. But that would only encourage her to continue to feel sorry for herself.

Beau yanked her up into a sitting position on the edge of the table and stood directly in front of her. His hands supported her weight, his nose a breath away from hers.

His voice projected so low and rumbling that Abby's body vibrated with terror when he spoke.

"Stop it! You can be anything you want to be. Do you hear me?"

She couldn't answer. She could only stare into the depths of his piercing eyes.

"There's no reason that you can't become a teacher. According to my research, you will be able to do considerably more by the time we're done. You'll even be able to drive again."

"Like that's ever going to happen." Her voice trembled.

"You know you're going to have to leave this house sometime, don't you?" he asked. His voice softened, his hold on her didn't.

"Why?" Her chin hitched up a notch.

"This is ridiculous," he professed. "You think you're never going to leave this house ever again? You're just going to stay here for the rest of your life and rot? What happens when your aunt and your father aren't around to wait on you?"

"I realize I'm going to have to leave someday," she added, frowning as her gaze dropped to the floor.

"Abby," he tightened his grip. "You will get better. You will walk again, and you will learn to drive again."

Salty tears slid slowly down her cheeks. "What if I can't? Then what?"

"Sweetheart, I'll be here with you every step of the way. I won't leave until you feel confident enough to walk on your own. Okay?"

He made it sound so easy. Fine. She could go back to school and get her degree, but what about the rest of her life—her other dreams?

"I'm not saying it's going to be easy. It's going to take determination and a lot of hard work to get to that point. But we'll get there, I promise you. Your dreams are still within reach." He leaned forward and gently kissed her brow.

Glancing up, she smiled through her tears. "Beau? How did you know I could still talk when I was convinced that I couldn't?"

He rubbed his hands up and down her arms. "Your mind tricked you into thinking you couldn't speak."

"I don't understand."

"Everyone has scars to deal with after a serious injury. Some take longer to heal than others, especially the scars we wear on the inside." Turning her head, she looked away. Beau placed a finger under her chin and tilted her face up to his. "It's very important that you keep seeing Dr. Berkman. It's possible that you may have to see her or someone like her for many years. Promise me and yourself that you'll continue seeing someone until they say otherwise." His lips were set in a thin line, his expression sober. But his eyes said she was capable of achieving things she hadn't even thought of yet. He believed in her.

"I will. I mean," she blinked by tears, "I promise."

"I think we've worked hard enough for today." He grinned and tweaked her chin. "What do you say we go back out by the pool and get a little sun before it's gone?"

"That sounds great to me." At the moment she couldn't concentrate on exercising if her life depended on it. Beau had just kissed her and promised to stay with her no matter how long it took for her to get her life back.

The hollowness in Abby filled with a contentment and warmth she had never felt before.

Chapter Twelve

Beau glanced at the clock radio next to his bed. Eleven PM. Each evening he barricaded himself in his room with textbooks and old research papers and charted notes of Abby's daily progress. Tonight he was having difficulty concentrating. Earlier he'd let his personal feelings for Abby get the best of him, and now he doubted his professionalism. Maybe an emotional drop-back was in order.

There was one thing he needed to keep a handle on; he could never be anything more to Abigail Pendergrass than her physical therapist. He was there to help her regain her life. A life that hadn't and never would include him. He needed to stay focused on the big picture—for both of their sakes.

Beau sighed and set his book aside; he was finished for the night. He stood and scrubbed his hand across his weary face. Crossing to the door, he reached for the light switch and heard a muffled noise. Opening the door he listened. The sound of weeping came from Abby's room.

He opened her door. Abby lay on her side with her back to the door, her face buried deep into her pillow, stifling her heart-wrenching sobs. He walked to her side and gently placed a hand on her shoulder. "What's the matter, sweetheart? Why are you crying?"

Abby buried her face further into the pillow and continued to sob.

"Tell me what's the matter. Maybe I can help." An unexpected tightness filled his chest, constricting his breath.

"You can't help," she wailed.

"Would you let me try?" Feeling helpless, he caressed her arm.

"You can't. Nobody can!"

"It can't be all that bad." He sat on the edge of her bed, reached over and carefully gathered her into his arms. She buried her face against his bare chest. He held her close and kissed the top of her head.

"Tell me what's the matter, darlin'." His hand gently stroked her back.

Several uncontrollable sobs escaped before she gained a small amount of composure.

Brushing away a lock of soft brown hair, he peered into her swollen eyes and repeated, "Tell me what's wrong. If you make me guess we'll be here all night." Moments passed in silence as the thought of holding her all night sent a surge of warm sensations through certain parts of his imagination.

"It's stupid," she replied between sobs.

"I doubt that. Whatever it is you can tell me."

"That's just it! I can't tell you!"

"Abby, you can tell me anything." He brushed his cheek across her forehead. "Try."

Unexpectedly Beau's body trembled as she slowly ran her fingertips across his chest, lighting small flames of desire in her wake. He willed his body not to respond to her touch but with little success. He only hoped that Abby's inexperience would keep her from knowing how she affected him.

Several seconds later, though it felt like an eternity, she spoke again. "I've never been this close to a man before," she whispered, her breath skimming over his bare skin. He didn't respond. "I've never *been* with a man ... ever."

She swallowed, and Beau felt the slightest touch against his chest. She was killing him, and she didn't even know it.

"I thought I'd marry one day and have children, but that's never going to happen now."

"You don't know that. There's no reason why you can't get married, and you might be able to have children, too."

She turned her face up to his as large tears rolled down her cheeks. "Who would marry me? Half a woman. A cripple? What could I possibly have to offer a man?"

"Don't talk like that. You have a lot to offer. You're beautiful. You're intelligent." He caressed her cheek with his hand. "Remember, you're not always going to be like this. You'll be walking soon." Her lips parted as if to protest. Fighting a strong urge to kiss her upturned lips, he swallowed, but his voice cracked as he continued, "Even if you wear a leg brace and arm crutches it won't matter. If he loves you he'll love you just as you are."

"But what about..." she started but turned away.

"What about what?" Beau placed two fingers under her chin and turned her face back to his. "Abby! What about what?"

Her throat convulsed, and the tears came again. "What if... What if I have no feeling? No desire?"

Damn. He wanted nothing more than to prove to her that she would and could feel desire. His hands ached to be filled with her small breasts. More than once he'd thought how much he wanted to feel her beneath him, her bare skin against his. He wanted to be the one to show her what she was missing, but he'd be committing professional suicide if he crossed that line. Besides, she deserved someone better than him, someone on her social level. He had nothing to offer her. Women like Abigail Pendergrass didn't marry penniless has-beens like him. She was out of his league. Heck, she was in a different division all together.

"When the time comes the right man will come along. I promise." She glanced up, her stare searching his for answers. "Maybe you should discuss this with Dr. Berkman at your next meeting."

Abby gazed into the depths of Beau's reassuring eyes and saw the right man. He was everything she ever wanted. Gentle, caring, loving and she wished she could stay wrapped in his protective arms for the rest of her life.

She laid her head against his chest. The gentleness of his hands and his warm breath against her hair made her feel safe, secure and loved. She loved him, but he didn't love her. He said she was good enough for someone else but not for him.

Unwilling to move out of his arms, she closed her eyes and relaxed against his chest. Beau's hands gently stroked her back, smoothing out her jagged edges. Soon she relaxed and drifted off to sleep.

Beau sympathized with her. He knew what it was like to want something you couldn't have. He wanted her, but she deserved her old life back, and that was a life he didn't fit into.

Her warm rhythmic breathing floated over his chest. He looked down, and for the first time realized he was only wearing boxer shorts. He'd been so concerned about her that he hadn't thought about putting on jeans before he left his room. He hadn't even noticed until now that Abby was dressed in a pink tank top and matching pink panties. What in the world was wrong with him? Had he lost his mind? He was going to lose his job if he sat there much longer. He cringed at the thought of what Lily would do to him if she found him like this.

In her state of slumber, Abby snuggled closer against his chest. One long slender leg brushed over the top of his. He should leave, but he couldn't make himself move. A few more minutes of heaven were all he wanted. Resting his head against the headboard, Beau closed his eyes. He didn't know which was worse, holding Abby and knowing he couldn't have her or the thought of leaving, knowing he'd never be able to hold her like this again.

* * * *

Beau awoke long before the sun rose to a quiet house. Perched at his desk now, he was surrounded by mountains of paper. He raked his hands through his hair for the third time in the last half hour. There were so many circumstances about an incomplete spinal cord injury that weren't real clear. He found some information about both aging and male and female sexuality while dealing with a spinal cord injury. The information was encouraging but overwhelming.

One report gave statistics and percentages on the rate of aging with additional medical problems, including cardiovascular disease, heart attacks and strokes. He was pleased to read that the death rates for patients with spinal cord injuries were only slightly higher than patients without the injury.

Overall, despite all of their medical complaints and documented diagnoses, individuals were satisfied with their lives. When asked about their quality of life seventy-four percent of the patients stated it was either good or excellent. Depression scores were lowest in those who had been injured the longest. And once again when compared with their non-disabled partners the spinal cord injury survivors in general reported less depressive symptoms. In conclusion, their relationships with their families and their need for learning had grown increasingly important to them.

Even though Beau found the aging information interesting, he found the article called "Sexual Functioning after Spinal Cord Injury" more intriguing. As he read he was pleased to hear that there was a good chance Abby would have all the feeling she needed and that there was a strong possibility she could become pregnant.

She would have to have the best gynecologist she could find, however, because there were potential complications associated with pregnancy and spinal cord injuries and a high risk of delivering by cesarean section.

To Beau this information was just what Abby needed. It should answer most if not all of her questions.

* * * *

Abby pulled herself on to her side, buried her face in her pillow, and inhaled Beau's lingering masculine scent. She nuzzled the pillow and sighed. She hadn't dreamt about the auto accident last night. She had slept in a cocoon of security undisturbed and awoke rested and eager to get started with her day.

Last night Beau came into her room, held her in his arms and wiped her fears away. He said that when the right man came along he would accept and love her just as she was. As far as she was concerned Beau was the right man for her. She just needed a way to make him understand that. Admittedly she didn't have much experience when it came to men, but somehow she would get her point across. She'd make him understand how she felt.

* * * *

The doorbell rang. Beau opened the door and stared at the woman across the threshold from him, a pinup girl right out of a Playboy magazine.

"Excuse my manners, ma'am. Won't you please come in?" He stepped back and motioned for her to enter.

"I'm Paris Jenkins, Miss Pendergrass' occupational therapist. I believe we spoke on the phone."

Closing the door, he turned and held out his hand "I'm Beau Winkelman." He wasn't at all prepared for a five-foot-nine voluptuous blond bombshell. Her low-cut turquoise suit matched her inquisitive eyes which danced in amusement. She wore a painted-on smile in kiss-me-red lipstick.

Her short blond hair that winged out on both sides of her head never moved out of place as she stepped forward, but her strong lilac perfume stung his nostrils.

Reaching out her hand, her nails painted in the same bright shade as her lips, she purred, "Very nice to meet you." Her stare slowly devoured him from head to toe.

"Yes. Well..." Although beautiful, she resembled a predator closing in on her prey, and he had no desire to be eaten alive today.

"Please come into my office and have a seat. Miss Lily will bring us some refreshments in a moment." He strolled to his desk and pulled out a chair for her. He cautioned himself to be strictly professional and not to show any encouragement or exhibit any form of attraction toward the woman lest she launch herself across his desk and consume him.

Paris trailed the ruggedly handsome man into a room which she guessed was once the formal dining room. She watched his muscles flex beneath a form fitting t-shirt and faded jeans as he swaggered across the room. His large hands wrapped around the back of a chair that he pulled out from under the table. Paris graciously sat in the designated chair and openly observed Beau as he rounded the large table and seated himself.

How charming. She placed her red leather briefcase on the table and opened it. Slipping on the diamond studded reading glasses that dangled around her neck on a silver chain she retrieved a notebook and several loose papers.

"From just the little time we spoke on the phone I've put together a list of things that I feel Ms. Pendergrass should be able to start with."

Over the top of her glasses she studied him as he skimmed over the list. He glanced at her with a questioning look on his face. "Of course, this is all going to take time," she added. "I don't expect her to be able to jump right into it."

"She can't *jump* right into anything." His voice held a bit of an edge. "To tell you the truth, I haven't even mentioned your visit to her yet. Miss Abigail has come a long way in a very short time though." He paused to read further. "I think she might already be able to do one or two of these on your list." He read aloud. "Transfer to her chair alone—

she did that one this morning. Dressing herself... Using the bathroom alone." He frowned. "Abby's strong-willed. She's also very competitive. I'm sure she'll approach these with enthusiasm." Deep lines marred his forehead. "This last one … driving again? I don't know. It's going to be pretty hard to persuade her to get back into a car."

He glanced at Paris, and she saw a hint of uncertainty in his eyes. She smiled, rose and said, "I doubt you would have any problem getting a young lady into a car. The front seat or the back."

"That may be true." He stood his brow still furrowed in a frown. "But Miss Abigail's not any ordinary girl—she's special."

Though she had no doubt he knew his way around women and she would love nothing more than to find out first hand, Paris was suddenly very anxious to meet the *special* woman who held this tall sexy southern gentlemen's heart in her hands. Before she could question him a woman pushed a young girl in a wheelchair into the room.

"Here we are. Looks like you have a visitor!" The older woman exclaimed, patting the girl on the shoulder.

The girl's gaze traveled from Beau to hers, giving Paris a thorough once-over. There was a hint of the green-eyed-monster in the young woman's eyes.

"Abigail," the older woman said leaning over. "Beau has a surprise for you. I'll let him do the introductions." She smiled, squeezed the girl's shoulder and then left the room.

Beau's demeanor changed. His frown vanished, and his face softened to a becoming grin as he rounded the desk. "Miss Paris, may I present Miss Abigail Pendergrass. Abby, this is Miss Paris Jenkins. She's an occupational therapist. Dr. Hanson recommended her."

So this was the princess of the castle who held this brawny knight's heart. She hadn't known what to expect, but it sure wasn't the scrawny little 'plain Jane' that sat in front of her now. The young woman wore tan slacks, a mint-green T-shirt and canvas tennis shoes. Her short brown hair hung straight. She wore no makeup or jewelry.

Paris smiled and stepped forward to shake her hand. "It's nice to meet you, Abigail."

"Call me Abby." Her voice sounded thin and vulnerable.

"Only if you call me Paris."

"We were just going over a light program that Miss Paris has put together for you. I think you'll find it challenging and interesting." Beau handed Abby his copy.

With hesitation Abby reached for the list. When she glanced up, he saw fear and panic flash in her eyes. Beau's heart went out to her. He knew she felt incapable of doing these things, but deep in his heart he also knew she could do anything once she set her mind to it.

Kneeling down in front of Abby, he took both of her hands in his. "Sweetheart, listen to me. Nobody expects you to be able to do everything right away. It's going to take time and a lot of hard work. We'll all be here to help you. I know you can do this."

Tears rolled down her face. Shaking her head, she stammered, "I can't..."

"Yes, you can. I'll be right by your side. We'll take it slow." She shook her head again. "Just this morning you transferred into your chair all by yourself. In no time you'll master everything on that list. Before you know it you'll have your old life back."

Beau raised Abby's hands to his lips and kissed the back of each one. "Sweetheart, let us help you get your life back."

Paris clutched her hands together, smothering the urge to throw the man across his desk and kiss him into the middle of next week. Besides looks and manners, sensitivity oozed from him as he spoke to the girl. And by the look on Abby's face, apparently Paris wasn't the only one that thought so.

Paris interrupted. "I'll leave these papers with you. You two can go over them before my next visit. We'll test your abilities and set up some charts and graphs then."

Beau rose and placed a protective hand on Abby's shoulder as she wiped at her tears with the back of her hand. Paris would give anything to have a man like him in her life, to hear him call *her* sweetheart and tell *her* everything was going to be fine.

She wondered if the girl realized what a treasure she had and if she had any idea how to handle a man like him. She shook her head. *What a waste.*

Paris walked out of the office toward the foyer where she stopped and turned.

Beau had followed her. He reached for the door and pulled it open. He honored her with a slow sexy smile and said, "Thanks, Miss Paris.

Sure was nice to meet you, ma'am."

His slow southern drawl made Paris's insides melt. She always thought she had a lot to offer a man. She never had any problems turning a man's head, but this guy had only one woman on his mind. She actually envied Ms. Pendergrass.

Paris laughed out loud as she drove away. It was quite evident Beau and *Miss Abigail* had strong feelings for each other, but did either of them know how the other one felt? It was going to be interesting working with these two.

Chapter Thirteen

Armed with a clipboard of information, Beau watched through the window of the great room as Dr. Berkman exited a classy white Mustang convertible. She leaned into the car to retrieve her briefcase, and he grinned at the pleasant view of her backside.

He pulled open the door before she could ring the bell. "Good morning, Dr. Berkman. Please come in."

"Good morning, Mr. Winkelman," she said, somewhat surprised.

Beau grinned at her expression then ushered her into the dining room. He rested his hand on the back of a chair and gestured for her to have a seat. A light pink washed over her cheeks as she perched on the edge of the chair.

Beau moved behind his makeshift desk, set the clipboard aside and retrieved a stack of typed papers. He turned and studied the petite doctor. Today her curly blond hair was restrained in a long braid that hung down her back. White slacks and a navy blue sweater concealed her shapely legs and figure. He could picture her in a skimpy cheerleader's uniform, her wild curls tumbling loose around her shoulders. *She sure is a sweet little thing.*

"Before your session with Miss Abigail," he said, tapping the loose pages on the desk. "I have an observation report for you." She appeared puzzled. Delighted with her reaction, he continued. "I mentioned to Mr. Pendergrass the possibilities that Abby may suffer from Survivor Guilt and or Post Traumatic Stress Disorder. I don't claim to be a psychologist, but in the past I've worked with clients that have suffered with one or both of these syndromes."

"I see. And I agree with you" she replied. "Unresolved guilt can intensify any traumatic experience and add depression and the sense of hopelessness to the situation. If a patient focuses on guilt rather than on their recovery this usually means they're unable to face other issues."

Satisfied they were on the same page he handed her the report and settled into the chair behind the desk. He studied her as she skimmed through the papers.

Despite the fact that she voiced her negative opinion in regards to his therapy at their first meeting, she wasn't looking down her nose at him today. He had expected a little eyebrow rising from her, but she merely nodded her head and hummed her agreement as she read. She was all right in his book.

Then she glanced up and smiled. "You may have missed your true calling, Mr. Winkelman. I'm very impressed with your observations."

"Thank you, and please call me Beau."

"Then I insist you call me Nicky," she replied. "This isn't a new concept," she added with a gentle smile, making Beau realize he hadn't single-handedly discovered the cure for cancer. "We touched on these syndromes briefly before Abigail shut down and refused to accept treatment. However," her bright blue eyes sparkled, "It's on the top of my to-do list and this," she held the pages up. "Your observation proves to me that you comprehend the severity of her disability."

Beau felt the blow of humility tackle his pride. Swallowing his pride, he took the fifteen-yard penalty with a large grain of salt. Then he remembered the information on aging and sexuality that he'd wanted to discuss with Dr. Berkman.

"Doctor, I mean Miss Nicky, I know you have several subjects you would like to speak with Miss Abigail about…" Beau retrieved another stack of papers. "But she seems to have some questions…" He felt the heat rise up his neck. "…questions that I have obtained the answers for but don't feel it's my place to discuss these types of topics with her. She needs to talk to another woman, a professional woman like yourself, about this." A look of panic flashed across her pert features.

He handed her his research papers. The top page was titled, "Women's Sexuality." The topics listed included sexual response treatment of sexual dysfunction achieving orgasms and birth control. As the young psychologist stared blankly at the papers, Beau turned and glanced out the window. With one hand he rubbed at the tension building at the back of his neck. Sex and relationships were subjects he'd always felt more comfortable demonstrating than discussing openly like some sort of debate panel.

"All I can do is broach the subject and see if she wants to discuss it." Nicky glanced up from the papers and met his gaze. And there it went, the raised eyebrow, the look that questioned his judgment that he'd been waiting for. "You really did your homework."

"I tried to reassure Abby the other night that she could have normal relations..." His voice trailed off as he recalled how wonderful she had felt in his arms. Clearing his throat, he said, "It would just be better coming from a woman. You know what I mean?"

"I understand. I'll see what I can do."

"Thanks."

Relieved, Beau stood and excused himself but swore he heard the woman's muffled giggles behind him as he walked out of the room. There must be something in the air that affected every woman that entered this house—bless their hearts—but for the life of him, he couldn't figure out what was wrong with all of them.

* * * *

Beau dove into the water and swam back and forth across the pool. Soon his muscles loosened up, and all his tension subsided. The water soothed both his body and his mind. The late morning rays filtered through clouds that reminded him of endless acres of Texas cotton fields.

His career appeared to be back on track. Abby continued to respond well to therapy, and today he had passed the ball to that cute little doctor who was willing to run interference for him. If Abby kept progressing at the rate she had been, soon his work here would be done. But the idea of leaving left a painful knot in his gut.

He paused at the edge of the pool. His gaze zeroed in on her bedroom window. One minute she drove him crazy with her constant fighting and complaining; the next her vulnerability surfaced, and all he wanted to do was cradle her in his arms and protect her. That couldn't happen. She wasn't his to protect. She never would be, and he would be smart to remember that.

He needed to stay on target. Focused on the one thing he could control in his life—his future. With Abby's rapid recovery and good references from Mr. Pendergrass and Dr. Hanson, his dreams of owning his own rehabilitation clinic could soon become reality.

With a confidence he hadn't felt in a long time Beau climbed the ladder and walked to the end of the diving board. *What a beautiful day. Life couldn't get any better than this.* He stretched his long muscular arms, reaching toward the sky. Filling his lungs with the salty air, he jackknifed into the pool. He swam several laps, reflecting on how fortunate he had become and how well everything was progressing. He wouldn't allow himself to think about the time he was no longer needed here and he had to leave. No, he was going to just enjoy himself.

When Beau finally surfaced, he couldn't believe his eyes. At the edge of the pool stood a hundred and twenty-five pounds of unmistakable trouble. He opened his mouth to speak but instead inhaled a gallon of water, erupting into a fit of coughing. Everything had been going too smoothly. He should have anticipated there would be a fumble.

Ginger's wild auburn waves fell loose around her shoulders. Her shorts barely covered her perfect backside and her tube-top covered even less. High-heeled sandals tap-danced along the edge of the pool as the rest of her bounced up and down with each step.

Unbelievable.

Beau's gaze traveled from Ginger to Lily who stood close by with her arms crossed over her chest, one perfect eyebrow raised in question.

Surrendering to the fact that he hadn't been hallucinating, Beau sank to the bottom of the pool. His life, his career and his future were over. *Lord, if you have any compassion, please let me drown here and now.*

He heard muffled screams and found himself being dragged to the surface. Ginger towed him to the edge of the pool and plastered kisses all over his face.

"Oh, Sugar, are you all right? Here, let me help you." Pulling herself up out of the pool she reached for Beau's arm, all the while her large breasts threatened to spill out of her tube-top. Beau glanced up and feared it wouldn't take much for those "bad-girls" to break free.

"No! I'm fine. Let go of me!" Ginger released him on command, her expression puzzled. Beau pulled himself out of the water. How on earth could this be happening? What was he supposed to do now? Maybe he could get her out of sight before anyone else saw her.

The door opened, and Dr. Berkman wheeled Abby out onto the patio, shattering any plans he might have conjured up if he could have even thought straight.

Beau sat on the edge of the pool and waited, but it didn't look like God was going to inflict a natural disaster on the Pendergrass estate for his benefit. He was on his own.

He stood and handed Ginger a towel in hopes that she would cover herself. With his hands, he raked back his wet hair and turned his attention toward the house in time to catch an amused expression flash across Dr. Berkman's face. The woman seemed to get a great deal of satisfaction at his discomfort.

"Um—Dr. Berkman, Abby, Miss Lily, this is Ginger ... Ginger Gonzalez," he stammered, trying to recall the woman's last name.

The women's polite smiles faded as Ginger happily announced, "I'm Beau's girlfriend from Texas. Nice to meet y'all."

Beau sighed and closed his eyes against the bizarre scene. This was never in the playbook. Opening his eyes, his gaze locked with Abby's. She hadn't said anything but appeared as surprised and confused as he felt.

What could she be thinking?

Dr. Berkman came to his rescue. "Nice to meet you, Ginger. I think Abby needs to get out of the sun." She didn't wait for a response but turned and wheeled Abby back into the house.

Confused and embarrassed at Ginger's unexpected arrival, Beau looked to Lily for support and understanding.

"Well, that was fun," Lily muttered as she approached Ginger.

"You can change your clothes in the guesthouse, dear," she said, pointing toward a small building set back in the trees.

Beau stared, dumbfounded. What was happening? He wasn't in Texas anymore. Somehow he'd landed in this strange place, and he had the craziest notion to click his heels together. Hopefully he'd open his eyes and find himself in some smelly old locker room, the whole experience just a bad dream.

"Thank you, ma'am." Ginger smiled politely and patted Beau's chest as she headed toward the guesthouse. "Fetch my bags from my car, won't you, Sugar?"

"Bags!" He turned toward Lily with no explanation. "I have no idea what she's doing here. As far as I'm concerned, our relationship was over when I left Texas."

"Well, then I'd say you're in a pickle, aren't you, S*ugar*?"

"You have to believe me. I never thought she'd follow me."

"Obviously, but she has. Apparently she wasn't under the same impression when you drove away and left her."

"What am I going to do?" he moaned, looking over his shoulder toward the guesthouse.

"You're on your own, Romeo."

Lily shook her head and walked away, leaving Beau to clean up his own mess.

Lily's imitation of Ginger set Beau's teeth on edge. Retrieving her bags, he headed for the guesthouse. What had she been thinking, inviting her to stay?

Beau entered the guesthouse and heard water running. Ginger's wet clothes were strewn on the floor like a trail of breadcrumbs leading to the shower. He dropped the bags and in two strides crossed the small room. Better to get this over with as soon as possible. He caught himself as he reached for the door. What the hell was he thinking? Ginger was in the shower. Besides, what was he going to say to her? He had better think about it first, come up with a foolproof game plan. Where he and women were concerned, nothing was ever foolproof.

Beau turned on his heels and headed for the nearest exit. *No woman other than Ginger could drop out of the sky and screw up my life any more than it already is!*

* * * *

After Dr. Berkman left, Abby sat alone in her room. What a fool she'd been. The doctor must have sensed her embarrassment; she had left right after returning Abby to her room and helping her back into bed.

During their session, Abby had gone on and on about how it felt to lie in his arms, her cheek against his bare chest. The way he had held her tight and stroked her back as she poured her heart out to him her deepest fears. And how he dried her tears and given her hope for a future.

They had talked about marriage and children, and Dr. Berkman had even given her several sheets of information about it to read. Abby swiped her arm across the bedside table, sending the sheets of paper flying. *She must think I'm a real idiot.*

Abby glanced out her window just as Beau entered the guesthouse. Tears streamed down her cheeks as she watched her future disappear behind someone else's door. Did they rush into each other's arms? Were they holding each other and laughing at her? He had told her she was beautiful, that she had a lot to offer. Had he even been thinking of her at the time, or had he been picturing Miss-Gee-Are-My-Clothes-Too-Tight the whole time she had laid in his arms?

Abby curled up on her side and allowed the tears fall. She would cry now, but it would be for the last time.

* * * *

Ginger realized Beau hadn't missed her at all. She had hoped that after not seeing her for a couple of weeks he would be happily surprised. Obviously she had been wrong. He left Texas in such a hurry; she had felt he had taken this job just to get away from her. The fact that he just dropped her bags in the middle of the floor and left confirmed her suspicions.

Walking out of the guesthouse Ginger found the patio deserted. With her hair dried and styled and dressed in a calico sundress, she chose a comfy chase lounge to sit on and wait for Beau to return. She knew Beau had his likes and dislikes. He would get over her little surprise visit soon enough and forgive her.

"There you are." The older woman smiled and walked toward Ginger. "I hope the guesthouse will be comfortable enough for you." She offered Ginger a tall glass of iced tea.

"Yes, ma'am. Y'all have a beautiful place here." Reaching for the glass, she replied, "Thank you," relieved the woman hadn't come to send her on her way. Ginger had planned on spending a week with Beau before she had to be back in Texas.

"Please call me Lily. Lunch is ready if you're hungry. You can eat in the kitchen with me, or if you prefer you may bring your plate out here." She gestured toward the table.

"I'd like your company." Ginger hesitated. "If you don't mind?"

"I'd like that, too," Lily smiled. "It seems I, too, will be dining alone. Abigail was resting when I checked on her."

"And Beau?" Ginger asked hopefully.

"He said he wasn't hungry then went to his room."

"Oh?" He was angry with her.

"He must have a lot of paperwork to do. After lunch I need to drive into town and pick up a few things. Would you like to come with me? The drive is beautiful, and it would give us a chance to get better acquainted."

"Thank you. You're so sweet." Ginger smiled and followed Lily into the house. She liked the old lady. Plus she was interested in finding out what the spunky little woman had up her sleeve.

* * * *

Beau planned to hide in his room all afternoon, burying himself in his books and research, but he kept wondering what Abby was thinking. He had never called Ginger or even mentioned her name. And Ginger ... well, sooner or later he had to talk to her. What had she expected by driving all the way up here? He rubbed the nagging pain in his neck. Lily had left him to swing in the wind, and Dr. Berkman seemed amused by the whole incident. Females—*she-devils every one of them, put on earth only to torment men.*

Beau opened his bedroom door and took a deep breath. *Don't show any fear.*

He found Ginger sitting at the kitchen table, drinking iced tea with Lily. "Ginger, can I talk to you for a moment?" Without waiting for her reply, he turned and headed toward the patio. A chair scrapped across the floor behind him.

"Ginger, how did you find me?"

She flashed him a shy smile and replied, "It's been weeks. When you didn't call I thought maybe something happened to you." She treated him to her well-practiced pouting lips. He didn't respond to her ploy, and she quickly switched plays. She stepped forward and slid both hands up the front of his shirt. He brushed them aside.

"I've been busy. This job takes up *all* of my time."

"Poor baby," she purred, moving closer.

"Ginger, don't! I think you should go back to Texas in the morning."

Although Ginger's pout was real this time, he could tell she wasn't ready to throw in the towel just yet. He'd bet she had her own playbook stashed someplace close by.

"Let's go into the guesthouse to sit down and talk for a while alright?" She turned and strolled toward the guesthouse, her seductive hips swaying back and forth. *She wasn't going to make this easy for him.*

The guesthouse seemed small and cramped. Her scent hung heavy in the air. Once he loved her tantalizing fragrance. Now her strong perfume burned his lungs and threatened to choke him.

Ginger poised on the sofa. Patting the cushion next to her, she summoned, "Come sit next to me."

"I'm fine." Beau frowned as he prowled the small quarters. "Ginger, I don't think it's a good idea for you to be here. You need to go back to Texas."

"Just how long do you think this job is going to take?"

"I'm not sure," he evaded "Abby has responded better to therapy than I expected."

"I'll bet." Ginger rose and closed the distance between them. Walking her fingers up his arms she paused at his shoulders before wandering across the front of his chest. In the past that's all it would take to get him into the game. Today her advances had only managed to make him angry.

"Didn't you miss me just a little?" She leaned into him, her lips parting for a kiss.

Beau stepped back and grabbed her by the wrists. "I told you we couldn't do this."

Ginger smiled "They can't see into the guesthouse. They'll never know."

"I don't care. You shouldn't have come here." His voice sounded much harsher than he intended.

"You said you would call me, and you didn't. I thought maybe something had happened to you."

"I'm a big boy, Ginger. I've been taking care of myself for a long time." He crossed the small room, putting as much distance between them as he could.

"Even big boys need taking care of sometimes," she cooed.

He watched as she moved in line for another scrimmage.

"Well, I don't. Not here and not now. I can't have you getting in my way and distracting me."

"So you did miss me." She grinned in triumph.

Did he? Beau raked his hands through his hair. Ginger hadn't crossed his mind once since he'd arrived. Hadn't she meant anything to him? She must have; she was pretty, sexy and fun. He thought he had feelings for her, but no, he hadn't missed her. Hadn't even thought of her.

"Listen, Ginger. This is my job. You can't just come barging in here and expect me to make time for you. This job is demanding. I work eight to ten hours a day with Abby. At night I have hours of reading and research to do. Do you understand what I'm saying? You can't stay. You have to leave." Not knowing what else he could say, Beau turned and walked out of the guesthouse.

* * * *

Abby reclined on her bed. Although it was late she had been unable to fall asleep. Out of tears, she'd settled on self-pity. Earlier she'd watched Beau enter the guesthouse. What made her think he would ever be interested in her, a cripple, only half a woman? He had more than a whole woman willing and ready, a woman who knew what to do with a man. No man would ever feel anything other than pity for her.

Her left leg began a painful spasm. She tried adjusting herself to get more comfortable, but the long hours of therapy had taken their toll. The harder she worked, the more her left side cramped and throbbed in agony. She struggled to sit up, cursed and attempted to rub her left leg. "I hate this! Damn it all to—"

"What's the matter, sweetheart?" Beau appeared in her doorway.

"Oh, go away, and stop calling me that!"

Without invitation, he crossed the room and threw back her covers. He perched on the edge of the bed and placed her foot in his lap. "Just lay back, and try to relax." One corner of his mouth hiked up in a slight grin as he reached for the bottle of lotion.

Reluctant, Abby lay back but doubted she would ever be able to relax around him again. His hands, which at first had been rough, were now soft from hours of massaging her. His gentle touch forced her quivering aching muscles to surrender. His hands felt like heaven as they stroked her into submission. How much more of this could she take? Irritated that her body came to life and responded so quickly to his touch, she tried pulling away.

"Hold still," he growled, his brows pulled together.

"Don't you have *someone else* to bother?"

His face relaxed. "I'm not getting paid to bother anyone else." Raising one eyebrow he gave her a slow sexy grin.

Insufferable man.

"If I pay you, will you go away?" she hissed between clenched teeth.

"Nope." Beau's voice rumbled soft and low. His gaze locked with hers as if challenging her. Uncomfortable, Abby turned away, avoiding his stare. Silence hung heavy in the air.

"I didn't invite her here," he offered in a low voice.

"Why should I care? It's between you and my aunt whether she stays or not." What did she care? He wasn't her man. Her man? What a joke.

"Miss Jenkins is stopping by tomorrow," Beau changed the subject. "I'm going to talk to her about fitting you for a leg brace."

Panic stricken, Abby struggled to sit up further. "So soon?" Her voice squeaked. She hoped he didn't notice.

"It'll be okay. Once you get the brace, we'll start off slow, using the support treadmill-training unit. We'll use it the same way we use it now. Someday you aren't going to need that wheelchair. You're going to be able to walk with the help of a leg brace and a couple of forearm crutches."

Abby glanced up and searched his face. Did he really believe what he was saying? Was he trying to convince her or himself? "I don't think I can work harder than I already am."

"The harder we work the sooner you'll recover."

And the sooner you can leave. Her stomach twisted at the thought of never seeing him again.

"Look how far you've come in such a short time. At this rate you'll be up and walking before you know it." He walked to the other side of the bed and continued with the massage. She wasn't ready to walk with a leg brace, and she wasn't ready for him to leave, but both knew it would happen with or without her consent. She wasn't a little girl who brought home a lost puppy. She couldn't keep Beau. She'd have to let him go. "I'm tired. Can we talk about this tomorrow?"

"Sure, sweet ... Sure enough."

Abby's throat tightened. She closed her eyes, attempting to ignore his thoughtfulness as he retrieved the blankets and draped them over her. He closed the door behind him as he left.

A gentle breeze floated in through the window, and she caught the scent of him—fresh air, soap and raw masculinity. Was this what the rest of her life was going to be like? She had gone from having anything her heart desired to not being able to give her heart the one thing it really wanted.

* * * *

Beau stood in the dark and stared out his bedroom window. He'd seen the panic in Abby's eyes when he mentioned the leg brace. They had been working so hard, and the time would come when she would be fitted for a brace and crutches. Why did she appear so reluctant? The sudden change in her baffled him. Had he done something or said something to upset her?

The cool evening breeze caressed his bare chest. Head pounding, he took a deep breath. The walls were closing in on him. He needed to get out of this house.

The pool was out of the question; he didn't want to be anywhere near Ginger. A run along the cliffs might clear his mind and help him sleep.

Letting himself out the patio door, Beau sprinted across the grass, making his way toward the trail that lined the rocky ledge of the cliffs. His long muscular legs ate up the ground, and the salty air stung his face.

Why did Ginger have to show up now? Abby had been showing significant progress. Now her self-doubt and insecurities would surface and drag her back down. She talked tough, but it was just a front to hide her apprehension, her fear. If only he could free her from her self-inflicted tethers.

The bright glow of the full moon reflected off the water, lighting his path. It was a beautiful moon, a moon to be shared. He had a strong urge to drag Abby out into the night and show her what she was missing. Prove to her that she was a real woman and that she could have everything she ever dreamt of. Frustrated, Beau pushed himself harder, each gulp of air burning his lungs. Abby's dreams—whatever they were—didn't include him.

His heart and mind battled over right and wrong. If he acted on his feelings toward Abby he'd lose his career and possibly his sister forever. If he didn't, he had a good chance of having a future as a therapist. But could he be happy without Abby?

Drenched in sweat, he finally returned to the patio. Bent over, he rested his hands on his knees. Sweat dripped into his eyes. With the back of his hand he wiped his brow. His chest heaved, and every muscle ached.

He glanced toward the guesthouse and drew a deep breath. He needed to get rid of Ginger—as soon as possible.

Chapter Fourteen

Abby awoke, reading seven o'clock on the palm tree-shaped clock radio that sat on her nightstand. The world outside her window was covered in sunlight. She listened for sounds of her aunt moving around in the kitchen and heard nothing.

She pushed herself up into a sitting position and reached for her bed jacket. Aunt Lily insisted she wear it over her new Capri pajamas. Gripping the bedrail with her right arm, she jockeyed her legs over the side and scooted to the edge. With the renewed strength on her right side, she put all her weight on her right leg and navigated herself into her wheelchair. Once seated, she exhaled a loud sign and smiled at her accomplishment.

She left her room and noticed Beau's door had been left open. Curious, she wheeled her chair to the door and glanced inside. A wave of longing and despair washed over her as she took advantage of the opportunity to gaze upon him as he slept.

His blond hair fanned across the pillow. The blue sheet draped the smooth tanned skin between his ribs and thighs. One arm was casually tossed over his head, the other across his abdomen. His broad shoulders and chest filled the small bed. His long muscular legs and feet protruded out over the end. The whole room, for that matter, seemed too small for him. He resembled Alice in Wonderland when she had taken the pills to make herself larger.

The cool morning breeze filtered through the open window but did little to cool the sudden warmth that engulfed her. She longed to crawl in and snuggle up next to him. Feel his bare skin against hers and his strong arms around her. But now that Ginger had intruded into her world it wasn't Abby he longed to hold.

The scent of soap, fresh air and sandalwood filled her senses. She took one last yearning look before her chin dropped in despair. Knowing she could never have his love, Abby wheeled away from Beau's door.

Ginger had ruined everything. Maybe it had only been her imagination but Abby believed Beau had been attracted to *her*. That his feelings were stronger than just simple affection. She knew now that having a life with him was only wishful thinking.

What Beau wanted—what he needed—wasn't a naive girl. She would be better soon, and he would have accomplished what he had come for. With his obligation met he would have no reason to stay. He and Ginger would return to their love-nest in Texas and pick up where they had left off.

She had seen the way Ginger looked at him. And he'd gone to the guesthouse last night. Her heart ached at the thought of him holding Ginger. Anything more than that sickened her. She wheeled her chair up to the kitchen table. A sudden headache pounded at her temples.

Lily entered the kitchen. "Good morning, dear. How are you feeling today?"

"I'm fine." Abby replied listlessly and wiped away a tear from her cheek.

"I love these cool mornings," Lily continued. "I slept like a baby last night. How about you?"

Without answering, Abby wheeled closer to the window.

"Are you hungry? Where is Beau?" Lily fluttered around the kitchen, chirping like a little magpie.

"I thought I heard someone out here." Beau yanked a faded gray T-shirt over his head. "Morning, ladies. Miss Lily, I'm hungry enough to eat a whole Longhorn steer this morning."

Lily giggled. "I don't think I have a Longhorn in the refrigerator, but I'll see what I can come up with."

"Thanks, darlin'. You're a peach."

Out of the corner of her eye Abby watched as Beau planted a quick kiss on her aunt's cheek and then followed her to the refrigerator. The metallic taste of hopelessness pooled in the back of her throat. His endearments came fast and free if he wanted something. Empty endearments—that's all they were too. They didn't mean anything. The sharp sting of disappointment pierced her heart.

A frown creased Abby's brow, and Beau wished he could read her mind. No, maybe that wasn't such a good idea. No man should be subjected to a woman's true thoughts.

As Lily busied herself in the kitchen and Abby gazed out the window Beau retrieved the list that the occupational therapist had left with him.

"Here," he said, placing the papers on the table in front of Abby. "I want to go over these before Ms. Jenkins arrives." Abby neither glanced at the paper nor responded. *So it was going to be one of those days.*

"I don't think you're going to have too much trouble with most of them. Heck, you've already mastered the hardest ones."

When she glanced at the papers, he settled into a chair across from her. He caught Lily's gaze, and her frown reflected her doubt.

Abby glanced up, and her expression appeared skeptical.

"Sweetheart, you've mastered the most important one of them all—communication." Scooting closer, he reached over and patted her knee. The patio door swung open, and Ginger sashayed in. Beau's train of thought ran off track and derailed.

Ginger was dressed to kill. She wore snug white Capri pants and a tight lime green crop-top that revealed her flat stomach. Her strong perfume filled the air, and she waltzed across the ceramic tile in three inch faux alligator sandals.

"Good mornin', y'all." She paused at Beau's side, leaned down and kissed his cheek. "Mornin', Sugar," she purred in his ear. Feeling his face flush, he shooed her away like a pesky fly. Then she placed a hand on Abby's shoulder and said, "Hi, sweetie." He caught a glimpse of her curvy hips as she pranced toward Lily.

"Oh, Miss Lily, something sure does smell tasty! My mouth is just watering in anticipation."

"You have perfect timing," Lily said as she wiped her hands on a towel.

Yeah, perfect timing, Beau thought.

"It's nothing special," Lily continued with an appreciative smile. "It's just scrambled eggs, onions, green peppers and ham."

Ginger gave Lily an affectionate hug. "It sounds wonderful. Can I give you a hand?"

"No, dear. Everything is ready. Grab a plate, and help yourself."

Beau returned his attention to Abby. A scowl marred her face, and with her right hand she jerked her chair toward the stove. What did he do? He shook his head. He would never understand women. One minute her eyes appeared sad and wounded; the next minute they were on fire and ready for a fight. He shook his head. Once again he was completely baffled.

Lily watched with amusement as Abby and Ginger sized each other up like two lionesses with a fresh kill as they both approached the stove. This could be interesting. Would Abby be intimidated by Ginger and back away? Or would she challenge her?

"Here, Miss Abby. Let me get that for you." Ginger's offer was made with a big friendly smile.

"I can get it myself," Abby snapped, propelling her wheelchair forward. *That's my girl.* Lily had done the right thing by insisting that Ginger spend her vacation with them. There was nothing wrong with her staying in the guesthouse. As far as she was concerned, a little competition was good for a person. She just hoped Beau wouldn't mess everything up.

Beau sat at the table, shuffling his papers, oblivious to the skirmish taking place behind his back.

Lily walked to the table with the milk and almost laughed out loud at his lack of awareness regarding the tension in the room. The man had no clue what was going on around him. She shook her head. Well, that wasn't anything new; most men didn't.

"Really, Miss Abby. It's no bother at all." Ginger's smile faded to a frown as she jumped out of the path of the advancing wheelchair.

"I said—I can do it myself!" With her plate resting on her lap, Abby proceeded to serve herself.

Beau turned his attention toward the commotion at the stove. "She's fine, Ginger. Leave her be."

Ginger took a step back, and Lily gave her a reassuring smile and nodded. With shaky hands, Abby gripped the serving spoon with her right hand and scooped a helping onto her plate. A large clump of scrambled eggs rolled off the spoon and flopped onto the edge of the stove and onto the floor. Lily forced herself to stay back and let Abby serve herself.

"I'll get that, Miss Abigail." Ginger reached for a napkin and quickly wiped up the spill. With a jerky movement, Abby wheeled her chair around and headed for the table.

Lily was aware of her niece's romantic feelings for Beau. She was even afraid Abby might have fallen in love with him. She had been right; Abby was acting like a normal jealous female.

They ate in silence, and Lily wondered if her niece would fight for what she really wanted or let her disability hold her back. Would Abby give up too easily and let Ginger walk away with her future?

* * * *

Strapped tight to the recumbent cycle, Abby forced her right leg to help the left one make several revolutions. Yet the visions of the redheaded bimbo flouncing around the kitchen kept invading her concentration. She was so mad; she wished she had run Ginger over with her wheelchair. And Beau hadn't been able to take his eyes off of the tramp all through breakfast.

Ginger acted so sweet and innocent when she offered to help Abby with her plate. The mere thought of that woman set Abby's teeth on edge. She wasn't going to give in or give up. Inexperience had never kept her out of the competition. She may not have as much to work with as Ginger, but she was going to throw her hat into the ring.

Beau stood several feet away, working with some free weights. Abby stopped and marveled at his body as he effortlessly curled the weights up to his shoulders, first one arm then the other. The muscles in his upper body bulged each time the weights were lifted.

He glanced up and caught her staring and asked, "Are you finished?"

Abby's tongue slipped out between her teeth, and she licked her dry lips. Sweat trickled down the sides of her face, pooled at the base of her neck and then slowly descended between her breasts. Knowing he watched her, she reached for a towel, closed her eyes and tilted her head back. With as much composure as she could muster, she slowly dabbed at her neck, first turning her head one way then the other.

She heard him set the weights on the mat and walk to her side. Her eyes fluttered open as he leaned over and unbuckled her straps. Placing one arm under her knees, the other around her back, he lifted her off the recumbent cycle. He held her in his arms, and a pained expression crossed his face before he set her down on the exercise mat and positioned himself in front of her.

His body fascinated her. Each muscle seemed to work independently of all the others. Just the thought of touching them made her mouth go dry. She licked her lips.

Beau cleared his throat and removed her tennis shoes. "If you're ever going to drive again you have to work up the strength in your ankle." He pushed his hand against the bottom of her foot.

"Who said I wanted to drive again?"

"I did, so quit giving me so much grief. I told you you'll be walking and driving before I leave."

"Who said I was going to let you leave?" she replied with a sassy grin, but he ignored her flirtation.

"Concentrate! Now push as hard as you can with your toes. That's good. Once more."

"How much longer? I'm tired." She reclined back on the exercise mat and closed her eyes. With all her strength, she stretched her arms over her head, drawing up her pink tank top, revealing her stomach. She had rolled up the hem on her little pink exercise shorts and now watched through lowered lashes as Beau gazed at her bare legs. She rolled to one side, and as she fought to hold her balance, she stroked one foot along the mat.

"M-M-Miss Lily..." he stammered, "...tells me you have a car in the back garage." His eyes worked their way up her body to meet hers.

"So? So what?" She struggled to rest her weight on her right elbow.

"So maybe I ought to look it over," he replied as he massaged the foot he still held in his hands.

"Why? What are you looking for?" Abby blinked innocently, and with only a small amount of effort she ran her left hand seductively over her hip.

His brows pulled together in a deep scowl. "I—I need to make sure that it will meet all of the U.S. safety standards." He released her one foot, reached for the other and roughly started manipulating it. "I want to see what modifications it's going to require."

He twisted her ankle a little too hard; Abby gasped and bit her lower lip. "Sorry." He glanced down at his hands as if expecting to find someone else's. "It's essential that you get one of those handicap stickers for parking."

"Hooray lucky me!" she said, shaking her head. *So much for attempting to be provocative. He didn't even notice.*

* * * *

Paris rang the doorbell, ran a hand over her red skirt and took in her surroundings. On her first visit, she'd been so captivated by the view of the ocean she hadn't noticed the beautifully manicured lawn. The door opened, and Mrs. Bendickson's smiling face greeted her.

"Ms. Jenkins, hello. Won't you please come in?" Lily stepped back to let Paris enter. "Beau and Abigail will be finished shortly. I'll take you out onto the patio where you can wait by the pool."

"Thank you. That would be lovely." Paris stopped at the doorway of the makeshift gym. They had plainly been in the middle of a serious conversation.

"Don't be like that. Do you realize just how lucky you are?" Beau berated the half-naked girl reclining on the floor before him.

Paris wondered the same thing. Not wanting to interrupt, she followed Lily through the house which was a unique mixture of European and Asian design.

"Here we go. Have a seat, and I'll fetch some refreshments. I'm sure they won't be too much longer." Lily then hurried back into the house.

Paris wiggled into one of the cushioned chairs. A large tan umbrella with white stripes and fringe blocked her from the sun's afternoon rays. Her gaze traveled from the regulation size tennis court and pool across the beautiful lawn to the ocean off in the distance. This piece of real estate was positively magnificent. Shaking her head, she wondered once again if Abigail Pendergrass knew how lucky she was.

Movement in the pool caught Paris's attention. A chestnut-haired mermaid surfaced and smiled up at her.

"Hello," she called as she emerged from the pool.

"Back at ya," Paris replied, interested in the woman who could easily be a swimsuit model in a men's sports magazine. The woman grabbed a towel and started toward her. Who was she? A friend of Abby's? Maybe a cousin?

"Hi, I'm Beau's girlfriend, Ginger Gonzalez," the mermaid replied in a slow Texas drawl as she reached out her hand.

"Nice to meet you. I'm Paris Jenkins, Abby's occupational therapist." How the devil did he pull this off, Paris wondered. "So how long have you been here?"

"Only a couple of days. I'm staying in the guesthouse."

"How convenient." Picking up the glasses that hung from a silver chain around her neck, Paris casually chewed on the end of them.

"What do you mean by that?" Ginger's eyes narrowed.

"Nothing really. Do you get to spend much time *alone* with Beau?" Her eyebrows rose in question.

"Well, no. Not really. Beau's very busy. He doesn't have much free time. Why do you ask?"

"Sorry, it's none of my business. I was just curious, that's all." Paris crossed her legs and tugged her skirt down. "How long have you two been together?"

"Close to six months now. Why all the questions, darlin'? Thinkin' on rustling him away from me?" Ginger flashed a confident smile.

"Oh, no. You don't have to worry about me."

"I didn't think so. You're not really his type. Beau likes *younger* women," she stated with a smirk.

Paris studied the not-so-much younger woman as she ran the towel over her wet body with slow deliberate strokes. From what Paris observed of Beau's professional behavior this hot redhead didn't seem like his type at all.

Just then laughter rang from the house. Both women turned and through the screen door saw Beau and Abby. Beau leaned down and kissed Abby's forehead. Then he said, "You did great today, sweetheart. It won't be long, and we'll be going out dancing." The screen door opened, and Beau walked out onto the patio.

Paris turned to Ginger and replied, "I guess you were right."

Beau lumbered toward them, a big lop-sided grin hung on his face. It bothered Ginger that *she* hadn't been the one to put it there. He had never given her the chance to get close enough to him since she had arrived. It's not like he never had any opportunities; he just never acted on them. He had been *too busy* with *Miss Abigail* to pay any attention to her. He was deliberately avoiding her.

A sick feeling came over Ginger when Beau called Abby *sweetheart* and then kissed her. Struggling with her emotions, she turned and strutted toward the guesthouse.

As Beau walked toward Paris, she couldn't help but appreciate his admirable characteristics.

"Miss Paris, I see you've met Ginger." He placed a tray of drinks on the table and handed her a glass. "Miss Lily's helping Abby change. She'll come fetch you when she's finished."

"Thank you," she replied and watched as he glanced toward the guesthouse. A puzzled expression momentarily crossed his face. He deposited himself into a chair and took a long drink from his glass. Paris smiled; he had no idea what bothered his *girlfriend,* and it didn't appear he was in too great a hurry to find out.

"Abby is doing so much better," he started. "We had a great session today. We talked about her driving again. She's still pretty terrified of the idea of getting back into a car, but I'll get her talked into it sooner or later." His eyes flashed with mischief.

"Did Miss Lily tell you that today at breakfast Abby filled her own plate? All on her own she wheeled over to the stove and helped herself. I knew she could do it." He leaned back in his chair. His chest expanded with pride.

"You've done a great job, Beau. You should be proud of yourself."

"It won't be long, and she'll be able to do everything for herself."

"That's wonderful, but I need to ask you something." Paris leaned forward, placing her elbows on the table. "I know it's none of my business, but did you really invite your girlfriend to come and stay with you?"

He squirmed in his seat. "No, I didn't invite her. She just showed up out of the blue. And we're not really together anymore." He rubbed the back of his neck with one hand. His brows furrowed in a deep frown.

"I told her to go back to Texas. Nothing's going on between us, and I don't think it's right that she stays here."

Paris was relieved. She liked Beau. He had made great progress with

Abigail, and he had a great future as a physical therapist. It would be a shame if he lost his job because of a little indiscretion.

The patio door opened, and Lily and Dr. Hanson walked out. As they approached the table, Lily turned toward Paris. "Ms. Jenkins, Abby's ready for you." Paris stood, said her goodbyes and followed Lily back to the house.

Beau stood to shake the older man's hand. "How are you, Dr. Hanson?"

"Fine. Please be seated." Both men settled into their chairs. "Before I forget, I checked with several of the therapists at the hospital to see which pool lift they recommended and ordered one for you. It should be here in a few days."

"That will be great." He was excited about having a lift for Abby, even though when it came time to use it she would probably put up a pretty good fight.

"The hospital has several orthotics practitioners," Dr. Hanson continued. "I mentioned Abby's case to Jacqueline Rae. She's young and very nice. I think Abby will get along well with her. I told her to expect a call from you to set up an appointment for impressions. I also gave her a written prescription for Abby's leg brace and crutches."

"Thanks, but Abby's hoping the impressions could be done here." Beau sighed. "I am going to have a hard time getting her into the car."

"Oh." Dr. Hanson frowned. "I hadn't thought about that." The doctor reached into his pocket and pulled out a prescription pad. "I'll write her a script for a couple valium. Give her one an hour before you plan on leaving the house." He smiled as he ripped off the sheet of paper. "This will help her relax and tolerate the ride. She'll cooperate for you."

Beau took the paper and placed it into his back pocket. "Thanks. This will make the trip easier on all of us."

With one problem under control, another sashayed toward them from the guesthouse dressed in a rainbow of colors, camouflaged as a pair of short shorts and a tight t-shirt. Both men stood as she approached, but Beau prayed she wouldn't say anything to embarrass him. Ginger stopped jiggling, and Beau introduced her. "Dr. Hanson, may I present Miss Ginger Gonzalez."

"It's nice to meet you, my dear." Dr. Hanson reached out and shook Ginger's hand.

"Ginger, Dr. Maxwell Hanson."

"It's very nice to meet you," she replied politely. "Beau, when you have a minute I'd like to speak with you. I'll be waiting in the guesthouse." She then turned back to the doctor. "Good day, Doctor." With auburn curls bouncing down her back and her rounded hips swaying, Ginger marched away.

Dr. Hanson cleared his throat. "Well, I mustn't keep you, boy." With a wink and a grin, he added, "I can see you have your hands full." Beau didn't return the smile, prompting the older man to ask, "Troubles in paradise?"

"Search me. I can't figure these women out." He started toward the house. "This place has too many women, and today they're all driving me crazy.

"Breakfast turned into a three-ring circus with Abby and Ginger juggling me back and forth between them. It didn't help that Lily just sat there smiling like she was privy to something but had no intention of sharing it with me. You know, Dr. Hanson, I think there's something in the water around here!" Dr. Hanson turned away and coughed in his hand.

At the far corner of the house he spied Lily in the garden on her hands and knees. Oblivious to their conversation, she hummed to herself and worked at pulling weeds from the flowerbed.

"Will you excuse me, please?" Dr. Hanson stood and headed toward Lily.

Beau shook his head. "Maybe it's the air?" He stood and ambled toward the house. In the hallway on the way to his room Beau overheard Abby and Paris talking.

"The biggest part of rehab is being educated about the type of injury you have and learning to compensate for skin that no longer has any feeling."

Abby didn't reply. Paris continued, "The amount of therapy needed depends on the person and how quickly they recover function and learn to deal with the residual defects."

The crazy blond really knows her stuff.

Beau settled on his bed, opened a notebook and scribbled down the information he heard from Abby's room as Paris continued. She mentioned daily living skills, like dressing, eating bathing, grooming and general health. He wasn't surprised the session came to an abrupt end after Paris brought up learning to drive an automobile again. He heard Abby remark she felt a headache coming on.

Paris smiled at Beau as she passed his open door. He lumbered to his feet and followed her into the kitchen where they met Dr. Hanson and Lily.

"I'll walk out with you, Dr. Hanson," Paris said slipping her arm through his. "I'm all finished for today."

The older man's grin widened. "That's the best offer I've had all day."

They all said goodbye and headed for the foyer.

* * * *

Once Dr. Hanson and Paris were outside, Dr. Hanson remarked, "That Beau is a smart man. I like the way he thinks." He patted Paris's hand. "Surrounding himself with beautiful women."

Paris grinned. "He may like pretty women," she said as she squeezed his arm. "But I'll let you in on a little secret—he only has eyes for one woman."

His brows shot up. "You mean Ms. Gonzalez? She's a yellow rose of Texas, all right."

Paris shook her head. "Nope, he's in love with *Miss Abigail*," she purred with a southern drawl.

Dr. Hanson stopped. A stunned expression crossed his face. Paris smiled and added, "Oh, she loves him, too. The only problem is—neither one knows it yet."

Chapter Fifteen

Beau paced the exercise mat, ready to pull his hair out. Abby sat in her wheelchair, her arms folded across her chest. She was trying his patience. He'd already explained to her the need to go to the hospital for her leg impressions. He sighed, and although his head ached, he attempted to explain it once more. "You're lucky that Monterey Bay General has a physical therapy department and an orthotics department."

"I don't see why they can't come here and take impressions of my legs," Abby complained.

"It's not just your legs. They need to fit you for special shoes. There are several different styles, and the orthotics practitioner needs to determine which one will work best for you. Besides," he stopped and leaned back against the desk. "We need to look at walkers and forearm crutches."

Several seconds of silence passed before Abby spoke, her brows pulled into a frown. "What're this leg brace and crutches going to look like?"

"Earlier I logged onto the Internet and printed off the type of brace that Dr. Hanson and I discussed." He retrieved the papers and handed them to her.

She examined them with a guarded expression then said, "Aren't they attractive?" The tone in her voice didn't quite hide her apprehension.

"What does KAFO stand for?" She turned her attention back to the papers.

"It stands for Knee-Ankle-Foot Orthotics."

This was going to be a challenge for Abby. Every day she had something new she had to learn to deal with. Putting her in a leg brace and forearm crutches meant removing her from her comfort zone once again. Beau ignored the sudden tightness in his chest.

He squatted down in front of her. "What's the matter, sweetheart?" He reached for her small hands and ran his thumbs over her knuckles. Abby glanced up, her tear-filled eyes pleading for reassurance.

"I promise it won't be as bad as you think. And just look at everything you'll be able to do that you can't do now! You'll be able to walk again and even drive. You can go back to school and become a teacher like you've always wanted."

Tears ran down her cheeks. She closed her eyes and shook her head. Beau gently reached up and wiped them away.

"Abby, what's the real problem?" He waited patiently then after several seconds lifted her chin. "What are you really afraid of?"

"Just the thought of getting back into a car terrifies me," she confessed in a frail feeble voice.

"It's all right." Beau grinned. "We've already thought about that. Dr. Hanson gave me a prescription for valium."

Indignant, Abby spat, "You were going to trick me again with drugs to get me into the car?" With the strength of a linebacker, she wheeled her chair around, knocking Beau over in the process. Her wheels barely missed his fingers.

Sprawled across the floor, he replied, "I wasn't going to do it behind your back."

"I'll bet," she spat, moving out of his reach. "Did you think I forgot how you tricked me before? I wouldn't put it past you to do something like that again!"

"It was Dr. Hanson's idea. He thought it would help you to relax— make it easier on you."

"Yeah, right." With her chin held high, she wheeled out of the room and yelled over her shoulder, "Dr. Hanson would never do anything so underhanded!"

"Of course not!" Beau hollered back. She disappeared around the corner.

"That was clipping and a fifteen yard penalty I'll have you know," he barked, scrambling to his feet. Tossing his hands up in surrender, he

177

grumbled, "I need a beer."

His throbbing temples promised a whopper of a headache was on its way. The kitchen was empty, but the lingering scent of Lily and her cooking still filled the air. She reminded him of his grandmother, loving, encouraging and firm but always fair.

Beau crossed the room and reached for the refrigerator as Ginger entered from the patio. In one of her tiny get-ups, she sashayed in his direction.

"I thought you were going to come out and talk to me," she asked dryly. She folded her arms across her chest which only accented her ample breasts.

Beau bit his tongue and rolled his eyes. He didn't need this right now.

Ginger took a step and placed her palms against his chest. "I thought we had something special. Was I wrong?"

Her soft amber eyes no longer affected him. "I'm sorry, Ginger."

"Maybe I should just leave?" Big brown eyes peered up at him, pleading with him to let her stay.

She stepped closer, and Beau took two steps backwards. "I told you this job is very demanding. Abby's fragile. Her whole future is at stake here. I just can't make time for anyone else right now. You understand, don't you?"

Ginger's hands dropped to her sides. "I understand more than you think." She turned and marched out.

Beau sighed. Although he hadn't meant to, he had hurt her. He'd seen the slightest flicker of pain in her eyes. He'd known Ginger for quite a while, and she had been a good friend. Sex always seemed to complicate things. Ginger just didn't understand what was at stake here for him or Abigail.

He opened the fridge and retrieved a cold beer. Now he needed a good place to go hide and drink it. He turned and found Lily standing in the doorway, watching him.

"How long were you standing there?" he asked, feeling the heat rise up his neck.

"Long enough. As far as I can tell, the score is girls two—Beau zero." She walked across the floor and placed a comforting hand on his arm. "What happened?"

"I fumbled at the scrimmage line." He placed the cold beer against his forehead.

"What seems to be the problem?"

"Women! They're both driving me crazy." He closed his eyes momentarily. "What am I supposed to do?"

Her heart went out to him. A house full of women had finally taken its toll. At first she wasn't convinced he was the man for the job. But he had showed them all that he could reach Abby, and for that Lily was grateful. He was good for Abby, and each day she thanked God for sending him to free Abigail from her emotional prison.

In her calm voice of reason she asked, "What does your heart tell you to do?"

Beau gave Lily a long hard look, and after several moments he answered, "Run for the hills!"

* * * *

The hour was late, but Dr. Voight didn't care. A little investigating into Beau's past had uncovered a juicy scandal, and he intended to confront the man tonight. He had enough ammunition to get rid of him for good. Winkelman and his sister were not going to stand in the way of his possessing Abigail or the financial security that came with her.

He turned off Highway One into the private driveway. A large stone monument highlighted by accent lights bore the name Pendergrass. Will smirked. "That will be the first thing to go when this place is mine."

As his old Buick approached the house he could see a man propped up against a tree, drinking from a can of beer. "It figures." Will pulled up in front of the house and shut off the motor. Beau made no attempt to move.

Without knocking or ringing the bell, Will marched into the house and froze. The house sat dark and quiet except for a dim light that shown from the kitchen down the hall. Something wasn't right.

Unsure of what he might find, Will cautiously crossed the threshold into the kitchen. The refrigerator door hung open, and the curvaceous backend sticking out definitely did not belong to Mrs. Bendickson.

The girl closed the door and jumped. "Oh! You startled me."

Will eyed the scantily clad and very sexy woman. "Not as much as you surprised me." He grinned with approval. "Who are you?"

"I'm Ginger Gonzalez," she drawled. "Who are you, Sugar?"

He studied the stunning redhead. *From Texas, I'll bet. That dog. Winkelman sent for a little side action.*

"Excuse my manners." He reached out his hand. "I'm Dr. William Voight." Not releasing her hand, he inquired, "Where is Mrs. Bendickson?"

"I'm not really sure. I haven't seen her all day."

"You haven't? Why? Where have you been?"

She pulled her hand free. "You sure ask a lot of questions." She turned and strolled out onto the patio.

"What's happened around here?" Will turned and headed for the stairs to Abigail's room.

The stairway was dark as was the second floor. Abby and her bed were both missing from her room. Panic ran cold in his blood. What on earth had he done to Abigail and her aunt?

Will ran back down the stairs. Ran into the kitchen and began yelling. "Abigail, can you hear me? Where are you?"

A light flickered at the end of the small hallway that led to the servants' quarters. He ran down the hall but then stopped. Abby sat propped up in bed, her cheeks streaked with tears. A pile of wadded-up tissues lay beside her on the bed.

"Oh, my God! Are you all right, Abigail?" With long strides, he crossed to the bed and sank down on the edge. She looked so distressed and fragile.

"Dr. Voight! I didn't know you were coming by." She wiped her cheeks. "What are you doing here?"

"Abigail, where is your aunt?"

"I don't know," she sobbed and reached for another tissue.

Although she had become stronger physically her emotional state appeared to be slipping. "What's been going on around here?"

"I've been working so hard. I'm sore and tired." She blew her nose. "Have you talked to Daddy? When is he coming home?"

"Don't worry. I'm here." He pulled her into his arms. "I'll take care of everything. Tell me what he did to you."

She leaned back and peered into his eyes. She looked so frail and weak. She hiccupped and gulped for air. "He was going to drug me," she wailed.

"I'll kill him!" He pulled her close again, his hands rubbing up and down her back. "I'll call your father and make him come straight home." She broke into a blubbering mass of tears. He should have insisted on staying in the house while George was gone. He would make George listen to him now.

After several minutes her crying subsided. "Are you all right now?"

Abby nodded and gave a big yawn. Will gently set her back against her pillow. She closed her eyes. "You get some sleep. I'll take care of everything."

Glancing down he suddenly noticed how she had been dressed. He marveled at the tight fitting t-shirt. Her small breasts—that would fit perfectly in each hand—were firm, the nipples hardened into little buds. It appeared there might be some nice perks in it for him after all.

Hearing someone enter the room behind him, jerked Will back to reality.

Lily stood in the doorway. "Dr. Voight! I thought I heard voices. How nice to see you."

Forcing his thoughts in a different direction, he turned and smiled. "Oh! Ms. Bendickson I didn't think you were home."

"Are you all right, Abigail," Lily asked.

"I'm fine. I'm just tired," Abigail replied with a yawn.

"You rest then. I'll check in on you before I head upstairs."

Lily turned to Will. "Why don't you come into the kitchen? I'll fix us both a nice cup of tea."

Confused, Will said goodnight to Abby and followed Lily into the kitchen.

"Won't you please sit down?" Lily motioned to a chair by the table. "It'll only take a second."

Will watched as she retrieved the teapot, walked to the sink, filled it and hurried back to the stove.

Beau sauntered into the kitchen. Ignoring Will, he walked toward Lily. "Can I give you a hand with anything before I turn in?"

Arrogant jock. The way he acted you would think he owned the place. That was going to change real soon.

"No, dear. Everything's under control."

"Then I'll say goodnight." He gave her an affectionate kiss on the cheek.

"Goodnight, dear. Rest well." She patted him on the chest.

"Yes, ma'am." Beau retrieved another beer, turned and disappeared down the same hallway toward Abby's room.

Totally confused, Will demanded, "Pardon me for asking, but what the heck is going on around here?"

Even after Lily spent the next hour reassuring Will that all was well, he remained far from convinced. Abigail didn't normally give way to hysterics. Something must have happened between her and Winkelman but what?

Will couldn't concentrate. The way she had been dressed more than piqued his interest. He had never considered her a desirable woman before. She'd always come across as Miss Prim and Proper. She'd felt soft in his arms, susceptible to him. If Mrs. Bendickson hadn't entered when she did he might have been tempted to find out just how nice she really felt and tasted.

The palms of his hands suddenly grew damp, and he wiped them on his slacks. If Abigail suddenly appealed to him she would appeal to other men—mainly Winkelman. Was that it? Had Winkelman planned to drug her and take advantage of her? Or were they already lovers? His fist hit the steering wheel. Jocks like Winkelman took anything they wanted. They had always cut him out and stood in the way of him having what he wanted.

Well, no more. Winkelman had to go. The stakes were too high, and Will wasn't about to give up on a year's worth of work. It was winner takes all, and that's just what he wanted—all of the cake, not just a slice.

It was obvious that Mrs. Bendickson favored Winkelman, so he hadn't mentioned anything about the man's plan to drug Abigail. She would most likely defend him. He would let her brother inform her that her wonderful Mr. Winkelman wasn't a saint.

As Will drove away the wheels in his mind started to spin as a new scheme started to formulate. He would take the information he'd dug up about Winkelman's affair with Mrs. Wentworth while in her husband's employment and embellish it a little with the facts, like one juicy redhead and the drugs Abigail mentioned.

It would be interesting to see what the old man thought about his football hero then.

Chapter Sixteen

Lily and Beau stood sentry as Abby popped a Valium into her mouth and took a gulp of orange juice. The pill appeared as reluctant to be swallowed as Abby was to swallow it. She needed a second drink to force it down.

It would be so much easier if they brought all the materials for taking the impressions out to her house instead of making her suffer the ride to the hospital. She didn't like the notion of being drugged, but the idea of getting back into a car scared her to death. Her eyes closed, and a shiver shook her body.

"There. It's gone" Abby stuck out her tongue for their inspection.

"That's my girl." Lily patted her arm, returning the juice to the refrigerator. Beau nodded turned and headed down the hall to his room. Behind his back Abby stuck her tongue out just for good measure.

Over his shoulder he replied, "I saw that."

An hour later he pulled Abby's red Mustang up to the sidewalk and shifted it into park. She didn't strike him as a muscle-car kind of girl, though he hoped riding in her own car would make the trip to the hospital more pleasant for Abby and more manageable for him.

Lifting Abby out of her wheelchair to place her into the Mustang, she wrapped her arms around his neck and refused to let go. His heart went out to her. "This is the only way," he whispered, settling her on the front seat. Once he freed himself from her death grip, he pulled the seat belt snuggly across her chest and buckled her in. Abby stared straight ahead, her chest rising and falling rapidly as she fought for control.

Beau folded and placed the wheelchair in the backseat. He

exchanged unsure glances with Lily, and she mouthed, "Drive careful."

Seated behind the wheel, Beau turned his gaze on Abby. "You're going to be all right, sweetheart. I'll drive slow, and if you get dizzy and need me to stop, just let me know."

He eased down the driveway. *So far so good,* he thought, watching her out of the corner of his eye. He turned onto the main road. She stiffened in the seat, and her eyes welled with tears.

"You're doing great. Try to relax. Breathe." He reached over and patted her hand. By her looks he feared she was about to lose it at any moment.

He switched on the radio and played with the knob until he came to a station playing a slow country ballad. Beau never considered himself much of a singer, but he sang along with the radio, hoping it would be an amusing distraction. After a moment Abby's hands unclenched, and she appeared to relax.

Even though her eyes looked a little hazy he could still see the fear in their depths. This was hard for her, and he knew she anticipated the worst. But he admired her strength and control. Abigail Pendergrass was a fighter, and deep down he knew she would be all right in the end— after he was gone.

"You're doing great, sweetheart. We'll be there before you know it." Another song started, and Abby slurred, "Sing."

One eyebrow arched, "So you like my singing?"

"Just sing."

"Yes, ma'am," he drawled as he happily obliged her.

It was a beautiful day for a drive up the coast. Before long they pulled up in front of the hospital in Monterey. Beau got out and retrieved the wheelchair. He opened the passenger side door and unhooked the seat belt. Abby fell into his arms.

"Easy now," he said, juggling her in his arms.

"You sing nice," she mumbled as her head fell back against his shoulder.

Beau shook his head, smiled and replied, "Why, thank you." He placed her in the chair, reached around and laced the support straps across her chest, securing her tightly in the chair.

Abby glanced up, smiled and melted back in the chair. Her eyes fluttered and closed. A flash of guilt shot through his chest. He wished it didn't have to be like this, but it was the only way.

The ride to the hospital hadn't been as bad as Abby feared it would be. She liked Beau's singing and the way his deep smooth voice made the melody flow like rich dark chocolate.

She floated on air as he guided her chair down the long white hallway. She inhaled the scent of antiseptic and flowers and laughed when she thought she smelled meatloaf. The surrounding noises whooshed in her ears.

They turned down a different hallway and met a group of people. Had they stopped? Was Beau talking to someone? Disconnected and confused, she couldn't understand what they were saying.

"Honey? Abby, sweetheart, this is Jacqueline Rae." Beau squatted in front of her chair, his nose appeared wider than his eyes, set back further on his face. "She's the orthotics practitioner."

What did he say? Abby struggled to understand. "Sweetheart, are you all right?" He spoke, and all of his words ran together.

The wall behind him was blue. *I like blue,* Abby thought. She smiled, and Beau patted her hand and stood. A pretty lady with wavy brown shoulder-length hair and soft brown eyes smiled at her. The lady turned, and Abby noticed her long white wings that almost touched the floor.

Beau removed Abby's restraining straps and slid his arms around her. When he lifted her up into his arms, she grinned up at him. "Sing to me again, Bo Bo."

"Behave yourself," he whispered close to her ear. His warm breath tickled her face. Laying her on the table, he started to move away.

"Beau!"

"I'm right here, sweetheart." He pulled a chair up next to her. "I'll be right here. I won't leave your side." One corner of his mouth curled up in his signature grin. She tried to imitate him, and he laughed.

"Just relax. You're doing fine." She closed her eyes. She trusted him completely. He would never let anything happen to her. Voices floated around her, and she envisioned dancers on a stage. A play. Swan Lake with Beau frolicking in white tights. A giggle escaped her lips.

"Honey, there is only one more thing left to do then we can go home."

Abby's eyes fluttered open. Beau's face hovered above hers. He looked like an angel. She smiled, "Hi, sweetart."

Jacqueline Rae giggled, and Beau shook his head. "I'm going to stand you up for this next impression. Don't worry. I've got you." He hauled her into a standing position, and the pretty lady pushed her foot into something mushy and cool which made Abby laugh.

"That's my girl. Now we're done. Are you ready to go home?" Still smiling, she tried to nod her head. Beau placed her back into the wheelchair and secured the straps.

It didn't take Beau long to get Abby secured in the car. But as he drove, her behavior continued to baffle him. Had she really been so affected by one Valium? She had seemed so out of it for the whole appointment. He doubted she would even remember their trip to the hospital tomorrow.

He had explained to Ms. Rae about the Valium and Abby's fear of getting back into a car again. She was very understanding.

Beau glanced over at Abby. She rested comfortably against the seat, her eyes closed, her lips slightly pursed. His gaze swept back to the road. She had handled this whole day like a champ. Yet he would have to inform Dr. Hanson how strongly she had reacted to the Valium. He glanced over and was hit again with a pang of guilt.

He drove just under the speed limit, enjoying the view along the coastal Highway. He liked driving Abby's bright red Mustang. The driver's seat went back far enough to accommodate his long legs and its low stance handled the curves nicely. With Abby's injuries limited to her left side he figured it wouldn't take much to modify the car to comply with the state's regulations. But he was sure Paris would insist on checking it out to make sure. Of course, Abby would have to practice getting in and out of the car and placing her arm crutches in the back seat.

"I watch you," Abby interrupted his thoughts.

"What?" Beau's head snapped in her direction. "You what?"

"I watch you." One eye closed in slow motion and then reopened as she tried to wink at him.

"You watch me?"

"Yeah!" Her eyes went big and round, and she fluttered her eyelashes at him. "When you're in the pool."

"You watched me swim? When?" His attention snapped back to the road. The sports car suddenly became too restrictive.

"When you don't know I'm watching," she added with an innocent giggle. "When you're mad, you go swimming."

"Abby, you're not making any sense."

"I make you angry on purpose. Then from my bed I watch you through my window." She grinned like a fool and licked her lips. "You didn't know that, did you?"

A little uncomfortable yet flattered Beau asked, "What were you thinking about when you watched me?" He knew what he would be thinking about if he ever got a chance to spy on her in the pool. He pictured Abby in a little bikini, her hair and body wet—

Abby reached over and ran her fingers down his arm. "I wondered what it would feel like to touch your wet strong slippery body." She licked her lips again.

Cotton filled Beau's mouth and his tongue wrestled with a swallow. Abby's fingers left a trail of fire down his arm, and he caught himself looking down to make sure his shirt hadn't gone up in flames.

"Do you want to know what else?" she whispered.

He wasn't sure he did. He had fought hard to keep his feelings benched and under control. She'd turned them loose with one innocent touch. She wasn't playing fair.

He chanced a sideways glance. Her head rested back against the seat. Her wanton gaze held his, her lips were moist and slightly parted in invitation. He wasn't going to make it to the house.

"I wanted to lick the droplets of water off every inch of your body." She brushed her hand across his thigh.

The tires screeched as the Mustang skidded to a halt. He cursed under his breath for almost missing the turn. He cranked the wheel and accelerated up the driveway. The car came to an abrupt stop in front of the house. If Abby's safety belt hadn't been secured she would have slid onto the floorboards like a wet fish.

"Are we home?" She blinked several times.

At that moment the front door opened, and Lily looked out and yelled, "Is everything all right?"

Beau lowered his window "We're fine. We'll be in shortly." Lily nodded, but a puzzled expression crossed her face as she closed the door.

"Let's go again," Abby wailed, grinning like she just rode her first roller coaster.

"I think you need some coffee or a nap," he suggested. "I know what I need," he added under his breath.

"A swim?" Abby giggled softly.

"Beau, what's the matter? What happened?" Lily asked as he wheeled Abby into the kitchen.

"Everything is fine." His guts were twisted in a tight knot. "But Abby could use a nap." Lily followed them down the hall. Beau picked Abby up out of the chair and placed her not-too-gently on the bed.

"She needs to sleep it off." He headed for the door then turned and walked over to the window and pulled down the shade. As he left the room Abby protested from her bed just above a whisper, "Spoilsport!"

* * * *

Hours later Abby drifted awake and savored the unfamiliar warm and tingling sensation. A fluttering deep in the core of her being caused her body to shudder once more with pleasure. Her heart slammed against her ribs. Her blood sang through her veins. She felt so alive.

Beau had been right with his prediction that one day when the time was right a special man would show her the secrets of love. The time was now, and the right man was just down the hall. She peered at the clock. Eleven thirty. She'd slept all afternoon and into the night, but it was worth it. She had dreamt of being in Beau's arms, of making love to him. Heat washed over her as she relived every glorious memory. Her body had twitched, trembled and still throbbed as his hands gently played her like a treasured instrument. Abby feared she'd lost this part of her life forever. That feeling desire was no longer a possibility. That intimacy would always be out of her reach.

She smiled. This was wonderful news, and she wanted to share it with Beau. Show him she was ready to experience love and able to feel everything he had to offer. She'd grown accustomed to his hands gliding over her body. Now her body would respond to his touch in a way she never expected it would. It was only right that she share her first time with Beau.

With a newfound energy she threw back the covers, scooted to the edge of her bed and then worked her way into her wheelchair. Taking a deep breath, she headed down the hall. Her heart slammed against her chest in anticipation.

Abby reached Beau's door and smiled. The moonlight cast his room in romantic shadows. He lay on his back, one arm flung over his head. His masculine scent filled the room, igniting the fire that burned deep within her.

She entered the room and quietly moved to his bed. Setting her brakes, she pulled herself up and out of her chair and then perched on the edge of his bed.

Eager to touch him, she lightly ran her fingers over his bare chest. His nipples hardened into little buds, and she smiled. She couldn't count how many times she had thought about doing just this. How she wanted to feel his arms around her, holding her, loving her. He'd held her in his arms before, but tonight would be different.

Bracing herself, she leaned over and dropped feather light kisses across his shoulder and chest. Beau's eyes fluttered open. Glancing up, she offered him a coy smile. "Is there enough room in there for me?" She giggled as his expression teetered between surprise and confusion. "Did I wake you?" she asked in a low voice.

He blinked and scanned the room. Abby reached up to smooth his furrowed brow. Beau flinched and lurched into a sitting position, the covers pooling at his waist.

Fearing he would bolt out of the bed before she could share her news, Abby fanned her fingers over his chest, pressing him back against the headboard. He opened his mouth to speak, but before he could she placed a finger against his lips. "Shhh. Don't talk." She reached up and brushed a strand of blond hair back from his face.

"I had a dream ... a wonderful dream." She traced a figure eight on his shoulder with her finger. "We..." She smiled shyly. "And I felt everything—still can..."

She leaned forward and brushed a kiss against his cheek then trailed little pecks along his neck. She swore she saw him draw in a sharp breath.

Beau's hands encircled Abby's arms, and he set her back. "Abby?" he said, his expression unreadable.

"I know! Isn't it wonderful?"

"Yes, it's wonderful—"

"My dream was so real. I could feel everything! You were right, Beau. I can love. Be loved as a whole woman." She leaned forward, placing her cheek against his chest, her fingers tracing patterns on his arms—strong arms that would hold her and show her things she had only imagined.

"Abby—"

Her senses were alive. She sighed and inhaled his scent which seemed different, stronger as if something had been added to it. Her fingers tingled where they grazed his bare skin. She listened to the melody of his heart as it pounded in his chest.

"Abby?"

Glancing up, she gazed deep into his eyes "Show me. Teach me. I want to know and feel everything. I want to be a whole woman, Beau."

"Abby, I can't."

"You can't love me?" she replied, shocked at the firmness in his voice.

"You don't know what you're asking."

She sat up straight. "I know what I'm asking, Beau. I want you to make love to me. I want to share this with you."

He closed his eyes and combed his fingers through his hair. He was so perfect, so beautiful. A humming started somewhere deep inside her belly. "Beau—" she leaned forward for a kiss.

Beau opened his eyes and in a stern voice he said, "Abby, go back to your room."

"What? Why?"

"Because this is wrong."

"It's wrong for you to love me?" *I don't understand*!

"Yes. It's wrong. Be a good girl, and go back to your room." He clenched his jaw together, and his mouth stretched into a thin line. He then folded his arms across his chest.

He was turning her down? She couldn't believe it. She had been rejected, dismissed like a disobedient schoolgirl. Banished to her room. Though Abby's eyes were filled with tears, she vowed she would not shed one. She pulled her gaze from his cold stare and reached for her wheelchair. With shaking arms, she settled herself back into her chair. Ignoring the shattering sound of her heart breaking, she released the brakes and headed for the door.

"Abby?" His voice was but a whisper.

She stopped at the threshold, swallowed her tears and raised her chin a notch.

"Abby, I..."

Abby gulped in a breath. "Go to hell!"

Chapter Seventeen

George paced his hotel room, replaying his phone conversation with Dr. Voight. The topic of discussion hadn't been at all what George expected. The phone call caught him by surprise, and he was still having trouble digesting the information.

He had no reason to doubt Will was telling him the truth. However, the accusations were incriminating and outlandish, and he had never been one to be impulsive. He needed to speak with his sister Lily before reacting.

As he reached for the phone, two quick knocks sounded at the door. It was Sarah's customary code. The door opened, and she entered, but her smile faded at his sober expression.

"George, what is it? What's happened?"

He wasn't sure he wanted to tell her. Yet he reminded himself she had been the one that assured him it would be all right to leave his daughter in Beau's hands—that he could trust Beau. The idea that she would outright lie to him was very unsettling.

"Sit down, Sarah. I need to ask you a few questions." She looked puzzled but took a seat on the small blue flowered sofa. He watched as she folded her hands and placed them on her lap.

He paced the small room, wondering how best to approach her. Over the past few weeks they had become close. He had even begun to entertain hopes of a long-term relationship with her. What he was about to ask and how she answered his questions would play a big part in how their future unfolded. If he was forced to choose between Sarah and his daughter, Abby's well-being would come first.

"Sarah, do you know a woman named Ginger Gonzalez?"

Her hands clenched into fists, and she moistened her lips before saying "I know of her, but I have never met her. She lives in Texas."

"How about Mrs. Jillian Wentworth?"

A frown marred her pale face "What's this all about, George? Did something happen?"

George's voice sounded harsh in his own ears when he demanded, "Do you know of Mrs. Wentworth or not?"

"I know of her, but again I've never met her." Her gaze darted around the room. "George, what's going on?"

"So you knew about Ginger Gonzalez and Jillian Wentworth when you approached me about hiring your brother?"

"Yes, but..."

"Does your brother take drugs?"

"No, of course not!" Her brows drew together, and she leaned forward slightly.

"Do you know that for a fact?"

"Well, no, not for sure, but he would never take them while on a job."

He watched her, trying to judge her reaction.

"Did your brother have an affair with Mrs. Wentworth while he was in her husband's employ? While he was treating their child, and she was still married?"

Sarah sunk back into the sofa. George wondered what she was thinking, but the fact that she hadn't answered his questions told him plenty.

"I received a phone call from Dr. Voight. He's been a good and trusted friend of the family."

He clasped his hands behind his back and continued. "He went to see Abigail, and as he drove up, your brother was sitting on the front lawn drinking beer. After he entered the house, he found a scantily dressed Ms. Gonzalez helping herself to my refrigerator. When he questioned her, she stated that she was your brother's girlfriend and that she was staying there."

Sarah sat quietly, the color in her face faded. She looked as if she might be sick.

"He went on to say that your brother had worked Abigail so hard she was lying in her bed crying and complaining about the long hours of exercise and the amount of pain she was forced to endure."

Sarah shook her head *no*.

George held up his hand. "Oh, it gets better. He claims that Abigail told him that your brother had planned on drugging her."

Sarah jumped to her feet. "He would never do such a thing! He promised me..." Her hand flew to her mouth to stop herself, but George saw the hurt and disappointment in her eyes. "He wouldn't do anything unethical or put Abigail in any danger." Sarah's chin raised a notch, and she held his stare as if daring him to call her a liar.

"These acts demonstrate a pattern of unprofessional behavior, and you chose to keep me in the dark about them. If it weren't imperative that I stay for these next two meetings I would fly home right now. As it stands I've instructed Dr. Voight to move into my home. He will monitor things until I can deal with things personally." Sarah didn't respond.

He walked toward the phone, picked it up and turned toward Sarah. Her eyes were filled with tears, her lips pursed with anger. What a disappointment. He thought they had the makings of something great.

"I believe we're finished."

Sarah walked to the door and let herself out. How could Beau do this to her? He had promised! She realized her job with Pendergrass Technology Incorporated and more importantly her relationship with George was over. She entered her room and started to stuff articles of clothing and toiletries haphazardly into her suitcase, tears pouring down her cheeks. Thirty minutes later she caught a cab to the airport.

* * * *

The phone rang, but Beau didn't concern himself with it. If Lily were out he'd let the machine answer it. At this particular moment he literally had his hands full.

"I've got you," he said, holding Abby tight to his chest. She lay rigid in his arms, making it more difficult for him to support her weight while he removed her from the freestanding treadmill. He had humiliated her with his rejection last night. He felt terrible and wanted to talk to her about it. Yet today she either ignored him or glared at him each time he pushed her or demanded her attention.

The long sleepless night had inflicted him with an excruciating headache. It tormented him to touch her and not show her how he really felt. If she had any idea what her touch had done to him she would have gone running from his room.

Abby's cheek brushed the side of Beau's face as he lowered her into the wheelchair. He felt a slight burning sensation, and by the redness in her face, she must have felt it, too. She jerked away and raised her chin. Her aloof demeanor irritated him. He was torn between pulling her across his lap and spanking her and laying her down on the gym mat and making love to her. Although she would benefit from either action both were out of the question. It was best to act as if last night had never happened.

"There you go," he said, taking two steps back. "Your legs are getting stronger every day. I don't think you're going to have any problems using the brace."

She still wouldn't look at him. "Abby, we need to talk" he said, hoping they could put the tension behind them.

"I don't want to go back to that stupid hospital," Abby stated, interrupting his thoughts. "Why can't they bring everything here?" She glared up at him; her anger lay just beneath the surface, waiting for the right moment to strike.

After her humiliation and loss of control, he would never get her to take the other Valium. He had no clue as to how he was going to get her back to the hospital for her fitting. He tried the reasonable approach. "You know you have to go back for a fitting and to check out which of the orthotics shoes are going to work best."

She grimaced. "I bet they're going to be real attractive."

"On you they'll be beautiful. Besides they're only shoes. Who's going to care?"

"Yeah, they're only shoes. And it's only a brace, and it's only crutches. Who's going to care?" She clenched her hands together on her lap.

He heard the tears behind her shield of sarcasm. He'd fumbled yet again. "Sweetheart, you're lucky to have come this far. It won't be long..."

"I know. I know," she waved her right hand in the air. "It won't be long, and I'll be up dancing and running marathons."

He wasn't in the mood for any attitude. His head throbbed as if it had been drop kicked fifty yards. Placing a hand on each of the armrests of the wheelchair he pinned her with his stare and growled, "Ditch the self-pity, Abby. You are not helpless. No one's going to coddle you anymore. You're an adult now. The sooner you accept your situation and deal with it the better off you're going to be."

He stopped and drew in a deep breath. "Sure, your life is going to be a constant challenge, but you have more spirit than most football players I know. You're brave, courageous and with a little self-discipline you could overcome any obstacle that might get in your way." He reached out with one hand and tilted her chin, forcing her to meet his stare. "Or you can stay locked up in this house for the duration of your so-called life. The rest of the world will continue to live with or without you. It's your choice." He pushed himself away from her chair and walked out of the room.

Abby drew in a shaky breath. She had been a fool to think Beau had any feelings for her. She shouldn't have been so surprised by his rejection. He'd summed it up when he said, "Who's going to care?" about her wearing grandma shoes and a metal leg brace. The crutches were just the icing on the cake. She didn't have to worry about anyone ever looking at her again. If they did it would only be with pity. Why did she think it would be anything else?

She wheeled her chair around to head for her room. As she came around the corner she ran into Ginger. The over-aged cheerleader blocked her way.

Ginger smiled and then stammered, "Sorry, I couldn't help but overhear. Beau's not really a tyrant. He can be pretty unrelenting when he gets something in his head. He's a little rough around the edges, but he means well."

Abby glared at Ginger, "I don't need consoling from you."

Ginger's body stiffened, and her hands flew to her hips. "I'm sorry. I was only trying to help."

"I'll bet."

Ginger's expression was serious, but had she been laughing at Abby behind her back all this time? Had they both been laughing at her?

"Sugar, you're misinterpreting his behavior. He's a man, and sometimes you have to have a decoder ring to figure out what they're really saying. It's not you that he's really angry with—"

"I don't need your help or your pity" Abby said with a snort and wheeled away. If Ginger understood Beau so well she was welcomed to him.

* * * *

A sharp knock penetrated Beau's door. He set aside his notes and answered it.

"It's your sister," Lily said, handing him a cordless phone. She turned and walked away. Puzzled by her concerned expression, Beau put the phone to his ear.

"Hello?"

"Beau? It's Sarah." Her voice quivered with desperation.

"Sarah, what's the matter?" He gripped the phone—his pulse sped up.

"George knows—" she sobbed.

"You're not making any sense, Sarah. What does George know?" The line went silent.

"Sarah?" He paced the small room, willing himself not to panic. "Sarah, where are you?"

"At home."

"In Texas?"

"My apartment in Monterey," she said between sobs. "I landed about forty-five minutes ago."

"Are you alright? Did something happen?" Beau reached for his shoes. "Hang tight. I'm on my way."

"No. Don't drive all the way up here. I just need to tell you—"

"What is it?" *Why do women have to talk in circles?*

"George knows about … about Mrs. Wentworth," she replied in a defeated tone.

Beau sat rigid on the edge of his bed. "So he knows about Jillian. What's the big deal? That happened two years ago. I'm sure you had a good reason for telling him." Although he couldn't think of one off the top of his head.

"I wasn't the one who told him." Her voice shook.

"Sarah, if you didn't tell him, who did?"

"George…" Another muffled sob. "George got a call this morning from Dr. Voight."

That bastard. Determined to reassure her, Beau said, "Mr. Pendergrass is an intelligent man. I doubt he'll listen to the ravings of a lunatic like Voight." He settled on the edge of the bed and ran his free hand over his face.

"You don't understand," Sarah continued sounding overwrought. "He also said you moved Ginger in."

Beau sighed. "Ginger just showed up one day. *Miss Lily* is the one who invited her to stay in the guesthouse." He rubbed the back of his neck. "I haven't … I haven't spent any time with her. Abby has my full attention."

"Beau, he said you were sitting on the front lawn, drinking beer, and that Abigail told him you were going to drug her. He said she was crying because you've been working her too hard, and she was in such pain! Beau, what the hell is going on?"

Irritated, he resumed his pacing. "I can explain everything. It was only one beer. I needed a break. And the medication was a prescription from her family doctor."

When I get my hands on Voight I'm going to wring his scrawny little interfering neck. The line went silent again.

"Sarah, I'm certain when Pendergrass arrives he'll see for himself that everything is just fine. Don't worry. It's going to be all right." Beau waited, but his sister didn't reply. Then he heard her sniffling. "Sarah. What's going on? Did he return with you, or did you come back by yourself?"

Several seconds went by before she whispered, "After he questioned me … I … I just left. I doubt I still have a job."

"That's crazy. Why wouldn't you still have a job? I got the feeling that he was kind of sweet on you." He relaxed and chuckled, but Sarah didn't reply. He had been only teasing but realized she may have been hoping for a relationship with him which she now thought was in jeopardy.

Anger at Voight's interfering rose up to choke him. It was one thing to run to Pendergrass with stories about Beau but another to drag Sarah through the mud with him.

"Sarah, don't worry. I'll straighten all of this out. Everything will be fine."

"I hope you're right."

Sarah had worked so hard for both of them, and he had disappointed her. If everything fell apart now, how was he ever going to make it up to her? "How about I come up there. We could have a couple beers and talk. How does that sound?"

"No, I'm tired. I think I'm just going to lie down. Goodnight, Beau."

The line went dead. Her heart was broken, and his ached for her. He hadn't done anything wrong, yet he had still managed to let her down.

Chapter Eighteen

The early morning sun cast its rays onto the beautiful Pacific coastline. Inside, however, tension hung like a blanket of fog.

The morning of Abby's fitting appointment had arrived. She wheeled herself into the foyer. Her arms felt heavy; her head ached with apprehension. *You can do this,* she told herself. Although scared to death, she was determined not to ask Beau for a Valium.

She sucked in a deep breath as he pushed the wheelchair to her Mustang waiting in the driveway. Without a word, he went through the motions of placing her in the car. Once he was settled in the vehicle, he reached for the ignition. Black dots appeared before her eyes as the car roared to life. She swallowed hard and pressed back into the seat. Beau spoke, and she turned her head. His lips moved, and his eyes reflected his concern for her, but his words were incoherent. She didn't dare open her mouth for fear that she might scream or lose her breakfast.

They pulled on to the highway. Abby saw a car approaching and closed her eyes. Her mind reeled back to how she psyched herself up against her opponent. She dug deep and found she no longer possessed the optimism and strength she once had. Replacing fear with anger didn't work either; it only brought her screams bobbing to the surface. She settled for concentrating on Beau's voice and the wind rushing through the open windows.

Abby was trapped on an evil roller coaster programmed never to stop. Every twist and turn sent waves of dizziness crashing over her. She prayed she wouldn't throw up. Once they reached the hospital and the torture ride ended, she sighed with relief.

Beau wheeled her through the electronic doors and down a long white hallway. They entered a small waiting room, and he talked to a person Abby couldn't see behind the deck. Another door opened, and he pushed the chair into a large room lined with tables. An array of crutches and arm and leg braces hung on several walls.

A young woman with long curly brown hair and a friendly smile walked over to them, and Beau introduced her to Abby as Jacqueline Rae. "It's very nice to meet you," Abby said automatically before recalling that she must have met her at the last appointment. She smiled and felt her face heat up. "I guess I should have said that it was nice to see you *again*, Ms. Rae."

"Please call me Jackie." She smiled. "Follow me, and we'll get started." She crossed the room and opened a door to another room. Beau wheeled Abby in to a light blue room. She glanced at a table and wondered if its strange looking contents belonged to her. Several posters and pictures of athletes adorned the walls.

"Do you want her on the table?" Beau asked.

Abby glanced toward Beau, and although she saw a flash of apprehension in his brown eyes, he offered a one-sided grinned and a wink.

"No, she's fine where she is," Jackie said, reaching for a brace on the table.

Oh, my God, Abby thought. *This is it.* The drumming of her heart echoed in her ears, and the black spots before her eyes returned. The therapist knelt before Abby's chair and removed her slip-on shoes then strapped the brace to her left leg. Next she placed the black orthotic shoes on Abby's feet and secured the Velcro straps. Abby watched her every move. The brace felt awkward and heavy. Would it really support her weight? She prayed she wouldn't fall and make a fool of herself in front of Beau and the woman.

The crutches came next. Jackie glanced up and smiled as she secured them to Abby's arms. The woman was saying something though her words never filtered through the cotton thick fog in Abby's head. She gave Beau some instructions, and he nodded in agreement.

Abby swallowed hard and drew on all her inner strength. Her leg was secured in its brace and unfashionable shoe, her upper arms strapped to the forearm crutches. Hysteria bubbled to the surface. If she swung her new appendages around in the air and screamed in agony people would mistake her for an alien.

Then the time finally came. Beau extended his hands and grasped her upper arms, helping her to her feet. Everything she had worked so hard for came down to this moment. She automatically reached out to him for support. His hands gripped her waist.

"You're all right," he whispered. "You're strong enough to stand alone."

She clenched her hands around the handles of the crutches. The room whirled once; she fought to stifle the scream that lodged in the back of her throat.

Still holding her, Beau nudged her feet slightly apart with the toe of his sneaker. A wave of panic washed over her as he positioned her upright, and his hands slipped away. She glanced down at her feet then back up to Beau's face. He nodded his head and pushed the wheelchair to the side.

"This is what all your hard work has come down to. You can do this, sweetheart."

Abby shook her head. "I can't." Her protest emerged not much more than a whisper. She feared that if she spoke too loudly she would topple and fall.

"I'm right here. I've gotcha if you start to fall. Move one foot then the next like at home on the treadmill. It's the same thing, just without the straps." He winked, nodded his head in encouragement.

Abby closed her eyes and took a deep breath. Could she actually do this? Beau's breath brushed her neck as he whispered words of encouragement in her ear.

"Remember how we practiced with the walker? Use the crutches the same way. Put most of your weight on your good leg and arm. Then slide your other foot forward."

With Beau at her side, she could do anything. But reality suddenly hit her like a hard slap in the face. He wasn't going to be with her forever. He had made it clear the other night that he didn't care for her in a personal way. Ginger was his girl; they would leave together when the time came.

Then she would be all alone. Again.

Abby swallowed her tears. Beau's words from the other day crashed down around her. *"Ditch the self-pity. You're not helpless. No one's going to coddle you anymore. The sooner you come to grips with your situation and deal with it, the better off you're going to be. Your life is going to be a constant challenge but you're brave, courageous, and you can overcome any obstacle that gets in your way. Or you can crawl back into the security of your comfort zone. It's up to you. The rest of the world will continue with or without you."*

She was an adult. And it was time to take back control of her life. She didn't need him or any other man. She could learn to take care of herself. She shook her head. Concentrate, she told herself. Stay focused.

Warily she lurched forward. Her right arm inched her crutch in front of her foot to maintain her balance. "That's my girl!" Beau's words propelled her forward as they moved together in unison. *I won't fall.* As if watching someone else, she moved her other foot and crutch.

"That's it. I knew you could do it."

Abby struggled through several more steps before her legs weakened under her. Beau was right there. He scooped her up in his arms with ease and swung her around. "You did it. You did it. I knew you could!" His eyes sparkled. "I'm so proud of you!"

He hugged her tight to his chest then gently set her down in a chair and knelt by her side. Abby's head spun. Had she really walked by herself?

"You were wonderful. Now I wish I would have brought a video camera." A joyous smile covered his face. Not his usual one-sided sexy smile but a genuine satisfied smile, and she couldn't help but return it.

Then without warning, Beau pulled her close and brushed her lips with a kiss followed by another hug. Confused, Abby watched as he stood and pulled Ms. Rae into his arms. "She walked! Did you see her? It won't be long, and there'll be no stopping her!"

Abby's gaze crashed to the floor. She should have been floating on air, but instead her elation sunk as she realized each step took her farther from Beau. He had done his job, and when her father returned, he would be gone. Out of her life forever. He and Ginger would go back to Texas, and he would never think about her again. Well, good riddance. What did she care if he left?

Today should have been the happiest day of Abigail's life. Beau had pulled her up out of the darkness and into the light. He had pushed her, challenging her to live again. To confront her fears and deal with them. To feel again. And she did. She felt pain, sorrow, closure and love. Her heart slammed against her chest—she loved him.

Beau folded up the wheelchair, placed it in the backseat and closed the door. He whistled as he circled around to the driver's door. He couldn't help it. Not only was he proud of Abby, for her success, he was proud of himself. Getting Abby to speak again had been a huge breakthrough. Getting her to walk had been nothing short of a miracle. If this accomplishment didn't put his career back on track nothing would.

After settling in behind the steering wheel, he turned the key. The country station on the radio belted out a classic tune. Beau grinned, chiming in with his own rendition.

They cruised through Monterey and Carmel. Beau's bare arm rested on the doorframe; he basked in the warmth of the afternoon sun. "Did you see the expression on Ms. Rae's face? I think you really surprised her today. Hell! You surprised me."

He grinned. "I'm so proud of you." Reaching over, he squeezed her hand. "I don't think anyone's made such a miraculous recovery as you have. You may have set a new record. I can't wait to see the look on Miss Lily's face when she sees you stroll into the house."

He glanced over at Abby. She still hadn't said a word, just sat ramrod straight in the seat. Beau tugged on the collar of his suddenly too-tight shirt and cleared his throat. "I really am proud of you." Still no reply.

"I know I've been hard on you these past few weeks." He licked his dry lips. "But I knew you could handle it. You're tough, and I knew once you made up your mind to walk again, there'd be no stopping you." Bewildered, he glanced once again at his sullen passenger. Nothing. "After a few more weeks of therapy, you'll be able to do anything you want."

Why wasn't she happy? Beau frowned, his index finger tapping on the steering wheel in rhythm with the song's beat. She should be in seventh heaven. She should be singing his praises, oozing gratitude.

His mind rewound. Had he said or done something to upset her? Nothing came to mind. Had he pushed her too hard today? At her first step, he'd seen both hesitation and panic cross her face. But she took that step and then another. To him, she appeared ready, determined.

Something was wrong, and as usual he didn't have a clue. Was she still trying to comprehend everything that had happened to her? Her life had dramatically changed over the past year. She'd gone from a vibrant young woman who was always on the move to a mute shut-in who had given up on life. She just needed a little time to get use to the fact that she was back in the game again.

Beau pulled off the coastal highway onto the long winding driveway. At the front door he turned off the engine and got out. He ambled around to the passenger side and opened the door to the back seat. Reaching in, he pulled out the crutches. Upon opening Abby's door he waited, but Abby neither spoke nor moved.

He took a deep breath. Speaking through clenched teeth, he asked, "Are you coming, or are you going to sit there all day?"

With pursed lips and staring straight ahead through the windshield, Abby snapped, "I'm tired. I want to use the wheelchair."

Beau shook his head. He didn't have a clue what her problem was, and he was starting not to care. "No. You can make it into the house from here. It's okay. I'll help you."

"I don't need nor do I want your help." She glared straight ahead.

Grinding his teeth to the point of possibly breaking them all off at the gum line, Beau jerked the wheelchair out from the back seat and snapped it open. After a quick glance at Abby's mulish expression, he gave the chair a shove with all his might. The wheelchair careened nearly fifteen feet across the lawn before it hit an unseen object and tipped over on its side.

"There. If you want it, go get it!" His words may have sounded childish, but he didn't care. She'd taken his good mood and stomped on it. The thought hadn't hit him until right then that she hadn't been the only one who accomplished something today. It was true that Abby had literally taken a huge step toward her recovery, but he had been very instrumental in it, and she'd intercepted his glory and bruised his pride. *Someone throw in a flag, and call a personal foul!*

"I can't believe you did that!" she cried, glaring up at him.

"I can't believe you're acting the way you are." He jammed his fists on his hips. "You should be happy. Ecstatic! At the very least, chipper!" He threw his hands up into the air. "I think I preferred you drugged. At least then I could understand where you were coming from!" He pivoted on his heels and stalked toward the house.

Lily peeked through the doorway, her gentle face contorted with confusion and anguish. Just how much had she seen and heard? Beau didn't care. He marched past her, ignoring her pleas as she called out to him. As he stormed passed the entrance to the great room he noticed Voight perched in one of the high backed chairs, an open newspaper in his hand. "Great! Could this day get any better?"

"Winkelman," Dr. Voight called from his perch.

Beau proceeded to his room and slammed the door. Within seconds, someone knocked.

"Winkelman, I need to speak with you." Dr. Voight's arrogant voice grated across Beau's raw nerves. He doubted the man would give up and leave. He yanked the door open; he apparently surprised the young doctor for the man took two hasty steps backwards.

"What? What on earth do you have to tell me that's so important?" He glared down at the doctor, crossed his arms over his chest, assumed his most intimidating stance and waited.

Will swallowed. His Adam's apple jerked violently, and his tone shot up an octave. "I'll be staying in the house until Mr. Pendergrass returns." He stood with his head tilted back so as to look Beau in the eyes. "I'm here at his request." He blinked several times. "I just thought you should know. That's all." Then he turned and walked away, dismissing Beau like one of his servants.

"Great." Beau grumbled and slammed the door.

Will smiled. That had gone better than he'd thought. He'd expected to have more of a problem with Winkelman. Satisfied, he strutted back to the great room and his paper. Entering the foyer, he paused as Lily pushed Abigail's wheelchair through the front door. At closer inspection he noticed both women had tears streaming down their faces. Will knelt down in front of Abigail. "Are you alright? What happened?"

Lily patted his shoulder. "She walked a few steps at the hospital today! Isn't that wonderful?" Her face beamed with happiness as she dabbed at more tears.

Abigail sat quietly, her hands folded on her lap. He studied her face and asked, "Are you alright?"

"I'm fine. Just tired." She glanced up at her aunt. "I want to go to my room. Now." Will stood as Lily wheeled Abigail past him. Something wasn't right. He could explain Lily's tears as tears of joy, but Abigail was hiding something behind her closed expression. Something had happened either at the hospital or on the ride home.

Will returned to the stately great room. He grinned as he sank down into one of the lush wingback chairs. Winkelman appeared to be screwing things up nicely without his help. The newspaper snapped as he opened it to the stock market report.

* * * *

How long could the man swim? Ginger had heard Beau hit the water ages ago. She'd been packing to leave but wanted to talk with him before she went. She'd come out of the guesthouse, sat down and waited for him to take a break, except he hadn't stopped swimming for almost eighteen minutes. What he was so upset about she didn't know, but she had a pretty good idea it had something to do with the princess with the poisonous tongue. She'd seen the way he looked at the girl. She'd recognized the glint of desire in his eyes. It was the look of respect and admiration she hadn't picked up on right away.

It wasn't going to be easy getting Beau out of her system. Ginger swallowed a sudden lump in her throat. Abby was a lucky girl to have a man like Beau fall in love with her.

She watched as his muscular body sliced through the water with ease. With each stroke his large hands and muscular arms emerged from the water. She shivered, recalling how her body had responded to the slightest touch from those wonderful hands.

Finally he stopped. He hadn't noticed her sitting there until he pulled himself up onto the edge of the pool. Water flew from his shoulder-length blond hair as he shook his head. Droplets trickled down the length of his tanned body, spurring romantic feelings she knew were only one sided. With a heavy heart she regretted what their relationship never became. Beau turned and locked his beautiful brown eyes on her. She mustered a slight grin and said, "Hey!"

"Back at you. What's up?"

"Just watching you swim."

"Yeah," he said dryly. "I'm really something to see I've been told."

He walked toward her and collapsed into one of the other chairs. Pools of water formed around his feet.

Ginger didn't understand his comment, but she agreed with his statement. "I'm heading back to Texas tomorrow."

"Really?" He rubbed his head with a towel.

"Yeah, I only came out here to make sure you were all right."

His hands dropped to his lap, and he sighed. "Sorry, I haven't had much time to spend with you."

"I know you're pretty busy. I guess I never realized how demanding this type of work really was. Besides, I need to get back to my own work," she added with a wistful smile. They both stood.

Beau shook his head. "I'm sorry, Ginger."

Ginger walked into his open arms. "I know," she murmured against his chest. He kissed her brow. They hugged for several seconds before she leaned back, looked up and said, "If you ever get back to Texas, cowboy, look me up."

He treated her with one of his slow sexy smiles, nodded and replied, "Yes, ma'am." Then he surprised her by leaning down and kissing her lips. A short kiss. A kiss from a friend. Their last kiss.

"I'll come in and say goodbye before I leave in the morning. Goodnight, Beau." Ginger walked away, realizing that she wasn't really losing Beau because he had never really been hers.

* * * *

Sitting in the dark, Abby tried to rationalize everything she had experienced that day. It appeared to be a day of firsts for her. She'd been excited and scared half out of her mind at the same time. She had taken her first step after thinking she'd never walk again, and she owed it all to Beau. She owed him her life.

He had been right by her side, and she knew he would never let her fall and get hurt. Then he had kissed her, catching her off guard. His lips were soft and warm. His kiss had ignited a fire deep inside of her. She'd had good reason to be afraid she'd fall and get hurt. She just hadn't realized it would be from falling in love with him.

She watched Beau and Ginger through her window. They stood by the pool and talked for a while then hugged and kissed. Had they made plans to meet later? Her eyes filled with tears. It was none of her business what they did.

Slipping under the covers she realized she'd acted like a child—no wonder her father had treated her like one. Why else would he have sent Dr. Voight to baby-sit her? What hurt the most though was that Beau thought of her as a child, too. He would never see her as a whole woman. A sob tore from her heart.

It wasn't fair. She had only just found love, and now it was lost to her.

Forever.

Chapter Nineteen

The tension in the exercise room was so thick you could have cut it with a Hail Mary pass. Beau glanced in Will's direction. The man had deposited himself in a chair by the door and leisurely paged through a doctor's magazine. The idea of being under constant observation ticked Beau off and made him feel restricted in what exercise he and Abby could work on. Any wrong move on his part would send Will scurrying to the phone to call Mr. Pendergrass to tattle.

Abby's white knuckled fingers gripped the handles of the walker. Beau hovered only inches behind her, ready in case she started to fall. Although she concentrated on putting one foot in front of the other whatever upset her yesterday was still wedged between them.

"You're doing great, sweet... Abigail. Nice and easy. That's it." A little voice in his head urged him to tackle her to the mat and kiss her senseless. He needed it as much as she did. Besides, it would be worth tossing his career out the window to see the expressions on both Abby and Will's face.

Abby felt a surge of electrical current in the air as Beau moved in close behind her. His warm breath floated across the nape of her neck. She knew if she turned their lips would collide. With each step she took he moved in tandem, but his hands never touched her. Her step faltered, and Beau's hard body brushed up against her backside, breaking her concentration.

"Are you alright?" His rich deep voice washed over her like melted chocolate.

She turned her head, their gaze collided, and she saw a smoldering look in his eyes that she'd never seen before.

"No," Was all she managed to say.

"Here, sit down, and rest for a while." Beau pulled a chair close and, placing his hands underneath her arms, helped her into it. He knelt in front of the chair, his hands instinctively going to her thighs, gently rubbing her legs. He glanced up, waiting for an explanation. A haunting scene replayed in her mind of him and Ginger kissing by the pool. She'd fallen asleep before he came in, her dreams troubled. Had he gone to the guesthouse and spent the night? Abby didn't care. *I don't,* she reminded herself fiercely.

Dr. Voight cleared his throat, and Abby's gaze shot up to meet his. He watched them with one brow raised. Could he possibly read her feelings for Beau?

Her gaze shifted back to Beau, and she wondered how she'd been stupid enough to fall in love with another woman's man.

Beau came to his feet and wiped his damp hands on his jeans. He needed a drink but doubted beer or water would do the trick. "I'll get you some water. You rest. I'll be right back." As he passed Voight, Will smiled up at him. Beau hesitated; he wanted nothing more than to knock the man offside—out of the game completely.

In the bathroom he splashed cold water on his face. She had brushed back against him, and he'd almost lost it. With a towel Beau dried his face and hands. He stared at his reflection and realized he couldn't ignore his feelings for her. He didn't want to.

Though she had been acting indifferent to him the past few days she'd made her feelings crystal clear when she came to his room. He studied his reflection. He could control his emotions, set his feelings aside temporarily and finish his job. But once her father returned, he would let his feelings be known.

* * * *

By the time George crawled into the cab at the airport to head home he was a nervous wreck. Dr. Voight's words had repeatedly echoed through his mind during his return flight. Winkelman was a womanizer, a letch, and George had left his daughter home alone with him. Why had Sarah lied to him? Hadn't she realized how vulnerable and innocent Abigail was?

He had phoned home several times, but no one answered. Sarah failed to show up at two meetings. He checked with the hotel desk, and they informed him she had checked out. He phoned her apartment but again got no answer, and now his cell phone was dead.

He drummed his fingers on his knees as the cab pulled into the driveway and made its way toward the house. He spotted Lily by the side of the house, working in the flowerbed.

Shoving a handful of bills into the yellow money tray, he leaped from the cab before it came to a complete stop.

Bolting around the side of the house, he nearly collided with Lily. He reached out a hand to help her up.

"George, what's the matter?" she asked, struggling to her feet, her face puckered in concern.

"Where's Abigail?"

"She's in the house," she replied, wiping her hands on her slacks.

"She's in there alone with that man?" George whirled around and sprinted toward the door.

"George, have you lost your mind?"

First he headed toward the small rooms off the kitchen where Dr. Voight had said Beau moved Abigail. How convenient for the jerk since Lily's room was on the second floor. He stopped at the first room and found it empty. He then hurried to the second. It too was empty. Turning to leave, a stack of papers on Abby's dresser caught his eye. The words "Sexual Response Sexual Dysfunction Achieving Orgasms and Birth Control" in bold letters at the top of the first page hit him like a fist to the gut. He spun around and saw his sister.

"George, what is going on?" Lily stood at the end of the hall, wringing her hands, her brows knitted together.

"Where are they? Where's Winkelman?" he demanded.

"I think they're in the dining room. George—"

He rushed past her and headed toward the dining room. He found Beau standing behind Abigail, the beast's large paws encircled her rib cage, her breasts brushing the tops of his fingers.

"Get your hands off my daughter!"

Beau straightened but didn't release Abby.

"Did you hear me? I said get your hands off her!" Beau leaned forward and whispered something in her ear then released her but didn't move away.

George froze as his daughter stood. Forearm crutches helped her keep her balance. He couldn't believe his eyes; it was a miracle. Abby glanced up. "Daddy!" Her eyes filled with tears, and she started to cry.

His fury returned. Dr. Voight had been right. Winkelman had pushed her too hard. Then she lost her balance and started to fall. Beau grabbed her under the arms; his fingers once again coming into contact with the sides of her breasts. George wondered how many other liberties the man had taken while he'd been away.

George rushed forward and reached for his daughter. He pulled her out of Beau's arms and gently glided her onto the nearest chair.

The two men exchanged challenging glances.

"You are never to touch my daughter ever again," George spat "Where is Voight?" He whirled to find Will standing by the door, a surprised expression on his face.

"What the hell is this all about?" Beau demanded.

George spun back around to face Beau. "I'll tell you what this is about. It's about who you really are … *what* you are."

Beau planted his hands on his hips. "You're not making any sense." His brows formed a deep furrow as his eyes sparked with anger.

"I'll make it real clear for you, Mister Professional. I know all about your affair with Mrs. Wentworth."

Beau's expression never wavered as he answered, "So?" George's blood hiked up to a full boil.

"Do you deny the fact that your girlfriend came here to be with you?" George jabbed his finger against the hard muscular slab of Beau's chest.

"Ginger has done nothing to keep me from doing my job."

"You honestly believe you're exempt from all the rules of propriety? What about this?" He threw the papers he'd picked up from Abigail's room into Beau's face. "Did you give these papers to my daughter without my permission?"

Beau bent down and picked up the papers. "Yes but ... but," he stammered.

"But this—you're fired. I want you out of my house now!"

"George! You can't be serious!" Lily shrieked from the doorway.

"I'm very serious. Where's your common sense, woman?" George stalked toward his sister and ignored her gasp and horrified expression. "Abigail is tired. Take her to her room." He shot a scowl at Will. "Where were you? Your job was to keep him from pawing her." A deep growl escaped his lips as he stormed out.

Beau studied Abby's blank expression. Her father had just accused him of abusing her—and she knew it. Still she hadn't spoken up. Why hadn't she denied it or at least defend him? Did she want her father to believe something had happened between them? Something had happened. He had let himself believe they could build a life together. He turned away from her and fought the bitter taste of betrayal that lingered in the back of his throat. What a fool.

Turning to leave, Beau found Will standing by the door. The Judas stood with his arms folded across his chest. Despite having George's anger turned in his direction, Will's eyes sparkled with triumph. Beau's hands fisted; the bastard had wanted him out, and he'd gotten his wish. He longed to wipe the smirk from the man's lips.

Lily's hand reached out and patted Beau's arm as he approached the doorway. "A terrible mistake has been made!" Her lips quivered, her gentle eyes searched his face for answers.

Beau engulfed her petite fingers in his and gently squeezed. Nodding, he murmured, "And I'm the one who made it."

She blinked back her tears. "I don't understand."

"I thought possibly..." He closed his eyes, and in that second, his heart hardened and crack like dry clay. "I was wrong."

Releasing her hand, he walked out. He had been used and betrayed.

* * * *

Twenty minutes later, Lily sat at the kitchen table, waiting for Beau. He entered, carrying the last box from his room. She stood when he placed the box on the table and walked into his opened arms for a hug.

"I tried talking to George," she muttered into his chest. "But all he did was mumble something about a phone call from Dr. Voight. I don't understand any of this."

"I don't either, but Voight made it clear from the beginning that he didn't appreciate me being here."

"Where will you go?"

"Probably back to Texas, but I have a few things at my sister's apartment to pick up first."

She released her hold and patted his chest. "I can't imagine what got into Abigail. Why didn't she say anything to her father? Why didn't she set him straight?"

Beau sighed. "I don't know. A lot has happened to her in the past few weeks. You just keep her up and moving. Don't let her crawl back into her hole again."

"I promise that I'll get to the bottom of this." He attempted to move away, but her fingers clenched the front of his shirt. "You're a good man."

"Thank you."

Reluctantly, Lily released her grip and smoothed the wrinkles in his shirt. "I'll worry about you. Call me so I know you're settled alright?"

"You're a peach, Miss Lily." He treated her to a lopsided grin and kissed her forehead.

Without a backward glance, he picked up his last box and walked out the door.

Lily's body shook with frustration. Heads would roll before the day was out!

* * * *

Ginger stood by Beau's truck. With her finger, she flicked the flap on one of the boxes. She offered a consoling smile as Beau trudged toward her carrying another box.

"How many are left?"

"This is the last one." He set the box beside the others on the bed of his truck. With his arms resting on the edge of the truck box, Beau's gaze dropped to his feet and the ground.

Ginger cleared her throat. "I went inside to say goodbye and overheard Mr. Pendergrass. I'm so sorry, Sugar. I hope my coming here hasn't damaged your career or wrecked your chances of getting your own clinic."

Beau sighed. "Don't worry about it."

"Is there anything I can do?" She rubbed her hand across his tanned arm. Arms that once held her tight but now only wanted to hold someone else. Beau glanced up. Although he attempted to smile his eyes couldn't mask his pain.

"I don't think so. I think it's best if we both just leave."

"What are you going to do? Where will you go?"

"I don't rightly know." He chuckled. "I guess I'm a free agent again."

"Well, I'm not," Ginger replied. "I have to head back today, but first I need to say goodbye to Miss Lily. She's been so sweet to let me stay."

Ginger walked into Beau's opened arms and hugged him tight, knowing it would be for the last time. Then suddenly she felt his body change from firm muscle to solid rock. She leaned back and glanced up. His jaw was clamped tight, his eyes mere slits as he glared toward the house. He loosened his hold on her and pushed her aside. Turning, Ginger saw Dr. Voight. An arrogant sneer marred his face as he marched toward them.

With one brow cocked, Will stopped directly in front of Beau. "Well, Winkelman, you knew all along that Abigail was out of your league. Next time don't set your sights so high." His sarcastic remarks set off warning signal in Ginger's head, and before she could react, Beau's fist struck Will's face with a loud crack, lifting the man off his feet and careening backwards.

When Will regained consciousness Beau was long gone. Ginger sat on the ground next to him, cradling his head in her lap. She combed his hair back from his face with her fingers. He glanced up, and she shook her head. "For a smart man, you're pretty stupid."

Confused, he blinked and winced with pain.

"Come on, Cowboy," she said, helping him to his feet. "I've got just the thing to fix you right up."

* * * *

Abby sat up in bed and listened as Beau drove away. He hadn't even stopped by her room to say goodbye. He obviously couldn't wait to leave. Free now, he and Ginger could get back to their old life. Well, that was fine with her. She fought to ignore the pain of her heart breaking in two.

He hadn't denied anything her father accused him of which meant he really did have an affair with a married woman. How many women did he have scattered across the country? She didn't care, she reminded herself.

All of a sudden, Abby noticed Ginger standing in her doorway. The beauty stood with her arms folded across her ample bosom. "What do you want?" Abby snapped, hoping Ginger wouldn't see her emotional pain. "I thought you would have left with him."

"I'm not the one he wants to be with."

Those weren't the words Abby expected to hear. She stared at the woman, trying to read her expression. Ginger raised one perfectly shaped eyebrow, and Abby wondered if she hadn't been trying to read her, too.

"Wow!" Abby smoothed the invisible wrinkles in her blanket. "Here I thought you had it all. His other woman must really be something if he left you behind to go to her!" Abby folded her arms across her chest, well aware it was much smaller than Ginger's and stared out the window.

"You don't get it, do you?" Ginger stepped to the end of Abby's bed.

Abby ignored her baiting comment.

"When I first got here I felt sorry for you." The first brick broke loose and fell away from Abby's emotional barrier. "You being in this terrible accident and all. Then I watched how hard Beau worked with you, and I saw how desperately he wanted you to walk again. At first, I thought he was only doing it for his career, but I was wrong." Another brick fell.

"What are you talking about?" She met Ginger's stare.

Ginger shook her head. "He didn't need you to walk again for him. He needed you to walk again for *you*. He wanted you to have everything you ever dreamed of. He wanted you to have your life back."

"Why? I was just another client to him. Someone he could bully and berate."

"Is that all you think you were to him? Just a client?"

"What else could I ever be to someone like him? Look at me? What do you see?" Abby said bitterly, raising her arms in the air.

Ginger smiled. "I see a beautiful young woman with her whole life in front of her. A determined independent woman who could walk, drive, go back to college … do whatever she wanted. All because of Beau. He gave you back your life, and you took his away. You let him down."

"He did this to himself. I didn't do anything," Abby stated, praying she didn't look as guilty as she felt. One more brick shattered.

"That's right, you didn't. You didn't do anything when your father accused him of taking advantage of you." Ginger's arms flapped wildly as she spoke. "Heaven only knows what he thinks Beau's done to you."

"He hasn't done anything to me … not in that way." Even though she had foolishly offered herself to him on a silver platter. What would her father think of that if he knew?

"He hasn't done anything to me in that way either since I've been here."

"You expect me to believe that? I saw the two of you by the pool last night. He kissed you."

"That was a goodbye kiss. I told him I was leaving today."

"I'll bet," Abby replied. Her head was starting to pound.

"Beau doesn't love me. I don't think he ever really did."

"I can't believe he would leave you for someone else. You have everything."

"I thought so, too." Ginger shrugged, looking a little hurt. "I don't have what he wants."

Not sure if she really wanted to know the answer, Abby asked, "What does he want? Who's this other woman he's so in love with then?"

"You, you dimwit." Ginger placed her hands on her hips and rolled her eyes. "He's in love with you."

Abby stared at Ginger as though she were crazy. "That's not funny."

"I'm serious, Honey. He loves you, and you just let him walk right out of your life."

"What do you get for telling me all of this?"

"Beau's my friend. I care about him, and I want to see him happy."

"If he loved me, he wouldn't just walk away from me."

Ginger folded her arms across her chest again. "Beau's a proud man. You hurt him by not standing up to your father. I'm sure he feels you betrayed him. Not to mention you probably ruined his career."

She couldn't be serious, could she? Panic rippled to the surface. "What can I do about it now?"

"You're the only one who can answer that," Ginger said, her voice laced with sympathy. Then she turned and walked out of the room. Another brick crashed to the floor.

What have I done? I let him down. I betrayed him.

A mixture of shock, panic and remorse washed over Abby. She had to do something—she just didn't know what.

* * * *

Lily walked into the kitchen and heard voices coming from down the hall. She was severely tempted to sneak down the hall and listen to what was being said. Instead, she paced around the room for several minutes before collapsing into a chair at the table. She prayed Ginger would be able to talk some sense into her hardheaded niece.

Moments later Ginger entered the kitchen. Lily sprang to her feet. "Well? Did you get through to her?"

Ginger sighed and shrugged her shoulders. "The only thing I know for sure is that it's time for me to leave. I think I've caused enough trouble around here."

"That's not true. You haven't done anything wrong," Lily professed. "It may not seem like it right at the moment, but you were a bigger help to my niece then you'll ever know."

"I don't see how," Ginger said with a confused look on her face.

"Are you going back to Texas?"

"Yes. I only took a few days off from work, and I need to get back."

Lily moved forward and pulled Ginger into a hug. "It was nice to meet you, dear. I'm sorry things didn't turn out the way you wanted them to."

"That's all right. We don't always get what we want, do we, Miss Lily?"

"No, dear, we sure don't." Lily knew Ginger spoke from experience. "I'm sure you'll find what you're looking for." Lily reached up and placed a strand of Ginger's hair behind her ear.

At the sound of the patio door opening, Ginger glanced up and smiled. Lily turned to see Dr. Voight standing in the doorway, holding a bag of ice over one eye. She turned around, and the redhead grinned and winked.

"Maybe sooner than you think!"

Chapter Twenty

Lily was dusting the great room when she heard a truck pull up out front. She opened the door before the surprised young man could ring the bell.

"Good afternoon, ma'am." He held a package wrapped in brown paper.

"Good afternoon. It's late to be making deliveries, isn't it?" she asked.

"Yours is my last one for today."

Lily signed for the package and thanked the young man. The package was addressed to Miss Abigail Sue Pendergrass with no return address. She walked through the house and down the hall to her niece's room.

Lily knocked once and opened the door. "Dear, are you awake? A package just came for you."

Abby was sitting up, gazing out the window. She didn't reply so her aunt repeated herself. "A package just came, but there's no return address. I wonder who it could be from?"

"Go ahead and open it, Aunt Lily," Abby replied dryly. Lily set the package down on the bed, peeled back the tape and carefully removed the brown paper. Without opening the flaps, she handed it to her niece.

The package was just shy of a foot long but weighed at least two pounds. Abby had no idea what it might be. Maybe her father had sent something to her and forgotten to mention it. As a matter of fact he hadn't been in to talk to her since the embarrassing scene he had made earlier.

Inside the package, wrapped in tissue, Abby found a trophy. She pulled it out and read the words engraved on the brass plaque. It said: Lifetime Achievement Award. Looking up at her aunt, she said, "I don't understand. Who's this from?"

"I don't know, dear. Is there a card with it?"

Abby handed the trophy to Lily and searched through the tissue paper, finding a note. Lifting it up, she read:

Sweetheart

You've worked hard and come a long way. This Lifetime Achievement Award is for all the things you have accomplished and all that you will still achieve. There is nothing you can't succeed at if you put your mind to it. I'm so proud of you.

Love, Beau.

With tears in her eyes, she handed her aunt the note. Lily read it and smiled through her tears. "Do you love him, too?" she asked.

Surprised, Abby asked, "What did you say?"

"I said do you love him, too?"

"Yes. Yes, I do," she replied sadly. "But he doesn't love me in the same way."

"What makes you say that?"

Abby's fingers toyed with the trophy. "Several times he acted as if he was going to kiss me then just before our lips met, he backed away. If he loved me why would he resist? I don't think his feelings for me were real." Abby wiped away a lone tear as it slid down her cheek.

"Oh, they were real enough, dear. But he must have had a good reason for backing off. Maybe it had something to do with client-patient relations or something," Lily replied.

"But why did he leave?"

Lily frowned. "If I remember correctly, he didn't have much of a choice. You pushed him away."

"What can I do now? It's too late. He's already gone." She tried hiding the hysteria that was building inside her.

Lily shook her head. "It's never too late if you want something bad enough." Lily turned and left, leaving Abby to make her own decisions.

Abby set the trophy on the nightstand and stared at it. She recalled the day Beau had gone up to her room and returned with an armful of her trophies. At the time he'd used them to taunt her, demanding to know what happened to her competitive spirit, but he must have realized how precious they had really been to her. None of them could ever mean as much to her as this one did. The card that accompanied the trophy plainly stated he had believed all along that she would walk again.

She should have stopped him from leaving. Instead she had permitted her jealousy to cloud her judgment. Now she sat alone in the darkness of her room, wondering if she was destined to be lonely for the rest of her life.

Carolyn's words echoed in her head. *"Someday you'll meet someone special, and you'll want to spend every minute with him."* Abby now understood what Carolyn had meant. Her heart tightened with a pain unlike anything she had felt before, and she knew she couldn't live without Beau. She didn't want to live without him.

Her eyes brimmed with tears as scenes from the past few weeks played out in her mind like a sad movie. The days he held her tight during therapy, all the while whispering words of encouragement. How his strong arms tenderly embraced her the night she confided her worse fears to him. He hadn't laughed but consoled her and comforted her while reassuring her that one day a man would love and accept her just the way she was. The day they drove to the hospital, he sang to calm her frazzled nerves. And the day he sat and watched Carolyn's funeral videotape with her, his soothing words convinced her to come to terms with her loss.

She would have never made it through losing Carolyn again without him. Although he had only been gone a few hours she ached with emptiness. She loved Beau, and she knew what she had to do. She just didn't know if she had the strength and courage.

* * * *

It was early evening, and George sat behind his desk in his study, tapping a pen on the highly polished surface. His sister had just left his office, and his ears were still ringing. She'd set him straight about what did and what didn't go on while he was away. Instead of trusting Lily's judgment, he had been a fool and listened to the jealous speculations of Dr. Voight. As his sister had been so kind to point out, he had messed everything up. He couldn't agree more. Not only had he alienated the woman who had restored his heart with love and joy, he had fired the one man who worked miracles on his little girl by helping her to walk and talk again, giving her hope and a future worth living for.

His little girl. No, Abby was no longer a little girl but a woman who needed the kind of love a father couldn't give her.

When the time comes to let her go, it isn't going to be easy.

George glanced up as his study door burst open, and Sarah stormed in. Her arms swung at her sides. Sparks flashed in her eyes as she marched toward him. He was never so happy to see anyone in his life before, though she didn't look too pleased to see him at the moment.

"You had no grounds for firing Beau after everything he's done for Abigail!"

He tried to speak, but she cut him off with a wave of her hand. "I admit I was wrong in keeping any information about Beau from you," she snapped, "but I had every intention of telling you..." Her gaze momentarily dropped to the floor then flashed back. "It's just—the time was never right."

George had never witnessed her protective side before, and he admired her courage. Her passion intrigued him.

"My resignation." She tossed a sheet of paper on his desk and headed toward the door.

Panic engulfed him. If he let her walk out of his house now, she would be walking out of his life forever. He wasn't about to let that happen.

"Sarah." George sprang to his feet and rounded the desk. "Wait!" She stopped, her back turned toward him, her hand resting on the door handle. He twisted her resignation in his hand. "I can't accept your resignation." She turned and with a stricken expression watched as he ripped the paper in half. The pieces floated to the floor.

"I won't..." He closed the distance between them and reached out for her hands. The hot rage he saw in her eyes dimmed to warm despair from his touch.

"I won't let you walk out of my life." He squeezed her hands gently. "I can't let you go," he whispered as he engulfed her in his arms.

Chapter Twenty-One

It was now or never. Abby stepped out into the morning sun and closed the front door behind her. She waited for some of the courage Beau said she possessed, but she didn't feel courageous; she felt terrified. If she faced and conquered her biggest fear, she could have a future with Beau.

She hadn't slept a wink but lay awake and cried for hours. She needed to reach him before he left town. She needed to explain. With great difficulty, she'd dressed herself and attached her leg brace and forearm crutches. Now she stood at the threshold of her past life ready to take her first steps into a new life of independence.

A life she knew she wanted more than anything. A life that could only include the one man who showed her she had so much to live for. The one man who knew she had the strength to face and overcome her nightmares. The man she had let down and turned her back on. She had to tell him she was sorry and that she loved him.

She'd fought against becoming self-reliant, too frightened to leave the protection and security of her father's home. Now she could take care of herself. She had to show Beau that he had freed her from her self-imprisonment.

With cautious steps, she took that first step off the landing. Abby's shoe scraped the sidewalk as she slid it forward. She mentally estimated the distance to her parked car. She could make it. She licked her dry lips. Each step was calculated slow and deliberate.

Once she reached the automobile she sighed. She reached for the door handle. Strapped to the crutch her fingers were too short to grip the latch. She repositioned herself and tried again. This time her fingers slipped off the handle, causing the tips of her fingers to sting. On the third try with minimal cursing, she worked the driver's door open. Stepping backwards, her shoe caught on an exposed rock, and she stumbled, nearly losing her balance. She teetered but caught hold of the car door, keeping herself from falling.

Previously the driver's seat had been moved back to accommodate Beau's long legs and that aided Abby as she fought to get in. She removed the crutches and placed them in the back seat. After several minutes of struggling, she finally settled behind the wheel.

Glancing up she saw her refection in the rearview mirror. "You can do this." She brought the seat forward until her right foot touched the gas pedal. Wiping her sweaty hands on her shorts, she took a deep breath and placed the key in the ignition. With trembling hands, she turned the key, and the Mustang roared to life. The sound of the engine vibrated through Abby's body, and she questioned her sanity.

The car radio was still set on the country station Beau had selected, and the singer's deep voice comforted her. Holding her breath, she moved the gear lever into drive. The sports car lunged forward, and she let out a scream. White knuckles gripping the steering wheel, she slammed her foot on the brakes.

Her head ached, and her heart pounded as if it were about to explode. She was certifiably crazy. She closed her eyes, took a deep breath and flexed her fingers.

"I can do this."

Gently she let up on the brake and crept down the driveway.

George strolled into the foyer and heard his sister whisper, "That's my girl. You go get him."

"Lily, what are you looking at?" George said, walking up beside her. "What's the matter? Why are you crying?" He glanced out the window and saw his daughter sitting in the red sports car. "What does she think she's doing? She can't drive!"

Lily wiped her tears away and smiled. "If she makes it down the driveway she can."

"Don't you care what could happen to her?" Panic-stricken, he headed for the door. Lily placed a hand on his arm. "I'm more afraid of what will happen to her if she doesn't make herself go."

Lily was right, but George's stomach churned with fear. Abigail was old enough to make up her own mind. He had to trust she knew what was right for her. Fear gripped his heart as he watched her ease her way down the driveway.

* * * *

Driving slowly and sticking to the edge of the road, Abby made her way north on the coastal highway. Her anxiety rose as she opened the window, hoping the fresh air would help calm her.

She caught her refection in the rearview mirror. "Try to relax. Don't panic and do something stupid." Her own voice lacked reassurance.

Then a car approached from behind. The driver honked for her to drive faster. She turned the wheel, and the front tire caught some gravel and pulled her toward the edge of the road. Her heart slammed against her ribs as she maneuvered the Mustang back onto the pavement. The car honked again then pulled around and passed. She released a long breath. "Don't worry about it. You're fine."

Abby eased along the road, the speedometer reading fifteen miles per-hour. The closer she came to the busy part of town, the more vehicles she encountered. The sounds of cars honking, motorcycles revving and radios blasting became overwhelming. She closed her window and carefully kept her distance from the other vehicles.

Pulling up to a four-way sign, she stopped. Her whole body seemed to vibrate with trepidation. She glanced at the other drivers. Were they all watching her, waiting for her to do something wrong? She waited her turn and then slowly pulled forward. A minivan coming from her right sounded its horn and barely missed her front fender. Abby's right foot hit the brakes. She froze in her seat, her hands clamped tight to the steering wheel. A lump rose in her throat, and tears slid down her cheeks. How long she sat there she wasn't sure. A tapping on her window caused her to jump.

"Ma'am, are you alright?" A man's voice asked through the window.

"Yes. Yes, I'm fine," she replied, though she couldn't make herself glance in his direction.

"Are you sure? You're as white as a ghost," the man stated. "Are you hurt?"

"Really, I'm fine. Just startled." She heard her own voice stammer with her reply.

"If you say so, lady." Then he walked away. Not wanting to draw any more attention, Abby looked around before pulling ahead.

She wasn't sure which apartment building Beau's sister was staying in but prayed she would spot his truck. If, of course, he was still there. There was so much she had to say to him.

She turned off the main road and within a few blocks spotted Beau's truck. Pulling into a parking spot, she turned off the engine. She watched Beau load boxes into the back of his truck until she felt steady enough to get out of the car.

Abby took a deep breath. It was now or never.

"You've made it this far. You can do this."

Opening the car door, she wrestled with her legs until they were both firmly planted on the pavement. Twisting and struggling, she reached into the back seat for her crutches. Only able to reach one she fastened the crutch to her arm, stood and then braced herself against the car. After a couple of tries using the first crutch as a hook, she finally caught the crutch that had fallen to the floor and pulled it out.

She secured the second crutch, then made her way around the door and pushed it shut. Leaning against the Mustang, Abby rested. It was a workout just to get in and out of the car, but she had done it, and she felt proud of all of her accomplishments. She'd taken life for granted before the accident. She'd taken people for granted, too, but never again.

Abby glanced up and caught Beau staring at her. The sound of the door slamming must have caught his attention. She took a deep breath and forced a smile. A frown marred his face, an expression she had grown to accept and love.

Her knees felt weak, and she prayed they wouldn't give out on her now. Tightening her grip on the crutches, she shifted her weight and took another step. Her arms shook with fatigue. Her mouth felt dry. She felt sick.

Another step and still he hadn't moved. He stood rooted in place and watched her slowly struggle to reach him. It was obvious he wasn't going to make this any easier on her.

With the next step, her crutch slid on a pebble, but she caught herself and didn't fall. *A few more steps to go,* she told herself. *You can do this. You can do anything, remember?*

Her right leg ached. Her arms hurt where the straps of her crutches dug into her tender flesh. Sweat trickled down her back and down the sides of her face. *Just a little further,* she thought and forced herself to move on.

Beau stood frozen in place. It was the hardest thing he had ever done. His guts twisted as he forced himself to just stand there and watch her struggle. He knew what it took for her to get into a car, let alone a sports car, and drive again. She must have been terrified. How she had made it across town and all the way up to Carmel was nothing short of a miracle. He'd known all along she could do it. Now here she was, walking by herself, though he shared the anguish he saw in her eyes.

Even though his heart was busting with pride, it was also breaking. It took all his strength to hold himself back from running to her. This was something she needed to prove to herself, that she could do on her own. She had worked hard and gained back her independence. She no longer needed his help. She could now continue on with her life.

One more step and she would be right in front of him. She took that step, stopped and smiled up at him, her pretty brown eyes brimming with tears.

"Hi," she said breathlessly. "I couldn't let you leave without saying goodbye. Mostly I wanted to thank you for everything you've done for me."

"Here, sit down." Beau pushed some boxes out of the way, turned, lifted Abby and placed her on the tailgate of his truck. Standing between her knees, his hands lingered on her waist. He took a deep breath and inhaled her familiar scent.

He wanted to forget everything that happened and take her in his arms. Instead, he took a step back and helped her remove the crutches. He placed them in the bed of his truck. Emotions were churning in his gut. What was she expecting from him? "Well? How was driving again?" he asked, trying to curb his emotions.

Abby laughed. A tear escaped and slid down her cheek. "It was horrifying! And there's a couple of drivers that aren't real pleased with my driving."

"But you did it. And you did it by yourself," he said with a slight grin. "I'm so proud of you."

"You were right." She held his gaze, then placed her hands on his arms, sending a jolt of electricity up both arms. "You were right about everything." A laugh and a sob escaped her lips.

He couldn't help but tease her. "Which right time are you referring to?"

"I'm serious," she said, squeezing his arms. "I was a spoiled brat! I acted disgracefully to my father, my aunt, the doctors, everyone at the hospital but mostly to you." Shyly her gaze dropped to her lap. "I'm sorry. I apologize for the way I treated you and for my childish behavior." Her head rose, and their gaze locked. "Thank you for putting up with me when you could have so easily given up and walked away." She smiled sweetly and ran her hands back up his arms.

It was clear to him; her feelings of gratitude were confused with those of affection. But his feelings for her were crystal clear. He loved her. He wanted to pull her into his arms and kiss her. He wanted to stay with her forever, but his past would always be there to haunt him. A constant reminder that he wasn't good enough. He had nothing to offer a woman like Abigail Pendergrass.

Abruptly Beau broke their contact by stepping back. Abby teetered forward, reached out and grabbed the side of the truck box to keep from falling off the tailgate. He was distancing himself from her and hadn't noticed. If he got too far away she would lose him forever. That wasn't something she was willing to let happen.

Beau picked up another box and placed it in the back of the truck. The muscles in his arms bulged as he wrestled the box into place. When he finished, he stood closer to her than he realized. Unwilling to let him move away, Abby reached out and touched his arm again. The slight scent of sandalwood—his scent, a scent she'd grown very fond of—tantalized her senses.

"I also wanted to thank you for seeing something in me that no one else did," she whispered.

His arm muscles flexed, and his eyes pinned hers. "It was always there. You just needed someone to point it out to you, that's all."

"You did more than just point it out. You made me open my eyes and see everything I was giving up. You gave me back my life, Beau." *And there's no way I'm letting you walk away from it.* "I want you to know that I appreciate that."

"You were willing to give up too much, and I couldn't let that happen. Your father and your aunt love you very much. You're very lucky. You have a lot to live for."

Abby slid her hand down to his, holding him in place.

"Your whole life is ahead of you, sweetheart. You can do and have anything you want. You've proven that today."

"There is one thing that I want." She reached out and placed her hands flat against Beau's chest.

"Abby, I'm sorry" he said, shaking his head. "I have nothing to offer you. You need to go back to your life. Go back and finish school. You can become the teacher you have always wanted to be."

He tried pulling away, but her fingers gripped the front of his shirt. She wasn't going to let him go. Not now. Not ever.

"I need to go, Abby!" He shook his head, and his brown eyes were dark with sadness.

"What makes you think I'm going to let you go?" She smiled and pulled him close. Her heart pounded wildly, and she wondered if he heard it, if he could feel it.

He stood between her parted legs, his hands resting on the tailgate of his truck as if he was restraining himself from touching her. Abby moistened her lips.

"Just one kiss," she purred, and she felt Beau's body stiffen. She slid her hands up his chest, laced her fingers behind his head and pulled him close.

The kiss was soft, and at his slightest hesitation, she deepened it. She wasn't going to let go until he surrendered.

Unable and unwilling to fight her any longer, Beau wrapped his arms around her waist, pulled her tight to him and took control of the kiss. His tongue forced its way past her soft sweet lips. How he had longed to kiss her like this! He wanted to take his time and kiss every inch of her body. Show her everything she had been missing. Then he remembered she wasn't his to do with as he pleased.

He broke free from the kiss. Abby's eyes flew open, and he saw raw passion and desire in their depths. He didn't know what to say. He tried pulling away, but she tightened her grip. "Abby, please. You need to let me go!"

"I can't, Beau. I love you," she whispered.

Stepping back, Beau tripped and pulled her off the tailgate. She screamed as they fell backwards onto the pavement with a thud.

Chapter Twenty-Two

Beau rung his hands and wiped his sweaty palms on his slacks. He'd never been so nervous in his life before. What was taking so long? Why wouldn't they let him see Abby or speak to her? He'd been worried sick about her all day. Earlier he'd gone to her door, but Lily wouldn't let him in. She had said that Abby was resting. His sister tried to get him to eat something, but his stomach was tied up in one big knot, and he feared nothing would stay down.

This was insane—why wouldn't they let him see her for just a second to make sure she was all right? He couldn't just stand around all day; he would go crazy. He paced back and forth across the small waiting room.

"Beau, try not to worry," his sister pleaded. "If there was something wrong they would have come out and told us." She rubbed her hand across his back. She meant well, but she had no idea what he was going through. He loved Abby with all his heart. The waiting was killing him. Something must be wrong.

* * * *

"I don't want to use the wheelchair. Why can't I walk?" Abby scowled at her father.

"The doctor said you need to save your strength whenever you can, dear," George replied with a smile.

"I know. I'm sorry. I didn't mean to snap at you. I just need to get out of this room. I'm getting claustrophobic." She felt as if she'd been trapped in the room for days, and she couldn't wait to see Beau again.

"The doctor said you have to be wheeled to the door. All right? It's just a little ways," he promised.

With her father's help, Abby lowered herself into the wheelchair.

A lot of things crossed her mind as her father wheeled her down the long hallway. Her car accident had changed her life forever. She had given up on her life and all her dreams. She resigned herself to the fact that she had no future and nothing to live for. Then Beau came into her life and turned everything upside down, and she would never stop thanking him for that.

They finally reached the door. George stopped and set the brakes on the wheelchair. He reached down and patted her shoulder. She smiled as he helped her to stand. He tucked her hand in his arm and kissed her cheek. "Are you ready, honey?"

Abby trembled, took a deep breath and nodded her head. The doors opened. With her father's help, she stepped over the threshold. Her eyes searched for Beau. If she could see him, concentrate on him, she could do anything. She spotted him, and although he smiled, she saw concern in his eyes. He knew how important it was for her to do this without his help.

"Ready?" her father asked again. Abby smiled and with a tight grip on her father's arm took that first step.

Soft candlelight illuminated the small chapel. Bouquets of red and white roses lined both sides of the aisle, and larger arrangements adorned the altar. Soft piano music came from somewhere in the background.

Abby ran a quick hand over her mother's wedding dress. Knowing that her mother watched from up above caused a warm comforting feeling to wash over her. Her eyes filled with tears. Every girl dreamt of walking down the aisle on her father's arm, and she had been no different. Beau had made that dream and many more come true for her. She loved him more than she thought was ever possible.

He looked so handsome standing at the altar waiting for her. It must have been hard for him to stay there. He took a step forward only to be pulled back by his best man who stood next to him. She had thought Beau was big and strong, but the three men who showed up on her father's doorstep two days ago were massive compared to him.

Abby couldn't wait to start their new life together. As she walked, she strived to keep her balance; each step came slow and calculated. She prayed she wouldn't fall, but she knew if she ever fell Beau would always be there to pick her up.

She was a vision—an angel. Beau had never seen anyone more beautiful in his life. Funny, a few months ago he would have never put *angel* and *Abby* in the same sentence, yet she was an angel to him and so much more.

His heart was being ripped from his chest as he watched the strain and pain each labored step caused her. She walked a few steps and then stopped to rest. She had refused to use her crutches, opting only to hold her father's arm. He had pleaded with her to use the wheelchair, but she insisted she could make it down the aisle. Her stubbornness and determination only made him love her more.

She walked arm and arm with her father like any other bride would. With her brace hidden under her long white gown she was determined to appear as a typical bride. Yet Beau knew only too well that there wasn't anything typical, common or conventional about Miss Abigail Sue Pendergrass.

Epilogue

Beau lounged by the same pool where he had spent many hours dealing with his frustrations by swimming in the cold water, except he hadn't felt the need of the cold water since he had married the source of his irritation. Married. He still couldn't believe it. If anyone had told him when he took the job that he would stay in California, marry Abby and open his own sports rehabilitation clinic, he would have told them they were crazy.

However, extraordinary things seemed to happen in California. Ginger and Dr. Voight getting together was one that still amazed him, but she did have a thing for misguided souls. His sister had married George, and Miss Lily and Dr. Hanson were due back from their honeymoon cruise next week. It was funny how their lives had changed in such a short time.

Beau closed his eyes, letting the sun's rays bathe his face. He wondered if life could get any better than this.

"I brought you a beer," George said, sinking into a nearby chair.

Opening his eyes, he grinned at his brother-in-law's exhaustion. "How's it going in there?"

"Sarah and Abby have joined forces and formed some sort of tag team system." George took a long drink of his beer.

Beau laughed. He could only imagine. "So, George, how does it feel to be a grandpa?"

"I have to admit I like it." George smiled and shook his head. "He sure is a cute little devil."

"He takes after me!" Beau professed proudly. Just then Sarah strolled up. "How are you holding up, sis?"

"I don't know what's more tiring, being a new mother or a grandmother! Those two little guys are wearing me out!" Turning to George, she added with a frown, "Your son is very demanding!"

George laughed and pulled his wife down onto his lap. "He takes after his father!" he stated modestly, kissing her brow as he winked at Beau.

The relaxed atmosphere was soon interrupted by Abby's sweet voice as she shouted from the patio door. "Can I get a little help in here?"

Sarah giggled. "Oh, I forgot to tell you," she leaned forward and tapped Beau on the knee. "It's your turn. You're it!"

Beau struggled to his feet with an exaggerated sigh. He couldn't help but smile at how proud his grandmother would have been of him, and how she would have loved Abby as much as he did.

"I'm glad you found a moment in your busy schedule to come in and help me," Abby growled as he entered the kitchen. She had her nephew propped up under one arm like a football and her son by the back of his shirt as both boys howled their protest. Her checks were flushed and fire sparked in her eyes as she held fast, determined to win the battle.

At the sound of his chuckle, both boys stopped struggling and reached out to Beau. He scooped them up into his arms. Little hands clasped onto his neck and shirt, and they smiled at their rescuer.

"They're both yours," Abby said as she turned away.

"Hey! Don't I get a reward for taking these monsters off your hands?"

Turning back around, one corner of her mouth hiked up in a smirk as

she sashayed up to him. Standing on tip-toes, she brushed her lips across

his and murmured, "That's all you get - for now, Sweetart."

About the Author

The saying, "You can take the girl out of the country, but you can't take the country out of the girl" describes this author. She likes to herd cattle in Montana, snowmobile in Wyoming, garden and write romance novels.

Her tales stem from a combination of past experiences and a lot of wishful thinking. She's written since 1996, but has been dreaming up wild adventures her whole life. She resides in east central Minnesota.

The women in her novels are country girls, who find themselves in strange predicaments with men, who definitely have the makings of true heroes.

Email: Lfnies1@yahoo.com
Website: www.luannnies.com

Other Works by the Author at Melange

Bearly Christmas Darling in Christmas Wishes 2012
Catrina's Cowboy

References

1) The Colorado Spinal Cord Injury – Early Notification System, the Injury Epidemiology Program Colorado Department of Public Health and Environment
4300 Cheery Creek Drive South, Denver, Colorado 80220-1530
"Understanding Spinal Cord Injury"

2) Craig Hospital Research Department – Contact Ken Gerhart
3425 South Clarkson Street
Englewood, Colorado 80110
Incomplete SCIs: "Down the Road" and "The Early Days"

3) Gale L., Florida VHL Family Alliance Home Page, "Paralyzed? Don't Give Up Too Soon!"

4) Mart, Krista, "The Long Road To Recovery - Rehab Proves Beneficial for Those With Partial Paralysis"; ABC NEWS.Com

5) Sipski, Marca L. (M.D.), "Sexuality and Spinal Cord Injury" By

6) Auto Accident Helpline – Roll-over Accident Injuries
www.autoaccidenthelpline.com

7) The Merck Manual of Medical Information – Home Edition
Section 6. Brain and Nerve Disorders
Chapter 65 Muscle Weakness, Chapter 69 Spinal Cord Disorders, Chapter 70 Peripheral Nerve Disorders, Chapter 75 Head injuries

8) Brown, David A. (PT, Ph. D.) Assistant Professor Northwestern University. "Body Weight Support Treadmill Training (BWSTT) Questions to Ponder and Studies to Propose."

9) Gerhart, Kenneth A. (M.S.), Charlifue, Susan W. (M.A.), Menter, Robert R. (M.D.), Weitzenkamp, David A. (B.A.) and Whiteneck, Gale G. (Ph.D.), "Aging with Spinal Cord Injury",
www.ed.gov/pubs/AmericanRehab/spring97/sp9706

10) Xing, Yingqi, (M.D.,MS) "Lower Limb Orthotics"
www.emedicine.com/pmr/topic172

11) Andrews, Cassandra, Stroke Recovery Systems. Inc. 8100 South

Park Way, Suite A-I, Littleton, Colorado 80120   "The NeuroMove
TM"

12) Kimberley, Teresa J. (P.T.), and Carey, James R., (Ph. D., P.T.),
"Neuromuscular Electrical Stimulation in Stroke Rehabilitation" &
"Breakthrough in Stroke and Spinal Cord Injury rehab!" Stroke
Recovery Systems www.NeuroMore.com

13) Bremmer, J. Douglas, (M.D.), faculty member of the Department
of Diagnostic Radiology and Psychiatry, Yale University School of
Medicine, Yale Psychiatric Institute, and National Center for
PTSD-VA Connecticut Healthcare System. "The Invisible
Epidemic: Post-Traumatic Stress Disorder, Memory and the Brain"

14) Lopez, Juan F., (M.D.), faculty member of the Department of
Psychiatry and Mental Health Research Institute , University of
Michigan, Ann Arbor. "The Neurobiology of Depression"

15) Fair View Orthotic Practitioner: Luke Rogers